Dear Reader:

Thank you for picking up this copy of *Sideline Scandals* by Pat Tucker, a phenomenal storyteller. Pat revisits the ladies from her *Football Wives*, members of the social club who are married to NFL coaches. Now she takes it up a notch with the same scandal and glamour.

Pat has a reputation for writing these tantalizing tales as well as controversial stories based on real-life issues. Her *Daddy by Default* and sequel, *Daddy's Maybe*, deal with paternity while *Party Girl* focuses on a Texas law when a person can end up on Death Row simply by being at the scene of a crime.

I hope that you enjoy *Sideline Scandals* and that you will also pick up Pat Tucker's novel, *A Social Affair*, co-authored by another phenomenal Strebor author, Earl Sewell. Their second dual literary effort, *Loyalty Among Friends*, is in the works.

As always, thanks for supporting the authors that I publish under my imprint, Strebor Books. All of us truly appreciate your support. If you would like to contact me, please email me at Zane@eroticanoir.com.

Blessings,

Zane
Publisher
Strebor Books International
www.simonandschuster.com

ZANE PRESENTS

SIDELINE SCANDALS

A Novel

Also by Pat Tucker

Sideline Scandals

Lachez (original ebook)

Football Widows

Daddy's Maybe

Party Girl

Daddy by Default

with Earl Sewell

A Social Affair

ZANE PRESENTS

SIDELINE SCANDALS

A Novel

PAT TUCKER

SBI

STREBOR BOOKS

NEW YORK LONDON TORONTO SYDNEY

Strebor Books
P.O. Box 6505
Largo, MD 20792
http://www.streborbooks.com

This book is a work of fiction. Names, characters, places and incidents are products of the author's imagination or are used fictitiously. Any resemblance to actual events or locales or persons, living or dead, is entirely coincidental.

ISBN 978-1-59309-479-9
ISBN 978-1-4516-9847-3 (e-book)
LCCN 2013933642

First Strebor Books trade paperback edition September 2013

Cover design: www.mariondesigns.com
Cover photograph: © Keith Saunders/Marion Designs

10 9 8 7 6 5 4 3 2 1

Manufactured in the United States of America

ACKNOWLEDGMENTS

I remain honored to be able to once again, give gratitude for some of the blessings bestowed upon me. As always, I'd like to thank God Almighty first and foremost. Next unlimited appreciation goes to my patient and wonderful mother, Deborah Tucker Bodden, my lifelong cheerleader, and the very best sister a girl could have, Denise Braxton, my patient and loving husband, Coach Wilson, thanks for your love and support.

Also, my handsome younger brother, Irvin Kelvin Seguro and Amber, the two best Uncles in the world, Robert and Vaughn Belzonie… Aunts, Regina, and Shelia…, my loving and supportive family in Belize, Aunt Flo, Elaine, Therese, my cousins, Patrick, Marsha, and Cassandra, and the rest of my cousins, nephews, nieces, and my entire supportive family, including my older brother, Carlton Anthony Tucker.

We don't share the same blood, but I love them like sisters: Monica Hodge, Marilyn Glazier, LaShawanda Moore, Lee Lee Baines, LaKeisha Madison, Tameka Brown, Kevina Brown. My love and thanks to Miranda Moore, Nikki Brock, Karen Williams, Jeness Sherell, Gloria Shannon, Keywanne Hawkins, Desiree Clement, Yolanda Jones, and the rest of those exquisite ladies of Sigma Gamma Rho Sorority Inc. and especially all of my sisters of Gamma Phi Sigma here in Houston, TX.

I'm blessed to be surrounded by friends who accept me just the way I am. ReShonda Tate Billingsley, thanks for your constant support, listening ear, and unwavering faith in my work. Victoria Christopher Murray, your kindness, giving heart, and willingness to help others are the truth!

Alisha Yvonne, your help with this story is immeasurable! Many, many thanks to Yolanda L. Gore, for helping to keep me on track, Markisha Sampson, Logan, Ron Reynolds, my KPFT Family, Marlo Blue.

Special thanks to my agent Sara, and a world of gratitude to my Strebor family, the dynamic duo Zane, and Charmaine, for having faith in my work. Special thanks to the publicity Queens led by Yona Deshommes at Atria/Simon & Schuster who help spread the word about my work.

But I saved the very best for last, ____________ ←(your name goes there!) Yes, you, the reader! I'm so honored to have your support. I know you are overwhelmed by choices, and that's what makes your selection of my work such a humbling experience. I will never take your support for granted. There were so many book clubs that picked up *Daddy by Default*, *Football Widows*, *Party Girl*, *Daddy's Maybe*, and *A Social Affair*, I wanted to honor some of you with a special shout out: The bible of AFAM Lit: Black Expressions book club! Johnnie Mosely and the rest of the wonderful men who make up Memphis' Renaissance Men's book club, Sisters are Reading Too (They have been with me from day 1!!) Special thanks to Divas Read2, Happy Hour, Cush City, Girlfriends, Inc., Drama Queens, Mugna Suma, First Wives, Brand Nu Day, Go On Girl, TX 1, As the Page Turns, APOO, Urban Reviews, OOSA, Mahogany Expressions, Black Diamonds, BragAbout Books, Spirit of Sisterhood, and so many more, I appreciate you all!

Also Huge thanks to all of the media outlets that welcomed me on the airwaves to discuss my work: "Inside her Story" with Jacque Reed, on the "Tom Joyner Morning Show," Yahoo Shine, Hello Beautiful, Essence.com, the *Huffington Post*, *Houston Chronicle* Guest Blog, Author Tuesday's presents, Northparan.com, The Book Depository.com, *Black Pearls* magazine, S&S Tipsonlifeandlove.com, nextreads.com, *The Dallas Morning News*.com, Interview KFDM-CBS Beaumont, TX, 3 Chicks on Lit, Clear Channel Radio News & Comm. Affairs, KIX 96 FM-KARK TV Little Rock, AR, KPRC NBC Houston, Beyond Headlines, Artist First Radio show, The Mother Love Radio Show, It's Well Blog Talk Radio March.

If I forgot anyone, and I'm sure I have, always, charge it to my head and not my heart. As always, please drop me a line at rekcutp@hotmail.com or sylkkep@yahoo.com. I'd love to hear from you, and I answer all emails.

Connect with me on Facebook, and follow me on Twitter @authorpattucker—I follow back!

Warmly,

Pat

SASHA

I turned my upper body to camera two, allowed my eyes to focus, and flashed my dazzling smile. This was when I was at my very best. The camera loved me, and I made sure to show my love right back.

Most of my time was spent at the KTLA Studios located on Sunset Boulevard, between Van Ness and Bronson Avenues. In addition to *The Sasha Davenport Show*, *Judge Judy*, was also taped there. Although my show was taped in one of the twenty-three studios, we only used a small section since I didn't have a live studio audience.

I glanced up at the lighting grid that was suspended from the studio's high ceiling. It held various colorful light fixtures, but the one that provided a spotlight for me, cast a soft yellow hue. It beamed down on me and kept me warm while we taped the show in the freezing studio. I loved what the lighting did for my complexion on tape. It helped add to my overall polished appearance, which I worked hard to maintain.

I had gotten used to the feel of the Vaseline that helped my lips glide effortlessly across my sparkling white veneers, so my smile was always camera-ready and perfect. I batted my real mink lashes and began to speak.

"So, I'm leaving y'all with this as we gear up for the next NFL season: There's tons going on behind the scenes. You have no clue!" I winked. "But that's why I'm here! I'm your girl, and you already know, I've got unprecedented access."

I crooked my index finger at the camera as if to summon it closer.

"Shhhh." I used that same finger to tap my pursed glossy lips.

"Between you and me, my sources have confirmed that Los Angeles Sea Lions Head Coach Taylor Almond's new staff will only consist of two familiar faces. That means only two of his assistants are returning! Can you say clean house?" I paused for effect and widened my eyes.

"Now, I don't know about you," I said, "but I, for one, knew this was coming. I mean, think about it. After all the drama that happened *off* the field last season, I can understand why Coach Taylor felt the need to make such drastic sweeping changes. Well, this year, we're gonna keep our eyes on a few key players, and hopefully, the coaches and their wives will leave the drama to the plays *on* the field. Stay with us. I'll be right back after this short break and a message from one of our sponsors."

"Sasha, you good? You've got two minutes," the director said through my earpiece. That was his way of letting me know I had time, if I wanted, to grab a quick glass of juice, water, or run to the ladies' room.

I looked up at the camera and nodded. I was gonna stay put.

"Okay. Cool," he said.

I needed to use the bathroom, but since we were nearly done taping the show, I figured it'd be smarter to wait. A couple of minutes later, the sound of the director's countdown stopped my thoughts. I focused in on the correct camera and waited to hear my cue.

"And we're back in five, four, three, two..." The floor director pointed at me, and on cue, I began to speak.

"Thanks for staying with us. Well, that's it for this week. Remember, I AM Saaaaasha Davenport! There's no one better. I am fierce, fantabulous, and very famous. Until next time, sweethearts, Muah!"

I made a wide sweeping motion with my arm and gave the camera my signature palm kiss. I smiled until the director yelled the magic words in my earpiece.

"We're clear. Great job, Sasha!"

The floor crew, which consisted of two camera operators, and a floor director, broke out in applause, and I hopped off the barstool we used for my closing monologue. *The Sasha Davenport Show* was going well, but lately I'd felt myself becoming bored. I needed more excitement. It wasn't that the thrill was gone or anything like that, but I felt like it was time for me to step things up.

Those were neither new nor sudden thoughts for me. From day one, my plan was to use this show as a stepping stone to bigger and better things. The problem was, I had become comfortable and stopped striving to get to the next level.

"Thanks, guys," I said as I made my way off the set. I cut through the control room, which is the nerve center of the television station, to get to the long hallway that led to my dressing room that also served as my office.

"Thanks, guys," I repeated.

I saw video of myself on one of the many monitors, but didn't stare too long because I didn't want anyone to think I was trying to nit-pick. The director, sound engineer, and video editor, barely looked up from their work as I slipped in. I knew the drill and left them to their work.

The moment I walked inside my office, my cell phone rang. I told myself that was part of the problem, too. Each time I began to think about what it might take to go to the next level, something distracted me, and I never revisited my plans.

I vowed not to allow that to happen this time as I greeted the caller. "This is Saaaasha," I sang.

"Sasha, you don't know me, but I've got some information that you might be able to use on that little show of yours," the caller said.

"Umph, well, if I don't know you, how did you get my number, and what makes you think your information is of any use to me and my *little* show?"

The woman's hearty laugh made me pull the phone away from my ear.

"Listen, I may not know you, but trust, dah-lin,' I know your kind," she said.

I didn't know whether to be offended or sit back and listen to what she had to say. "You know *my kind*, huh? And what *kind* might that be?"

"Well, honestly, I didn't think it'd be this hard. But whatever. If you wanna play it like that, I'll hold on to my information. I guess you'll have to run to play catch up and chase the story like everyone else once it breaks," she said.

People like this caller made me sick. I made a mental note to check my producer slash assistant because I didn't have time to be bogged down with this kind of foolishness. Everybody and their mama thought they had a line to some good exclusive hot gossip, until they realized I didn't pay for that type of information. And I was certain this time was no exception.

"Besides, I shoulda known you was one of them ol' stuck-up—"

"Oh, no you didn't!" I snapped and cut her off. "How did you say you got my number again?"

"I didn't say," she answered.

I frowned. By now, I was pissed and wondered what could be done about these freaks who thought it was cool to pay $39.95 to get anybody's cell phone number off the Internet. I was about to check her when there was a quick knock at my door before it opened. My producer, McKenzie Fields, slipped into the dressing room.

"Hey, what's wrong?" she asked.

I guess the scowl on my face must've told her immediately there was a problem.

"You know what, I don't have time for games. If you have a legitimate show or story idea, you need to go through the proper channels like everybody else. Regardless of how you got my number, here's a bit of advice, it is tacky and classless to use a stranger's number out of context," I said.

McKenzie moved closer. "Who are you talking to?" she asked.

The caller screamed, "I know your ball-chasing, gold-diggin', opportunist behind ain't trying to give me no lessons on class and tact!" She laughed. "Especially when we know you ain't got an ounce of either one!" She laughed louder like it was all she could do to try and catch her breath.

I sucked my teeth and pressed the END button on my cell phone. Then, I turned my anger to McKenzie. She needed to handle this kind of mess. I had other things on my mind, and filtering out the fans from the freaks was way beneath my pay scale.

"McKenzie," I said.

"Who was that?" she insisted.

"Yeah, that's exactly what I wanted to talk to you about." I pointed toward the chair. "Sit, please."

JERRI

I stretched my long, chocolate legs along the length of my chaise longue and yawned. I wasn't tired as much as I was bored, but what could I do? I looked down at the thick, black rubber band around my left ankle and rolled my eyes. It was a constant reminder of a time I wanted desperately to forget. My life was not supposed to take this path.

"Let me do you all night long."

Marsha Ambrosius' velvet voice filled the room. I perked up a bit when I heard my cell's ring tone.

"Hey, wanna do it all night long, baby."

Although I wanted desperately to snatch the phone, I needed to wait a respectable amount of time before I answered. I didn't need anybody thinking I was desperate simply because I was down temporarily.

I grabbed the phone before voicemail kicked in.

"House of beauty. This is cutie," I sang as I answered the phone.

"Damn, you sound real delicious," Ed said. "What you doin'?"

Edward Keal would not have been my first choice to help cure boredom, but I knew I'd have to settle. The girls were off in Vegas, and my ass was trapped in the house.

"I was sitting here thinking about *you*, daddy. What's up?"

"Just checkin' in on you. I know how lonely it can be when a butterfly's wings get clipped," Ed said.

Ed got on my nerves for many reasons. One of which included the fact that he felt he had to remind me that due to my house arrest, I couldn't venture any farther than the end of my driveway. On some days, depending on the weather and the signal to this little black box that reported my every move, I was able to venture a few feet farther.

"How'd you know I was lonely? You wanna come over and lick my—"

"Baby, I'm outta town," Ed said before I could finish my offer.

I rolled my eyes.

"You outta town?"

I didn't even try to hide the irritation in my voice. I wanted to ask, "Then why the hell did you think you should call me?" But I held my tongue. Ed was a third-string running back for the Sea Lions, but I believed greatness could happen at any time, so I kept him on the back burner just in case. Who knew how this thing would end with Jason.

"Yeah, babe, my agent set up a meeting to see if there's interest here in B-More," he boasted.

My mind instantly thought about all the reasons I'd never leave L.A. for Baltimore. But there was no way I would say that to him. I needed to keep him on ice in case my plan A, B, or C didn't pan out.

Ed wasn't hot. He was mild, but his earning potential was what kept him on the ticket. My girls and I used a scale for rating men and how they looked. It began at "hurt," which was the equivalent of needing a brown paper bag. That didn't mean he wasn't doable, but we probably wouldn't admit it, even under oath. "Mild" meant he was worthy of public appearances, but only at night when the lighting made said appearance deniable, if necessary. "Medium" meant he was claimable under the right circumstances and events. Then "hot" was self-explanatory.

Anything beyond "hot," which was rare, but possible, meant potential threesome worthy. Beyond "hot," involved impeccable good looks, swag, an outstanding body and filthy rich to boot. There hadn't been too many of those running around. But when they showed up, it was usually on a field and carrying a ball.

I had nowhere to go and nothing to do, but I still felt like being on the phone with Ed was a waste of time and energy. If I wanted a cocktail, he couldn't bring me one. If I wanted company, he couldn't come see about me either.

"Hey, why don't you holla at me when you get back? I need to take this call on the other end," I said quickly.

The shock in his voice told me he wasn't ready to get off the phone, but I was done with the conversation the moment I learned he wasn't in town.

I picked up the remote and surfed channels until that bored me, too. I had watched all of my favorite shows, including the episodes of *Scandal* that I had TiVoed, so I clicked the TV off.

The more I sat around, the more I thought about the fact that my girls were in Vegas living it up while I was stuck in the house, and it made me sick. At first, I was embarrassed about the thought of having to do community service, but the more I thought about it, the more I realized it was a great way to get out of the house for a long period of time.

When I heard the alarm disarm, I rolled my eyes. I grabbed the TV remote and clicked through the menu so I could look at the security cameras.

Heat climbed my neck and face, while I watched with pure hatred as that punk bitch walked in and dropped his bags. He stopped at the table in the foyer and picked up a stack of mail. The house was more than eight-thousand square feet, three stories with walnut flooring, vaulted ceilings, an elevator, a theater, and a three-car garage with living quarters above for the staff. But still, it wasn't big enough for the two of us.

I wondered when he had arrived back in town. Obviously my prayer that his plane would crash didn't come to fruition again, but I'd have to live with that.

A few moments later, I clicked the monitor off and decided to read a book. I needed to get away, and since I was confined to my house, a good book was my next best option. I couldn't wait for Thursday to roll around so I could go meet the director at the center where I was scheduled to do my community service.

This was so not how my life was supposed to go. My life as Jason Nelson's wife was supposed to be fabulous. Instead, I was living a real-life nightmare.

I got up from my chaise and walked to the bookshelf. I grabbed a book and settled back down on my sofa. A great story always helped me forget about being confined to the house, the misery that had become my life.

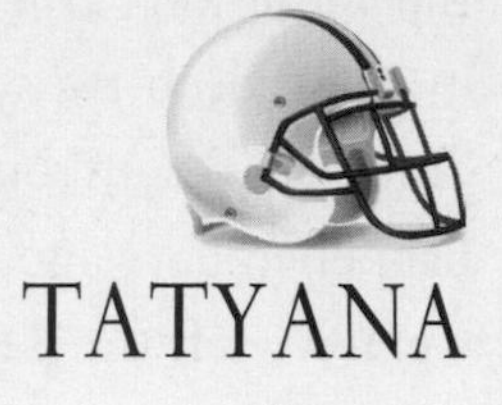

TATYANA

I stood at the bottom of our cascading staircase and shuddered despite the warmth in the massive room. My left eye twitched. I frowned at the handwritten letter as I read it. My eyes took in the words, and although I was well-educated, I simply could not comprehend. Antics from desperate women were nothing new, but this was something else, and it was completely out of order. I felt like the room was beginning to close in on me. Things like this only helped to fuel my desire for less time in the spotlight. The glare had become far too bright.

My husband of almost ten years was none other than Dax Becall, the star quarterback for the Los Angeles Sea Lions, so trust, I had literally seen just about everything under the sun when it came to desperate women.

After I read the foolishness for the second time, I walked toward the back of the house and out to the outdoor kitchen for privacy. I picked up the phone and called the only person I trusted, other than my mom, who lived in Houston. "Hey, Pamela, girl, you busy?" I asked.

Pamela Evans and I used to be NFL cheerleaders together back in the day. People said we looked so much alike, we started saying we were cousins and it stuck. She was very pretty.

"Since y'all packed up and moved to *La-La Land*, how can I be busy when you call?" Pamela asked. Pamela always spoke in a sing-song voice that made everything she said sound lighthearted. But there were true emotions behind her words.

It had been two years since Dax was traded to L.A, from the Houston Texans, but Pamela still behaved as if the trade and move happened days ago. I knew exactly how she felt though, because when we left the Texans, I thought I was going to die. I couldn't think of anything I'd like about Los Angeles until we moved.

The weather was almost always perfect. And beautiful people were everywhere. It was difficult to be depressed for long in L.A.

"I wanted to read something to you," I said.

"Read something like what?"

"This letter I got. You got a sec?"

"Yeah, go ahead," Pamela said.

"Okay, it's kinda long, but here we go. '*Dear Tatyana. My name is Simone, and I know I'm going to get into a world of trouble for this, but woman to woman, I felt like I had to reach out to you. I'd want someone to do the same for me. Anyway, I was really pissed at Dax when it dawned on me that he has still not talked to you about us like he said he was going to do. You see, I'm the other woman he's been seeing, and I am not just some random chick he's been having sex with. I care about him and he cares deeply about me.*'"

"What the hell?" Pamela interrupted.

"Oh, girl, you ain't heard nothing yet," I warned. "There's tons more." I continued, "*...he cares deeply about me. I have been telling him that it's time to come clean with you about everything, and I thought he agreed, but now I know he was telling me what he thought I wanted to hear.*"

"Um, where did you get this doggon' letter? And Simone? Who is this trick?"

Pamela kept interrupting and that made it hard to keep my place.

"Let me finish!" I stressed. "Okay. '*As it stands now, we talk and text each other every day. Mostly our messages are really sexy. We talk about the things we are going to do to each other the next time we hook up. I've saved some of them just in case you ever want to see them for yourself. Just so you won't think our relationship is all about the incredible oral and hot toe-curling sex we have, I also know tons about his life. That means we talk a lot. Like he told me how now that you've gotten older, you don't like sex the way you used to. He also said that although he loves his kids, Benson, Tempest, and Cole, he hates the way you use them as an excuse not to give him sex when he wants it. Maybe it's my youth he enjoys, but I have told him I will never deny him sex no matter how tired I am, and I think he really appreciates that!*'"

"Okay, this is way too much. Are you serious?" Pamela huffed.

"Wait, girl, let me finish! I'm almost done. Okay, she says, '*I'm not telling you any of this to hurt you, but to show you that I am a real person. Although I didn't want you to find out about us in this way, I am tired of waiting on Dax to do the right thing. He says you will try to keep him from his kids, but woman to woman, I'm hoping that you will realize we never set out to hurt you, so you should step aside because that's what he truly wants. I'm giving you my cell number in case you want to talk. I'd love to meet with you so that I can answer any questions you might have. You can check Dax's cell bill, and you will see that my number shows up frequently. Also, I want you to know that when Dax and I are married, I will love your kids like they are my own. I may only be twenty-three, but I'm far from stupid. Again, I'm reaching out to you because if the shoe was on the other foot, I would want someone to tell me. I hope you'll agree: Forcing a man to stay in a loveless marriage for fear of not seeing his kids is so not a good look.*'"

"Not a 'good look?' 'I may only be twenty-three but I'm far from stupid'? You have got to be kidding me!" Pamela screamed.

"Girl, I wish I was," I said.

"So, what are you gonna do?" Pamela asked me.

"You know a part of me is wondering who in their right mind would do something like this. I mean, I don't put anything past any man, even mine, but who writes the wife a friggin' letter?"

"Ah, obviously someone who is twenty-three and far from stupid." Pamela chuckled.

"Can you believe that?"

"Where did you get that doggon' letter?" she asked.

"Oh, that's the best part. It was sitting in the mailbox, and it had my name on it."

"No shit?"

"No shit," I said as I glanced over the letter again.

"Girl, I'd start burning his shit right now! You don't like sex since you've gotten older? And she will never deny him sex? Oh, but my favorite part has to be the fact that 'I may only be twenty-three, but I'm far from stupid.'" Pamela busted out laughing.

"It's so crazy it's nearly comical. Who does this type of foolishness?"

"Girl, what are you gonna do?" Pamela's voice sang.

"Pam, now you know good and well, if I ran to Dax every time one of these crazy broads did something stupid, I would've left him long ago," I said.

What I didn't tell Pamela was the fact that I had already told Dax I thought it was time he transitioned into a career off the field. He didn't have to leave sports, but I envisioned something far more private, away from Sunday, Monday, and Thursday night lights. I thought he'd fit right in with Keyshawn Johnson and the others on *Sunday NFL Countdown*. But Dax wasn't trying to hear it.

"Umph, so, you're telling me you're not going to do anything at all? You're not even gonna check for her number? What if it's true? What if he is screwing some chick who's ten years younger than you?"

"What do you expect me to do?" I asked.

"He would be walking in to find all of his shit shredded or piled up on the front porch or on the lawn, or at least what was left of his shit."

"Yeah? And what if I was wrong? What if she's some freak who gets off on stalking players? Trust me, if Dax is really bold enough to convince his sidepiece that they have a future together, he's got bigger problems than little Miss Far From Stupid," I said.

I could imagine the contorted frown that Pamela's pretty features had probably taken on. There was no gray area for her when it came to a situation like this.

"Umph! Well, you better than me, cause I would be working overtime to track this little *jump off* down, and then I'd take him for everything he's got," Pamela said.

I didn't want to take her back to another time, years ago, when she was in a similar situation, and I don't remember a single match being struck. Also, Pamela had a way of being able to tell everyone else exactly what they should do about their problems, but she was unable to solve any of her own. Despite this, I still loved her like the sister I never had. I simply exercised extreme patience with her shortcomings.

"Well, we know before all was said and done, you'd be in somebody's jail somewhere. But, seriously, enough of that. What's up? Are you coming or what?"

"Yeah, you know I'm coming. I'm dying to meet these women you're always talking about. A Football Widows Social Club?"

"Girl, you're gonna love Sasha and the girls! You watch her show?"

"Yeah, I do, and I have to admit, she seems kinda cool. But

what made you decide to join a social club after all this time in the league?"

"I guess I'm a little bored. The kids are getting older and they act like they need me less and less. I figured this group could be my own little something." I shrugged. "I don't know, to sort of give me a life."

The truth was, I needed to try and make connections of my own. What if Sasha could help Dax get his own talk show? I wasn't sure who the other ladies knew or what kind of connections they might have. To me, joining the club was a smart, strategic move. Once I got to know everyone better, it wouldn't be long before I'd be able to parlay my membership into something beneficial for my family.

"Umph, well, you *had* a life here in Houston," Pamela chided. "You didn't have to go buy your friends at some lame-ass social club!"

"Girl, you know I ain't never had to buy a friend. But you're right, I did have a life in Houston. And now, I've had to get one here in L.A., so make sure you have your butt on that plane next month, so there won't be a bad misunderstanding between me and you!"

"Yes, ma'am!" Pamela said. "But on the real though, I say you at least need to look into that situation. That's not something you should let slide."

"I hear you, my cousin. I hear you."

And I did hear her, but the truth was, I had other things on my mind, and a plan had been brewing long before I got wind of that letter. My mama taught me long ago, when you present an ultimatum, you've gotta be ready to deal with the consequences. I wasn't ready just yet.

ELIZA

Satisfied that there were no bugs beneath my desk, I rose to my feet, dusted off my pants at the knees and walked over to unlock my office door. My office was a comfortable size. It was practical, nothing fancy, but it was my space. Everything was neatly in order, wooden file cabinets, a matching hutch, and a large flat screen monitor as well as a TV. I had a small sofa and a wooden end table with a pastel-colored lamp that sat atop a colorful rug.

I handled the press for the Sea Lions. It was my job to assist with setting up interviews as well as make sure the players and coaches received good press. Because of my job, I had lots of connections with reporters, producers, talk show hosts, and show bookers. I was what most people called a workaholic because my job was my life.

I had been trying to get a few of the players on a local talk show that was nationally syndicated, but the show's producers hadn't called back yet.

My boss was the worst, but since I loved my job, I tried my best to ignore her. The best times at work were the ones when she was traveling or simply out of the office. Unfortunately for me, this was not one of those times.

No sooner had I sat down on my chair, than she strolled into my office. Her presence wasn't what bothered me most. It was the fact that she always felt the need to barge in on me while she was on the phone. She never knocked. She simply opened closed doors and strolled in.

Poppy McDaniel was the epitome of a hardnosed bitch. She was tall, about six feet, with a slim but muscular body. She was a serious runner, and I knew she took part in two major marathons each year. I think she might have played basketball at UCLA, but I wasn't sure. As a former athlete, she maintained a nice figure, but didn't look too masculine like some other female athletes.

However, where some people thought their shit didn't stink, Poppy didn't give it much thought. She knew for certain her shit didn't stink, and she had no problem letting anyone know. It was also hard to read her sometimes because she began most of her sentences with the same catch phrase, "Yes, absolutely."

I asked her about it one time, and she said it gave her the upper-hand because people thought she was agreeing to their suggestions even when she wasn't. It made no sense to me whatsoever, but it worked for her.

"Yes, absolutely, my assistant is working on booking Dax and Dwight." She eased her bony tail onto the edge of my desk.

I wondered how much longer I'd have to endure her latest performance.

"Shut the front door!" she yelled.

Suddenly, her head whipped in my direction. Her fair complexion began to turn colors, her big blue eyes widened more, and her thin pink lips formed a perfect "O." "You wait until I talk to Eliza about this. We were promised an exclusive. I know there's no way in hell Eliza would book them on something like that! We are not sending our players unless they deliver what they promised!" Poppy yelled.

I braced myself for the load of crap I knew was headed my way.

In a most dramatic fashion, Poppy pressed a button on the device that clung to her hip, hopped off the desk and threw her hands on to her hips. I figured if I remained calm, she'd follow suit.

"I just heard from a very reliable source that *you* were not able to book Dax and Dwight with Sasha Davenport!" Poppy yelled. "For the exclusive!" she added.

"I've made contact," I stammered.

"Yes, absolutely, you've made contact!" she said sarcastically. "What the hell does that mean? You've made contact? When are they going on? And who will they be on with? What kind of contact did you make?"

Her hair danced out of her signature little blonde page boy as she snaked her neck. I hated when white people behaved in ways they thought *we* as black people could relate to. None of my friends snaked their necks while talking, but I knew this was not the time to point that out to Poppy. Besides, she was far from a friend.

I used my index fingers and rubbed my temples. I took a deep breath and prayed everyone else was so busy with their projects that they were unable to focus on the drama going down in my office.

"Poppy, I know I can get them booked. I'm not worried about it. I, um, I was going to pitch them as an exclusive, but I need to first get the pitch together," I said.

The truth was Sasha's producer, McKenzie Fields, was probably pissed because she wanted to use one of the suites last season for a particular game, and I couldn't make it happen for her. But I wouldn't dare tell Poppy that.

Poppy screamed. It was a piercing-running-from-the-killer-in-a-horror-movie scream. I cupped my ears and sighed as two co-workers rushed to the doorway.

"Get out!" Poppy screamed at them. "Yes, absolutely, get the hell out!"

They scrambled away nearly as quickly as they had appeared.

"You'd better get in your car and drive down to that damn studio. I don't care if you have to camp out all day and all night for the next seven days. But you'd better get both Dax and Dwight booked on that show for two weeks from today or else!" Poppy screamed.

As she yelled her orders, I scuttled around the office, picking up things I might need. I accidently grabbed a small envelope when I reached for my purse. I couldn't imagine anyone who'd give her a "thank you" card, but whatever. I tossed her card back, grabbed my purse, my laptop and my iPad and hightailed it out of there.

"If you even think about coming back here without news of that confirmation, heads are going to roll!" she screamed at my back.

I felt like an ass as I scurried out of the office with my head hung low. Everyone knew Poppy was a bitch, but there was little I could do unless I wanted to risk my career. She was well-known in the industry, and this business was incredibly small.

Publicity managers in the NFL knew other publicity managers, and the league was even smaller, especially for women. I wasn't the only black woman on Poppy's team, but I was the one with the most seniority and despite what she said, I technically, was not her assistant.

Everyone pretty much hated Poppy and almost always talked about her behind her back. When she traveled or worked away from the office, we actually had great times. When she showed her face, the team's morale sank instantly.

I had no idea how I would get those guys booked, and booked, by themselves nonetheless, but I knew I had to get it done. As I waited for the attendant to bring my car, I thought about the best way to get the guys on the show. It shouldn't be that hard because Dwight and Dax were super star athletes.

It hit me suddenly, the club!

That was where I needed to go, not the studio!

SASHA

I needed to do something that would take me to the next level. Lately, it was all I thought about. I'd been doing the show for almost three years now, and it was fine, but I wanted more. I wanted my own, and I had to figure out a way to get what I wanted. Sometimes it took another person to help you see the light.

Just yesterday I walked out of the Gucci store on Rodeo Drive and a woman nearly knocked me down.

"Saaasha, that you?" she asked.

"Every day," I sang.

"Girl, I'm Maxine, and, girl, I sure do love your show!"

She was dressed in a bright fluorescent-green, oversized T-shirt and ill-fitting white leggings. Her hair was big and curly, and I wasn't sure if she was really tanned or had a mocha complexion.

She tossed a hand on her hip like she was about to read me the riot act, but instead, she said, "But me and my girls were talking the other day and all of us think you need to be on that show. You know, the *Real Housewives of Atlanta*!" She snapped her fingers, and that showed off florescent nail polish. "No, maybe that *Love and Hip Hop Atlanta*!" she screamed. "You could go on there and teach that Josieline a thing or two," she said.

"Um, really?" I crinkled my nose at her comment. "I, for one, think I'm way too classy for either of those gigs," I joked.

Maxine busted out laughing like we were old friends.

Tourists were a regular fixture on the immaculate Rodeo Drive. Many were there to gawk at the expensive cars that lined the street, window shop, or people watch. Most celebrities tried to avoid encounters with their fans, but not me. I loved mine. I knew that was why they tuned into my show the way they did. They helped to keep my ratings high, and I never forgot that.

As we posed for pictures, I couldn't take my mind off what she said. NeNe Leakes didn't have nothing on me. And now she was about to be a real bona-fide actress on a sitcom! Why shouldn't I be headlining my own show? Look at those lowlife chicks on *Basketball Wives* and those *Hollywood Exes*. The drama in my life made theirs look like middle school on a good day.

Take my social club for example. Every time you turned around, some mess popped off in there. That country bumpkin may not have had an ounce of style, but she had a point. Maxine was right, I was destined for greater things, and I needed to make something happen while my stock was still hot.

Before I got back in the car, I imagined a camera crew following behind me and capturing my every move. My show was already in syndication, but a reality show could lead to so much more; a clothing line, and who knew what else? That Snooki chick was like a household name. Even the president knew who she was.

Yes, I needed my own reality show, and I needed one fast.

Once I was behind the wheel, I was stunned to catch a glimpse in my rearview mirror. Maxine was speed walking as she took pictures of my car. Now if that wasn't some real star, celebrity-type shit I didn't know what was.

Once I got on the freeway, I dialed my agent.

"Marteen Carrington," she answered.

Marteen was a thirty-something-year-old heiress who was

hell-bent on making a career for herself. Her family owned a successful winery, but she wanted no part of the family business.

"Marteen, I've experienced an epiphany; sort of like a real spiritual flash that's bound to change my career and eventually my life," I said.

"An epiphany, huh?"

I completely ignored the sarcasm in her voice. She often took a while to see my visions, but once she got on board, she was completely committed, and I liked that about her. It just took some time to get her on board sometimes.

"Yeah, that's what I said. Anyway, I think we need to get me my own reality TV show. Once we do that, we can look into merchandising and get my clothing line and my perfume line off the ground," I said.

"Why stop at clothes and perfume? What about shoes and luggage?" Marteen said.

If she was kidding, I ignored that. I was on a mission.

"I think we should hire a production company so they can start shooting right away, and we can try to shop it. I know Bravo or VH1 would probably get into a bidding war," I said.

"Sasha, slow down. You make it sound so simple. I say if you're serious, why don't I find a few producers and set up a meeting? Let's do our homework before we jump in with both feet, fair?"

"That sounds good. Can you reach out to some people and try to set something up by the end of the week?" I asked.

Marteen was good at what she did, but I also knew if I didn't stay on top of this, it would fall to the bottom of her priority list, and I didn't want that.

"This week?"

"Yes, Marteen. I'm serious about this. The show's doing really good right now. I think my ticket is really hot. I say this is the best time to test the waters. So, if you can get a producer to meet with us by the end of the week, we can get the ball rolling."

"I can't make any promises, but I'll make some calls, and I'll let you know as soon as I find someone," she said.

"Okay, that sounds good, so let's touch bases in two days," I said.

"It may take a bit longer than that," Marteen said.

"Well, if you start making calls now, I'm sure we can get someone before the end of the week. I mean who wouldn't want to consult on the *Seriously Sasha Show*?"

"Oh, you even have a title?" Marteen chuckled a bit.

"Marteen, I'm serious about this," I told her. And I meant it. We ended the call once she promised to get on the producer meeting right away, and my mind raced with tons of new ideas. Why hadn't I thought of this before?

"Seriously Sasha!" I squealed and exited the freeway more excited than I had been in a very long time.

JERRI

I watched the woman as she scribbled something on her clipboard, and I rolled my eyes. She made me sick, and I didn't even know her that well. She wore a navy pants suit made of polyester with a pink button down shirt under her blazer. It looked like it was too small for her, and I doubted she was able to button that jacket. There was nothing feminine about her, and I couldn't stand that about her either. I knew she was only doing her job, but still.

"Have you checked in at the center yet?" Beverly Sanchez asked. She barely looked up from her notes. I wondered what she had written on that clipboard, but not enough to ask. I really wanted her gone. I had plans.

"Um, no, not yet." My eyes shifted as I reached for the nearest lie.

The truth was, I had called over there, but when they told me Sasha wasn't there, I didn't leave a message, and I hadn't called back.

"Mrs. Nelson, your participation is not optional." She cut me off before I finished my elaborate lie. "This is not to be done at your leisure." Her hazel-green eyes locked on to mine. "This is one of the conditions of your probation. If you can't hold up your end of the deal out here, we'll have to violate you and send you to jail," she said.

"You didn't let me finish." I frowned. "I talked to someone over there who said it would be okay, but I need to wait for Ms. Davenport to call me back and sign off on everything," I said.

One of her bushy eyebrows jumped above the rim of her glasses. She needed a wax job and not only on her eyebrows either.

She blew out a breath like she was exasperated. "Look, the gig is up. These people are your friends; I get that. I really don't give a rat's ass what you do over there. I'm surprised the judge approved this, but it is what it is. All I know is that if you think for one instant that I'm going to allow you any special privileges because of *who* you are or *who* you know, you're sadly mistaken," she hissed. "If Sandra didn't have stars in her eyes, you wouldn't even be on my caseload."

She tried to mumble the last part, but I heard her.

I listened to her because I had to. It was obvious to me that she was jealous of me and everything I had, so I played it cool and let her feel like she was getting it all off her chest. I could only imagine what ran through her mind when she pulled up to our eighty-three hundred-square-foot home. It sat behind a circular brick driveway on a sprawling lot.

When she walked across the gleaming-white marble floors and stopped near one of the huge white columns that stood outside the family room, I waited to see what she would do.

She glanced around and that's when I decided to help.

"It's over there; behind the staircase." I pointed in the direction of the oversized French chest.

Before she moved again, she looked toward the custom-made, wrought-iron staircase that cascaded beneath a massive chandelier. Envy seeped from her pores, and inside, I laughed wickedly. I wondered what she would've thought had she come in through the front entrance. She turned and pulled herself over to the corner where the receiver to my ankle bracelet was kept. I flipped my middle finger at her back.

"Remember the five-hundred-feet stipulation." She pressed buttons on the receiver, then jotted something down on her clipboard. "I'm not sure how the two of you function like this, but as long as you abide by the rules of your probation, I won't have to violate you." She turned back and faced me. "Looks like everything is in order here," she said.

I wanted to add, "Just like it was the last time your colleague visited," but I knew I couldn't.

"I should have confirmation from the Football Widows Social Club in a couple of days," I said.

"By close of business Monday," she corrected.

I simply nodded. If I had argued, she'd surely stay longer, and that, I couldn't have.

Later that evening, showered, and freshly changed, I had the music pumping, and the chef had laid out quite a spread. There were warm and cold hors d'oeuvres, seafood, and a variety of cocktails. I was more than ready for some company. Being stuck in the house all day every day was no joke.

"Here I come!" I yelled when the bell chimed. I snatched a jumbo shrimp and bit into it as I rushed to the door. I pulled it open and blinked at the sight before me.

Vanessa and Natasha stood on my doorstep looking fabulous.

"I knew you was here. What took you so long?" Vanessa asked with her squeaky voice. Her signature blonde locks were now a darker honey-blonde color. The designer T-shirt she wore hugged her double Ds and the matching designer jeans finished her expensive look. A size twelve had never looked better.

"I can't wait 'til this mess is over. We talking about going to Jamaica, and you can't even roll," she said.

Natasha nudged at her with an elbow. She looked just as good as Vanessa. Her shoulder-length, bone-straight hair sported its signature part down the middle of her head, and her face was flawless. Natasha wore a fitted mini-dress that made her long, golden legs look even longer.

"We brought you something back from Vegas," she sang.

Where Vanessa was the pessimist, Natasha, or Nat, was the optimist who always smiled and looked for the bright side. The three of us were thick as thieves and rarely took steps without each other. That was, of course, before I got caught up and locked down.

"C'mon in. I'm so glad to see you guys," I squealed.

And I was glad to see them. It felt like forever since they had hopped a plane to Sin City and left me behind. It wasn't because they wanted to, but my probation officer wouldn't sign off on the trip, so I was stuck at the house.

"Umph, you did all this just for us?" Vanessa asked as she stepped in and focused on the spread. "Looks like you 'bout to feed an army! I'm hungry, too," she said.

"Is *he* here?" Natasha asked, looking around the room.

"He's always here," I said, rolling my eyes dramatically, waving the thought away with a dismissive hand.

"He still ain't shit!" Vanessa said.

I was not in the mood to talk about my soon-to-be ex, Jason Nelson. I felt like he was the one behind all of my misery, not to mention my current situation. "Let's forget about *him* and enjoy ourselves," I said.

Vanessa had already plucked a wineglass from the table, filled it, and started to sip.

"You okay?" Natasha asked.

"Better, now that you guys are here," I admitted.

And I had not exaggerated. I was going mad. Regardless of how fabulous the house was, being forced to stay inside made it nothing short of a fancy prison.

"Aaww, well, we can spend the night if you need us to. I made sure Vanessa didn't make any other plans for tonight," Natasha whispered.

Natasha threw her arm around me, and we walked together toward the towering seafood centerpiece.

"How'd you get Vanessa to agree to that?" I asked.

At the tower, she grabbed a plate. She glanced at me and smiled.

"You know how Nessa can be, but I reminded her that we had partied enough in Vegas."

I giggled. I couldn't wait to hear all the juicy, dirty details.

We stacked our plates, grabbed some drinks, and made our way to the sofa where Vanessa was seated.

I looked between the two of them and smiled.

"Okay, start at the beginning, and tell me everything! I want to know what you guys did, who you did, how you did it, and I don't want you to leave a single thing out."

TATYANA

I hated to go to LAX. The airport was too damn big. The way the oversized buses pulled in and out of traffic like they were compact cars, you were never sure what or whom you might hit. I was nervous anytime I picked someone up from that airport.

If I had thought better of it, I would've ordered a car service and saved myself the stress and hassle. But, I didn't, so I had to deal with it. I pulled up in front of the United Airlines sign and slowed to a stop. Suddenly, I jumped when I heard the loud, piercing shrill of a whistle in my ear.

My head whipped to the left, and an officer blew his whistle at me again. "Keep it moving," he said as he used his arms to motion in the direction he needed me to move. I was pissed.

It was sheer chaos. Traffic closest to curbside was at a complete standstill, but other cars zoomed by on the outer street to the left, and people darted out into the streets like they were equipped with bumpers. The scene was just as busy and confusing as always at LAX.

I looked toward baggage claim one last time, then reluctantly pulled away from the curb. I didn't want the cop bursting my eardrums with his whistle. I hated to have to circle the massive airport again, but I also didn't want a ticket. After I exited the airport, I drove until I found the sign for a place to park.

I pulled into the cell phone lot, parked, and waited for Pamela to call me. As I sat there, my mind went over the newest letter I had received. I was beyond tired. I wasn't naïve enough to think this sort of thing couldn't happen if he wasn't a superstar athlete, but I couldn't help but feel like it wouldn't be so widely accepted if he switched careers. Maybe I was wrong, but that's how I felt. I still hadn't said a word to Dax, but I was eager to show everything to Pamela so we could pick it all apart and try to figure out what was really going on.

The only reason I kept the details fresh on my mind was so Pamela and I could begin to comb over everything on our ride back from the airport. She would be able to help me figure something out. When my cell phone finally vibrated, I cranked my car and headed back to baggage claim.

Traffic seemed worse than it had been less than an hour earlier. Cars were still bumper-to-bumper, and we were going nowhere fast. The massive buses continued to bogart their way in and out of the traffic jam with little regard for the other vehicles.

"Pamela, I'm trying to make my way to you. It's a zoo out here," I said into the phone.

"Girl, there's no place else like LAX," Pamela said. "I'll wait right here, under the number seven sign by United," she said.

As I eased my way forward behind other cars, I was eager to get to my friend. It had been months since we'd visited. When I finally pulled up and saw her standing next to her matching designer luggage, I threw the car into park and pulled my door open.

"Pamela!" I screamed and rushed into her wide open arms.

"Taaatttyana, it's been too long," she sang.

We hugged, jumped up and down and squealed with laughter.

"Girl, this place is crazy," I said as we broke our embrace.

"Yeah, *everybody* wants to come to L.A.," Pamela mocked.

I stood back and stared at my friend. She was still as gorgeous as ever. She was a slender but curvy five-nine. Her figure resembled something like the shape of a Coke bottle. Pamela was heavy on top, with full perky breasts, a barely there waist, and voluptuous hips that looked to be precisely the right size. She looked just as good, if not better than she did back in the day when we shook our pom-poms and everything else on the sidelines.

"Girl, you still holding it together," I said as I reached out for another hug.

"Oh, don't praise me. Praise Dr. Camille Cash in Houston," Pamela said with no shame.

Dr. Camille Cash was a talented plastic surgeon who was speed dial number 4 on Pamela's cell phone. Pamela fell back into my arms, and I caught a whiff of her hair and perfume. She smelled good and expensive. I was glad to have my girl in town.

We pulled back, and she looked at me with such love in her eyes, I wanted to break down in her arms and cry like a big ol' baby. It wasn't that I was sad, but I had a plan, and none of this crap was part of the plan.

"It's been way too doggon' long," Pamela said.

"I know, right?" I sobbed. I tried to wipe the few stray tears that escaped from my eyes.

"Tatyana, you okay? You couldn't have missed me *that* much. We only talk just about every doggon' day!" Her hands flew to her hips like she dared me to question that fact.

I chuckled and reached for her suitcase.

"I'm fine, girl. I'm fine. I'm so glad to see you, that's all," I lied.

Pamela gave me the look that told me she didn't buy my claim as she grabbed the handle to the other suitcase and marched it toward the back of my Mercedes jeep.

Once we were on Sepulveda Boulevard, I struggled to keep it all together. I never realized how much the mess with the letters had bothered me until I finally had someone to talk about it with.

"So, whaaaat's up?" Pamela sang.

"I can't say I know where to begin," I said as I focused on the road ahead.

"Well, let's see. We've talked about the letters. What we haven't discussed is when you're gonna confront the bastard!" Pamela growled. She had always been so dramatic. And Pamela always went hard when it came to a man, or at least someone else's man.

"I don't wanna play myself or my hand too soon. I need to move carefully before I strike," I said.

Pamela's oval-shaped eyes glanced at me sideways as her top lip curled upward. "This is *me* you talking to," Pamela said.

"No, seriously. You know I don't move hastily. I'm trying to see how far this trick is planning to take it," I said.

"Remember the days when being a side piece was nothing to be proud of? Nowadays these doggon' desperate women wear their position like a badge of honor." Pamela shook her head. She shrugged. "Honestly, I'm not sure what you should do. I mean, you have a life with this man. You gave him three kids. What are you supposed to do; let some little hooch come and slide into your place?" She snickered.

"Not without a fight," she concluded.

It was like she was in the discussion alone. She'd ask a question and before I could utter a word, she'd answer herself.

"Is the Cheesecake Factory okay?" I asked. "In Manhattan Beach?" I added.

Pamela turned to me and smiled. "Girl, I don't care where we go. As long as we can throw back a few drinks and catch up before we get to the house, it doesn't really matter," she said.

That's when I remembered what bothered me most about my girl. She could never make a decision. But I shook that off and decided to relish in the joy of having my girl near.

When I pulled up to the restaurant, it looked like a party was underway. People were crowded outside the front door with cocktails in hand. Music played from outdoor speakers. I started to find someplace else, but decided we'd give it a shot because of the outdoor seating. Before we made it to the front door, I noticed several groups that lingered inside near the podium.

Pamela and I made our way up to the podium where the workers were taking names.

"Hi," I said.

"How many in your party?" the young woman asked. Her mouth was filled with braces and colorful miniature rubber bands.

"Ah, two. How long's the wait?" I asked.

"Oooh, wee." She glanced down at her list.

I turned to Pamela and asked, "It seems busy. You wanna stay or go somewhere else?"

She shrugged. "It's up to you," Pamela said.

I blew out a breath and turned back to the young woman at the podium.

"Looks like it's gonna be at least an hour, maybe an hour and a half," she said.

The place was packed. Sounds of music, laughter and chatter mingled in the air.

"How about the patio?" I asked. "Or the bar," I quickly added.

"Uummm, let me see." She looked down at her list.

In my mind, I instantly started thinking of nearby restaurants.

"Actually, the wait for the patio is only fifteen minutes," she finally said.

She should've said that in the first place.

I rolled my eyes and forced a smile when she presented the square restaurant pager to me. I snatched it and followed Pamela toward the bar.

"Wanna have a drink while we wait?" I asked.

Before she could answer, I turned toward the bar. The moment we placed our orders, the square pager began to light up and vibrate like crazy. Pamela and I exchanged knowing glances.

"Uuugghhh, that was not fifteen minutes," I said.

"Oooh weee, that was kinda fast," Pamela sang.

When the bartender turned, I held up the restaurant pager and smiled.

"It's okay. I'll send it to your table." He smiled.

I mouthed a grateful thank you, then we went to see the hostesses.

Once seated outside beneath a tall heating lamp, I was glad we'd opted for the patio. It was much quieter, less crowded, and Pamela and I could actually hear each other. As the imitation palm trees swayed overhead, we eased into our cushioned seats.

"Now this is what I like most about L.A.," Pamela said.

"What's that?"

"It actually starts cooling off in the evenings out here. You know in Houston, it's probably still one-hundred degrees outside," she said.

When the drinks finally arrived, I was settled and ready to start dishing.

ELIZA

I felt like a low-life stalker as I sat behind the wheel of my car and waited. My alarm clock had gone off at five in the morning, and I was out the door by five thirty. I avoided traffic because it was early, so I had plenty of time to think about what I would say to Sasha.

By eight, I was more anxious than the day before when Poppy had all but pushed me out of my office under the threat of certain unemployment. When I saw two women walk into the storefront that housed the Football Widows Social Club, a little after ten o clock, I was relieved. I was more than a little pissed that it had taken so long for them to show up, but still I was relieved.

I pulled myself together the best I could, got out of the car, and walked over to the door. I pushed the door open and stepped inside. A chime followed by a computerized voice announced someone at the door, and a human voice called out.

"Just a moment," the voice said.

I walked around and looked at the pictures on the walls. Most were of Sasha surrounded by children. There was one of Sasha with the Sea Lions' Cheerleaders and another with her being held up sideways by players as she allowed her microphone to dangle by the cord. It was actually cute.

"May I help you?" a voice said.

I turned around and saw a petite, light-skinned black woman. She looked at me suspiciously for a moment.

"I'm Josie," she said.

"Oh, I'm Eliza Carter." I flicked a business card in her direction. "I handle publicity for the Los Angeles Sea Lions. I'm working on a project, and we thought we'd reach out to see if you ladies wanted to partner with us," I said.

Another woman eased herself around the corner.

"I'm Danielle." She smiled.

"Hi, Danielle, I'm Eliza. I was telling Josie here that I handle publicity for the Sea Lions. We're working on a project, and we thought the Football Widows Social Club might want to partner," I lied.

Danielle, a leggy brunette, who looked like she was getting ready for a yoga class, grinned extra hard.

"We love the Sea Lions around here," she said.

"We sure do," Josie added. "Most of our members are either married to players or are dating players," Josie informed me.

I wasn't sure where I was going with my lie, but I kept talking hoping the next person to walk in or pop out from somewhere would be Sasha. Nearly thirty minutes later, as the ladies and I talked about the special camp the Sea Lions would sponsor for young ladies at the center, I became impatient.

As we talked, I kept thinking it was actually unfortunate that it was a lie because the project actually sounded pretty good.

"So, we will have some of the cheerleaders come by and make sure they take part in the event," I said.

"Oh, that's a great idea. You know the players will come out for the photo shoot, but it's the cheerleaders who will really bring this home," Josie said.

Danielle got up. "I should've been taking notes long ago. You know Sasha's gonna want details." She walked around a corner.

When she returned, she had a legal pad and her iPhone in hand.

"I'm gonna call and see where Sasha is right now. I think this is great, and as you can see, we love doing activities with the kids," Danielle said.

I wasn't sure if she was being facetious or not, so I let it slide. When she dialed a number then brought the phone to her ear, I stopped talking.

"Sasha," she said. "Hey, are you coming by the office today?" Danielle asked.

Of course I couldn't hear what Sasha said, but I was hopeful.

"Oh, okay," Danielle continued. "Because there's a lady here who works for the Sea Lions and she wanted to know if we'd like to—"

When Danielle stopped talking nearly mid-sentence, my heart plunged to my toes. What if Sasha wasn't interested? What if Sasha told her to get rid of me? Sasha was all but a local celebrity, especially among sports fans. She had built a pretty solid reputation for herself in terms of her community service projects and even her talk show.

"Okay," Danielle said.

Suddenly, the call was over. I was speechless. I didn't want to ask what Sasha had said even though I desperately wanted to know.

"Sasha'll be here in like ten minutes, I think she'll love this idea. Can you wait?" she asked.

"Oh, yeah, of course. Is she the one who would ultimately decide?" I asked.

Josie shrugged. "Well, we all kinda decide what projects to do, but since Sasha is technically the founder and the president of the group, she has the final say."

"Yeah." Danielle nodded.

I had never met Sasha Davenport before. I caught her show a few times because publicity was my job, but I wasn't sure what to expect from our meeting.

When the door swung open, and she floated in, I wondered if she'd see through my BS.

"Hi, I'm Saaaasha," she sang. "Do you watch my show?" she asked.

"Actually, I do," I said.

Her smile grew even wider.

I quickly ran down my idea about the Sea Lions' sponsored event and was suddenly struck by a brilliant idea.

"You know what? I'm thinking about this right now," I said. "What if we had the two players come on your show and talk about the project! I mean, this was all their idea, so we could do something like an exclusive, where we announce the formation of the project live on your show."

Sasha cocked her head to the side, and I held my breath. If she saw through me, I'd be screwed for certain.

But when her eyes grew wide, and a frozen smile hovered on her lips, I released that trapped breath.

"Wait. Who are the players?" she asked slyly.

"Dax Becall and Dwight Sampson," I said slowly.

That smile on her face quickly spread into a massive grin, and her eyes seemed to twinkle.

"Oooh, I'd love to have Dax Becall," Sasha said dreamily. "Um, I mean on the show," she quickly corrected.

Danielle and Josie laughed at her slip of the tongue.

"His wife, um, I mean Tatyana Becall, you know, she's a member of the club," Sasha said.

"Yeah, so is Roxie, Dwight's fiancée," Josie said.

"Oh, yeah, that's right," Sasha added. Her excitement caused a wave of nervousness to wash over me. It was obvious that I now had to come up with an actual project, school the guys on it, and generate a buzz around it.

I'd make this project a success if it killed me.

SASHA

I couldn't wait to meet with Marteen and her producer friend. Ever since she called to say he agreed to the meeting, my mind had been working nonstop. I was fully prepared to hear this guy out, but I had tons of ideas of my own.

My cell rang at the end of the show.

"Hey, Marteen." I was so excited.

"You should probably take a car service. Traffic is maddening," she said.

"Okay, can you send someone over? I wanna change before I meet you guys," I said.

"Sasha, don't take forever. Sebastian is very busy, and he's meeting with us as a favor. You cannot be late," she stressed.

"Marteen, you know how excited I am about this. You know I'm gonna be on time for this meeting," I said.

"Well, I'm sending a car, but you can't keep the driver waiting, and trust me when I tell you, he will not think being fashionably late is cute!"

"Marteen, if you let me off the phone, I can be on time for sure!" I snapped.

I heard what she'd said about not being late, but I didn't want her friend to think I was some ordinary chick. He needed to understand that I *am* somebody, and if he knew how to spot real talent, he'd try to jump on my bandwagon, too.

My phone rang again, and I answered in the middle of re-doing my makeup.

"Saaasha Davenport," I said.

"Yes, your driver, Carson Rivers, at your service. I'm waiting outside the building, ma'am," he said.

"Oh, you're here already?" I asked. "Okay, I need a couple of minutes," I said.

"Uh, ma'am—"

I cut him off because I knew he was about to start fussing like Marteen.

"I'll be out in ten minutes, Carson," I said and quickly hung up the phone.

I wanted my appearance to be perfect. I dabbled with my makeup a little longer and changed my top three times. When the third selection didn't look as good, I put the first one back on. After I decided on the outfit, I looked at my reflection in the mirror. I wore a burnt-orange pencil skirt with a bright-purple strapless top.

Black shoes didn't look good, so I switched to a nude pump then decided a strappy sandal would do better. The sandal looked okay, but I really needed a higher heel.

My cell rang again. This time, I didn't answer because I knew it was either Carson, the driver, or Marteen, who would be stressed. I dug through the closet and found a pair of brown stilettos that polished the look.

Once I approved of the final image I saw in the mirror, I snatched my bag and flicked the light off on my way out.

As I walked out, the driver shot me a glance of relief.

"I tried to call you back," he said as he held the back door open for me.

"Yes, I was on a conference call on the other line and couldn't click over," I said.

The driver was a professional. He didn't bother me with useless small talk which I appreciated. I needed to get my mind right and chitchatting with him was not gonna do it. Once we had been on the road for fifteen minutes, I dialed Marteen's number.

"Sasha, I told you, you could not be late," she huffed.

I shook my head. Marteen could be such a worrywart sometimes, but she didn't realize this was my moment, and I was not about to be stressed out.

"We are stuck in traffic," I said to Marteen, "but we'll be there as soon as we can."

Marteen sounded pissed, but what could I do? I had to look the part if I expected to sell this guy or anyone else on me as a reality TV show star.

Traffic in L.A. was always maddening, and especially because I needed to be somewhere, it seemed worse.

"So, lemme get this straight," Carson, the driver, said.

I didn't understand what was so difficult.

"You want me to go in ahead of you, press this button on your iPhone, and then do what?" He looked perplexed.

When he announced we were five minutes away, I told him what I needed him to do.

"It's like me walking in to music. This is a very important meeting, and I want to make a great first impression," I said.

"But you think playing this music will help with the first impression?" he asked. His bushy eyebrows shot upward, like he was confused.

"Are you gonna do it or what? The job pays fifty dollars, if you're interested," I said.

Carson looked like he was considering my offer.

My phone began to vibrate. I didn't even bother looking at it because I knew it was only Marteen. I was really only about thirty minutes late, and that wasn't hardly my fault.

I convinced Carson that he would be passing up easy money if he left it on the table, and that's what he would've done if he decided not to help me out.

Reluctantly, Carson took the phone from me and walked toward the building's front door. He pressed the button as I instructed, and he stood at the door while sounds of Beyoncé's "Upgrade U" flooded into the air.

Finally, I sashayed into the room and wanted to dash back out when I saw the look in the eyes staring back at me. Marteen was visibly upset, and her producer friend looked like he had an attitude, too.

"Hi, I'm Saaasha," I said and smiled like I didn't see their long faces.

Marteen rolled her eyes, but I could see her producer friend softening up a bit. He wore a bright pink shirt, a necklace with a seashell, and a matching bracelet. His face was well-manicured with eyebrows that could rival any woman's.

"Sebastian, this is my client, Sasha Davenport," Marteen said.

"Sasha, you are too much," Sebastian finally said and broke into a grin.

Once he smiled, Marteen began to come around.

"I told you to be on time," she scolded playfully.

"Traffic," I said. "How you expect me to do something about that?"

Marteen gave me a sideways glance and turned her attention to her producer friend. "I'm sorry she's late. Thanks for staying," she said, like I wasn't standing right there.

"Oh, Marteen, it's not that bad. We were stuck in a little traffic, but I'm here now. Let's not make a huge thing out of this," I said.

Marteen retreated a little more.

"So, Sasha, Marteen tells me you want to talk reality TV shows," he said. "And the song was cute." Sebastian winked.

I loved it. A man who was quick on his feet and straight to the point.

"I do," I said.

"Well, honestly since Marteen called last week, I've spent some time looking you up. Your show is great. There have been a few episodes where I was like that's nice, and that will probably help somebody. But honestly in this climate when it comes to reality TV, you would need to trash it up quite a bit. In addition, you look great. You seem popular, and you know your sports. But between you and me, you're not quite reality TV material just yet."

My heart plunged. Air whooshed out of my lungs and I cringed. I was mortified.

"Not reality TV material? Are you serious?" I said.

"See, I told you. You don't really get it. You would need a completely different hook," Sebastian said.

"A different hook? What do you mean?" I sat poised as he explained himself.

"Your show—there's no drama. It's nice that you want people to know where and when to find you, but if you want to take things to the next level, then I suggest you trash it up a whole lot more, and while you're at it, find yourself a superstar husband, preferably a bad-boy."

Sebastian's voice peaked, then dropped at the appropriate times. That gave his phrases a different tone. He did one of those pregnant pauses and capped it with his perfectly arched eyebrows twisted upward.

But our eyebrows rose, too—one from Marteen and the other from me.

"'A superstar husband,' and 'trash it up'?" I twisted my face.

I didn't have a question about what he suggested, but I wanted to be clear that he thought both were needed to get what I wanted.

"Sasha, no one wants to see the perfect life on TV. Most people want to feel good about themselves, and, honey, if your life is perfect, that simply lets them know they've gotta be doing something wrong."

"How could something be wrong with them if my life is perfect?" I asked.

"Well, a perfect life on reality TV translates into a boring show and low ratings. People want to see the mess and drama because it helps them feel better about their own lives," he stressed.

The conversation wasn't going the way I had envisioned, but I didn't want him to see my defeat.

"So, I need a husband in order to get my own reality TV show," I muttered. "He's not my husband, but I do have a bad-boy friend named Tim."

"That's cute. And no, what I said was, you should find yourself a superstar husband, preferably a bad boy."

His eyes started to twinkle, and he smiled. "Remember, this is a business. People want to see how different your life is from their own. It's an escape."

"So, I need a superstar husband, and it can't be a fairytale?" I said.

He shook his head vigorously. "You're not getting what I'm saying. Sure you can do the whole fantasy, happily-ever-after thing, but people want drama. They want over-the-top, crazy, mad drama. They want it even when they don't realize it's what they want. They crave it. The more of that you give them, the more they'll tune in."

"I'm not sure about this," Marteen said.

I had expected her to speak up a long time ago. The minute he started going on about the drama and the whole bad-boy thing, I knew what she thought before she even uttered a word.

"I mean, why can't she simply find someone and they date and marry with the whole world watching? I don't get why that can't be enough," Marteen stated.

Sebastian gave Marteen a poor-child look that nearly made me chuckle aloud. He sighed dramatically, then said, "Think reality shows. Now think of the ones that do really well. You know how you can think of those—because your mind goes to the drama and the foolishness. You won't think 'Oh, that evening they spent around the TV or at Bible study.' That isn't what's going to stay with you. The drink splashed in someone's face, the mistress crying because she's pregnant, the tumbling on the floor—that's great TV, and that's what has people talking around the water cooler the next morning," Sebastian said.

He turned his attention back to me.

"The choice is yours. Keep doing what you're doing, with Tim, which is fine, or position yourself to move to the next level. It's that simple." He shrugged.

As far as I was concerned, Sebastian had just given me my new marching orders, and he wouldn't have to tell me twice.

JERRI

The loud, booming noise at the door jolted us all into a sudden silence and made us focus on the door. I was more startled than I realized. My heart began to race.

"What the hell?" Vanessa asked.

Natasha put her wineglass down, and I sprang from my seat.

I was confused, but I turned the music down and rushed to the door. As my heartbeat thumped loudly in my ear, I wondered what in the world could be wrong.

"Open up! LAPD," a voice barked, after another thunderous knock on the door.

My eyes widened, and I frowned at the thought. What the hell were the cops doing at the door? Had something happened up front? We hadn't heard a thing!

When I pulled the door open, two uniformed officers stood with frustrated expressions on their faces. Little did they know, I wanted to see them far less than they had wanted to see me.

"Mrs. Jerri Nelson?" one officer asked.

"Ah, yes. Is there a problem, Officer?" I asked. I wasn't as nervous as much as I was confused.

"We received a call from your, er, er, husband—" The officer had an awkward expression on his face.

"Estranged husband!" I corrected as I cut him off.

"Okay, *estranged* husband. But Mr. Nelson says the noise is too much," the officer said and shrugged.

Shock numbed me from head to toe. I felt my pulse escalate. I was livid. I went from zero to sixty in one second flat. My hands flew to my hips, and my face contorted into a frown.

"He called the damn cops saying the *noise* is too much?!" I screamed.

The other officer motioned with his hands as if he could bat away my anger and my words with the mere motion of his hands.

"Ma'am, we are simply doing our job. He says it's too loud. We need you to keep it down," the cop said. "There's not a major issue here," he added.

Now I understood the expressions they'd greeted me with. What kind of cockamamie bull was Jason Nelson trying to pull now? By now, Vanessa and Natasha had rushed to my side.

"No, he didn't," Vanessa snarled.

"That punk!" I snapped.

One of the officers rolled his eyes and exhaled. The two of them looked familiar, because they'd been by before, and neither looked like they wanted to be at the door having this conversation.

"Ma'am, please calm down. Mr. Nelson has every right to relax in peace and quiet. We understand that these arrangements and the circumstances surrounding them are unique and could be stressful to you both, but we don't want any problems here. If you turn the music down, and you ladies promise to keep the noise at an acceptable level, I think we can all get along fine this evening," he said.

"So, he gets to call the friggin' cops on me, and I'm supposed to what, sit here, smile, and say it's okay?" I rushed back inside. "Oh, but no, this shit ain't going down like this. I'm about to go over there and give him a piece of my mind right now," I said as I struggled to step into my shoes.

"Ma'am. Please. Let's remember the restraining order. We

intend to fully enforce it if we have to. Now Mr. Nelson is asking that the noise be kept down. You two share this property, so I suggest you simply adhere to his request and we can all enjoy an uneventful night."

Natasha came and stood next to me.

"It's not worth it, Jerri. It's no biggie. We're good. Let's enjoy our evening. All he's doing is trying to get under your skin. He wants you to go off. Don't trip," she said.

I knew I couldn't afford another infraction. The last thing I needed was my probation officer Beverly riding my ass over another arrest. I wondered if the officers would have to report this call.

Anger rippled up my spine. I turned away and took a deep breath. I tried to pull myself together. I knew Natasha was right, and I knew the officer was right, too, but I felt like that was a shitty move on Jason's part.

I sulked back to the front door, sucked up my anger, and told the officer what he wanted to hear.

"Okay, Officer. We'll turn the music down, and we'll make sure to keep it quiet."

He did an awkward smile and nodded slightly.

"That's what's best," he said. His eyes wandered around behind us, and I was glad when he tipped his hat, turned and left.

"Can you believe that shit?!" I screamed the moment I closed the door.

"What a loser," Vanessa said.

"He's just pissed that we're over here having a good time. It's like he wants you to suffer at all times. What's it to him if we are a little loud. This mansion is so massive, I can't believe he even heard us," Natasha added.

My mood had changed to sour, and I couldn't imagine how I'd recover. I was pissed, embarrassed, and downright livid. Thoughts of the officers talking about me and our living arrangement only added fuel to an already-blistering fire.

I had no idea why he couldn't leave well enough alone. I didn't want to be sharing a house with him no more than he wanted to share one with me, but the longer this divorce dragged on, the longer he and I would have to remain reluctant roommates.

Pre-nup my ass! If he thought he was gonna get rid of me without paying, he'd soon find out how wrong he was. I had given him some of the best years of my life, and that was worth far more than he wanted to give. But I wasn't really worried. I knew my time would come. Jason would pay dearly if it was the last thing he did.

For as long as he ran with that ball, I'd make certain I got a cut of his earnings. And the more he and his wicked lawyer tried to give us the runaround, the longer this thing would take.

I turned the music back up, refilled our drinks, and the party was on again.

It was more than a struggle though. Each time Vanessa talked about being on the dance floor, I wanted to kick the wall, but I knew that wouldn't do anything but hurt my foot. Besides, I knew I didn't need any more trouble. I had enough, considering I still hadn't gotten into the Football Widows Social Club. The last thing I needed was my probation officer breathing down my neck for something else.

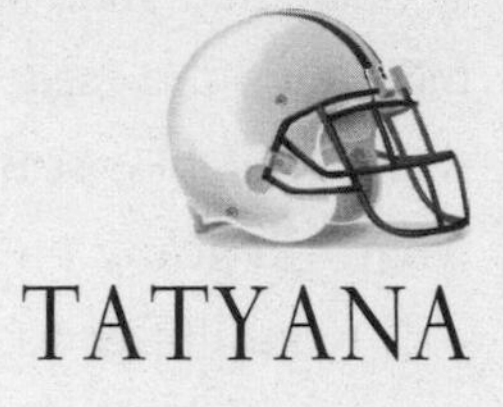

TATYANA

A blank stare best described the expression on Pamela's face. As she contemplated whatever had her bewildered, I took that moment to savor the last of my crispy crab bites. Several beats passed, and she still hadn't spoken. I gave her a look that said the floor was hers, but still she sat silent, so I sipped my lemon drop martini and waited.

"So, you're saying you've been getting letters from some hooch for nearly six months, and not once did you think to confront your husband?" Pamela asked.

"You remember when you was with Logan?" I asked sweetly.

Because I knew her so well, I didn't miss it when her left eye twitched slightly. She crinkled her nose and sniffled as if her allergies had surfaced.

It was a harsh and painful memory, but I had to drive this home for her. Back when we were NFL cheerleaders, Pamela fell hard for a superstar running back. It didn't take long for him to get into her too and soon it became exclusive. Well, they were hot and heavy for a while before it became obvious that they weren't as exclusive as she thought.

It wasn't the fact that he was running around, but the fact that there was this one chick in particular who insisted on taking Logan away from Pamela. Back then, the chick would sell pictures to gossip sites and celebrity papers.

When those pictures popped up, Pamela would suddenly behave as if she had glaucoma. That was years before Facebook; it might have been the early days of MySpace. Although the pictures never went viral like scandals do today, everyone in our circle knew what was going on.

"I would offer to meet with her. I mean, she's offering to show you proof, isn't she?" Pamela finally said.

She ignored my comment about Logan, and I understood her reason for doing so, but she still didn't get it.

"Pamela, hear what I'm saying. I'm not dumb enough to think my very popular, handsome, rich husband is faithful. I've heard about those road trips—a chick in each city, the crafty women who find their way into hotel beds—but why confront him if I'm not ready to pull the trigger?" I asked.

"So, you allow him to live a double life at the expense of you and the kids?" she asked.

The kids were actually headed to Houston. The moment summer hit, they were sent off to my mother, and that gave me much-needed alone time. The time was supposed to be for Dax and me to relive our single days. And by single, I meant before children. But because of his off-season commitments, endorsements and youth camps, sometimes the off season felt as busy or crazy as the season itself. I never complained because I understood the lifestyle, and it was one I had accepted long ago.

I stopped talking when a new waitress came to our table.

"Kali went on her break, so I'm checking up on you two for her," she said. "Are you ladies doing okay?" she asked. She was a frail, thin, model type with bushels of red, curly hair.

"We're good." I smiled. I looked at Pamela, "You want another drink?"

Pamela's eyes darted to her empty glass. She wrinkled her nose. "Ahhhh, not sure." She shrugged.

"You can bring us another round," I said.

The waitress rushed away, and Pamela and I resumed our conversation.

"So, how long are you gonna allow this to go on?" she asked.

"First off, we don't know for sure that *anything* is going on. But what I do know is I'm not about to jump the gun. If it turns out that this is some overzealous fan or someone who would like to take my place, what kind of fool would I look like jumping every time someone claims they're sleeping with Dax?"

"So, you're just gonna turn a blind eye?"

She could be relentless. Some of the very things I loved about Pamela were the same ones I hated. But just like sisters and cousins, we might have had our moments, but we always found our way back to each other.

After we finished up at the Cheesecake Factory, Pamela and I headed to the house.

"Will he be around much?" she asked.

"Nah, you know he has tons to do with the onset of summer. Once we see the kids off, I figure we can go spend a few days in Vegas—do some shopping, and of course hit up a couple of spas."

"That all sounds perfect." Pamela beamed. She turned and looked out of the window. "I've always liked the Echo Park part of this city," she said. "I don't know—all of the trees, hills and greenery makes me feel so refreshed."

"It's nice," I said, as I turned the car toward my neighborhood.

"You guys ever thought about hiring security?" she asked.

"It's really quiet up here. For the most part, only the residents venture this far. There's an occasional tour bus here and there, but otherwise, it's really quiet and mostly secluded."

"Umph," said Pamela.

"What?" I didn't mean to sound as irritated as the question came out.

"I don't get it," she began.

"What is it that you don't get?"

"If it's so secluded up here, then how is it that this girl is able to leave these letters for you? If you had security, you'd have a description of her and we'd have a better chance of tracking her dumb butt down."

"Really, Pamela?" I questioned.

Her expression was a frown when she turned to look at me. "I'm serious, Tatyana. I'm worried about you. I think you need to take this far more seriously than you're doing right now. You don't want to be blindsided by this kind of thing. Believe me, when this kind of scandal makes the headlines, you need to have a contingency plan in place. I mean, what if he and this chick are planning to run off together? You don't want to be the last to know," she stressed.

"Blindsided? Scandal in the headlines? Contingency plan, and them running off together?" I asked. I shook my head as I turned down the curvy, tree-lined street that led to our sprawling estate. "Pamela, it's too damn much! I think you are taking this way too far," I said.

Pamela turned away again. But this time, she shook her head as if it was all she could do to throw some pity my way.

That's when it became incredibly obvious that mystery chick was not the only one who underestimated me. So did the one female I was closest to in this world.

ELIZA

I hated Monday mornings. They were hellish for everyone in the Sea Lions' public relations office. I was never the first one present, but I prided myself on being at least forty-five minutes early every day. Not only did I need to get my projects lined up for the meeting with Poppy, but I needed to get my mind right to deal with her.

As I walked into the spacious section of the building that housed our offices, I savored the light and friendly atmosphere.

"Elisa, top of the morning to ya!" Bill, an older white guy, greeted me enthusiastically.

I heard the light chatter and laughter from the moment I stepped off the elevator. The way it floated in the air told me no one had seen or heard from Poppy. When Poppy was absent, everyone worked with a different sense of ease and determination.

"Hi, Bill," I said as I rounded his cubicle and made my way to my office door.

"Mary, how was your weekend?" I asked.

Mary Rodriquez was the administrative assistant for our section. She was in her early twenties, but let Poppy tell it, she had a questionable reputation with the players. Regardless, I liked her. She had this weird obsession with Hard Rock Café, but I didn't have lunch with her often, so no biggie to me.

"It was good," she said. Her accent was thick, but in the three years she'd been with us, we'd learned to understand her. Well, most of us had. One of the reasons Poppy tried to treat me like I was *her* own personal assistant was because she never had the patience to deal with Mary.

"She's such a slut!" Poppy said. "When I was twenty-three, I wasn't loose like that!"

"She's young—having fun," I said.

Poppy looked at me like I was a retard.

"If you call bed-hopping or shuffling around the locker room on your knees fun, I guess." Poppy shrugged.

Outside of Mary's personal life, I thought she was cool.

Mary lowered her voice and changed her expression. "When is *she* coming in today?" she asked.

"Not until noon," I said.

Like a Jack-in-the-Box, Mary popped up from her seat and announced in her thick accent, "She Devil alert: Noon!"

A thunderous applause filled the room, followed by cheers.

I laughed as I walked into my office and unloaded my folders and files. Someone even turned up the radio station a little.

So far, I had made contact with Sasha Davenport. I arranged a meeting with the two players, and she insisted on being present. I found that kind of odd, but figured maybe that was how she prepared for her shows.

After I checked up on a few Sea Lions-sponsored events, I looked up when someone knocked softly on my open door.

"Excuse me a moment, Eliza," Bill said.

"Hey, what's up?"

"I wanted to see if you had a moment to go over the press release about Craig Shepherd," he said.

I smacked my forehead.

"Yeah, I'm sorry. I've been so focused on this thing with Dax and Dwight, I forgot all about Craig. Sure, you wanna send it to me, and I'll get it right back to you?"

"Sounds great. I want to have all of my projects done before the meeting at one," Bill said. "I'll email it right over." He turned and went back to his cubicle.

A few minutes later, a ding on my computer alerted me to the email he sent. I opened the document and glanced at it. There were a few typos. I corrected the kicker's wife's name, and I reworded Bill's first and second paragraphs. I also used track changes to suggest he add the logo for Craig's foundation on the release; then I sent it back to him.

Only a couple of my files were up for show in the meeting, but I liked to keep my mind fresh on them all because Poppy was known to try and throw a curve ball.

SASHA

I looked around the room at the members of the Football Widows Social Club. My mind raced with possibilities, but my thoughts had nothing to do with our next project, or even topics on the agenda.

How would I be able to find a superstar husband when all of those were already taken?

Most of the stars came into the league with baggage from college. Those coeds started working on the studs early on. The minute the big man on campus broke out, they'd begin to plot. I couldn't blame them, but that made it near impossible for the rest of us. I had been doing my homework since the meeting with Sebastian and Marteen. I knew who my man was. I knew exactly how I'd get him, but there wasn't any easy path to accomplishing this goal.

"Sasha?" someone called out to me.

I shook my husband-search thoughts from my mind and tried to focus on the meeting. I looked at the woman who called me.

"Yeah, what's up?"

"I was asking whether we were gonna take part in the canned food drive?" Stacy Brooks asked.

She was the club's secretary and married to one of the running backs on the team. At that moment a crucial piece of the puzzle to my dilemma strolled in late and slipped into a chair near the back of the room. Tatyana had a woman with her whom I had never seen before. I wasn't sure why I hadn't thought about this before. But now that Sebastian's words were in my head, it made total and complete sense.

I knew her husband would be perfect. He was gorgeous, rich and had a body that was out of control.

"Oh, yeah. We can do that," I said.

I stopped talking and focused on Tatyana. Once she had settled into her chair, I stared until she locked eyes with me. When she mouthed the word "sorry," I answered Stacy's question.

The rest of the meeting moved quickly. Sherry Watson, the treasurer, announced the names of members who were in violation for missing our last function and how much each owed.

All kinds of thoughts overflowed my mind. Suddenly, I couldn't wait for the meeting to wrap up so I could call Marteen. But just as quickly, a thought overpowered me, and I came to my senses. This was not the kind of thing Marteen would sign on for. I needed to proceed with caution. There were only a couple of people I could share this plan with, and Marteen was not one of them. The wheels were already in motion, but I had to steer carefully. And the last thing I needed was naysayers on board.

By the end of the meeting, I was so focused on all I needed to do that I nearly slipped into my office without talking to Tatyana and her friend.

"Sasha, this is my good friend Pamela. She's visiting from Houston for a couple of weeks. Hope you don't mind that I brought her along," Tatyana said.

I flashed a quick, fake smile to her.

"I really like your show," Pamela said.

As if she'd say she hated it.

"Most people do," I said.

Pamela's eyebrows jumped, but I didn't care. My response must've affected Tatyana more because her eyebrows curled into a frown and she stepped closer to me.

"Sasha, is everything okay?" she asked in a failed attempt at a whisper.

"You know it's against the rules to bring strangers to our meetings, especially while we're discussing club business," I said.

Tatyana's features looked like she'd break down in tears any moment. The color drained from her cheeks. I knew she was weak. This would be easier than I thought! I smiled to myself.

"Uh, I guess I wasn't thinking. It didn't dawn on me to call and ask somebody," Tatyana stammered.

"It's not me really, but the others. There have been so many times when they wanted to bring someone and because of our rules and bylaws, it's not permitted," I said.

When I recruited her, I made note of her husband's status. As the star quarterback for the Sea Lions, he was as high profile as one could get. I thought she'd be cool to have around. But once Sebastian laid the plan out for me, she became far more valuable than I'd ever imagined. Each time I looked at her, it was to size her up. Her weakness confirmed for me that she had seen her best days and needed to take a backseat.

As I talked to her, I noticed her Bama-looking friend as she watched us. I didn't understand why these women didn't see the need for looking their best when they stepped out. Tatyana and her friend were pretty, but they were both plain. Nothing was worse to me than a woman who didn't know how to work her assets.

Mentally, I reminded myself that her slipping would be my come-up.

She could turn into a fat, sloppy pig right before my eyes, and it would do nothing but make my job that much easier.

"Wow, I guess I wasn't thinking," she grumbled under her breath.

Before she could bore me with more meaningless words, I pivoted, edged past her and her friend and sashayed away.

JERRI

Saturday mornings were never the same when my kids were gone. But that was the beauty of camp. Jason and I had shipped them off for eight glorious weeks, and although being free of kids was a great feeling, I had to admit, it made my situation even lonelier.

I had a few text messages from my Ed who had made the team in Baltimore, but there was nothing thrilling about that, so I ignored him and his lewd messages. I got up and looked at the schedule posted on the corkboard that sat atop my dresser.

"Damn, it's just eight-thirty!" I hissed.

Since it wasn't after nine in the morning, I had to call for access to the kitchen or wait until Jason was done before I could go in. Saturdays belonged to Jason and Sundays were mine.

At times the arrangement made me sick, but I was determined to stay the course. He and his lawyer were probably banking on me giving up.

We were already in a difficult situation before Jason filed for divorce, but the fact that we couldn't reach an agreement made this nearly unbearable. I said *nearly* because I was not about to leave my dream house, and apparently, he felt the same way.

I contemplated going back to bed, but decided to shower and wash my hair instead. Although he was supposed to be out of the kitchen by nine, if he thought it would irk me, he'd hang around just so I wouldn't be able to go in there.

If anyone had told me five years ago that I'd wind up trapped in a bitter divorce and sharing a house with my estranged husband, I'd swear they didn't know Jason or me. We were the couple that was gonna make it. We had met on the campus of San Jose State University and fell in love instantly.

I was a freshman, and he was a sophomore at the time. Jason Nelson was a star running back who could do no wrong off the field because of his skills on the field.

We married right after he was drafted into the NFL during the second round. I was already pregnant by then. Immediately after the birth of our daughter, we thought it would be cute to have another baby right away, so we did.

If there was a poster girl for the young, dumb and naïve, it would've been me. I believed every word that came out of Jason's mouth. If rumors swirled about him and another woman, he'd simply explain it away, and I took his explanation as the gospel. I desperately wanted our marriage to work.

Memories of one of the women bold enough to challenge me were as fresh as if they'd happened a few seconds ago. One in particular had remained with me for years. I could feel my pulse increase as I ventured back in time.

"Mrs. Nelson, the kids are down, is there anything else you'd like before I retire for the evening?" Gina, our live-in nanny, asked. She was an older Guatemalan woman we had hired through an agency, and she was great with the kids.

"No, Gina, I'm good. Thanks for asking," I said.

After Gina walked out of the room, I glanced at the clock and wondered what was taking Jason so long to call that night. It was as if I had summoned him with my thoughts. The phone rang the minute I looked away from the clock.

"You're gonna live a very long time," I said as I answered the phone.

I didn't get to travel much with him because it seemed like I was pregnant for most of our marriage. We were still newlyweds, and I knew it would begin to take its toll on our relationship, but what could I do?

"How my babies doing?" Jason asked.

"We're missing you."

"We'll be back by noon tomorrow," he said.

"So what are you guys doing tonight?"

Back then Jason played for the Falcons, and they were at an away game in San Diego. The kids and I were home in Atlanta with the nanny.

"A bunch of the guys are going to some party at a club, but I'm beat. I'm about to soak in the tub and lay it down for the night," he said.

That sounded odd to me, but I didn't want to come across as insecure. The last thing I wanted was for him to worry about whether I was worried while he was on the road.

"It's kinda early, huh?" I asked.

"Yeah, but you know after the beating we took, my body is still trapped on East Coast time, so I'ma let them have it tonight," he said.

It wasn't that I didn't trust him, but I knew he could be a little too friendly with other females at times. I glanced at the clock again. It was midnight, which meant it was only nine out there. I couldn't wrap my mind around him being in for the night that early. And if he really was, who was he keeping company with?

"Well, I'm about to go to bed myself," I said. "I was waiting up for your call."

When Jason yawned, something made me want to keep him on the phone even longer. I felt like the yawn was nothing but him being completely "extraed" out. He was doing entirely too much.

"Well, 'night, babe," he said. He even sounded groggy. It all came off as an act. But I was nearly three-thousand miles away, so I resolved that there was nothing I could do about the uneasiness I felt.

After we got off the phone, I changed from my bathrobe into nice pajamas. I gave myself a facial and brushed through my hair. I listened to some soothing music and told myself that since more than an hour had passed, perhaps there was no shoe dropping.

I finally lowered the music and turned off the lights to go to bed. My mind fluttered with all kinds of thoughts about what and *who* Jason might've been doing.

When I squeezed my eyes tightly shut, I felt another woman in his presence. I was lightly sleeping, but still I was so angry that I felt my fists clenching.

Sleep never came easy for me when Jason was on the road. But this uneasiness was different than anything I'd felt before. My shoulders were tied into knots, and the queasiness would not leave the pit of my belly. At first, I couldn't tell if the buzzing was happening in my dream, but when it wouldn't go away, I got up and reached for my phone.

Who was calling at 4:45 in the morning?

I grabbed the phone and rubbed my eyes with the back of my hand. My eyes focused on the images on my phone. The text messages that accompanied them left me mortified.

He may be yours in name but as you can see he's mine too

That message was under a picture of Jason's thick, slippery dick as it lay lifeless on his thigh. I didn't know if the cum at the tip was pre-cum or leftovers.

In the next picture, her little pink tongue sat at the tip of it. I wanted to cry.

And if that wasn't enough, another picture captured her fingers sprawled across his pubic area like she was grabbing at his balls.

I was beyond livid. I dialed his number, but there was no answer. I sat there in the dark, furious. But what could I do? He couldn't lie and say it wasn't him because I knew his crotch better than I knew my own! Whoever she was, she wouldn't answer his phone, but the second I stopped calling, she began her slide-show again.

The next picture I got was her legs intertwined with his. His dark-chocolate limbs locked with her mocha-colored flesh burned me like a searing brand. When she showed a picture of his lips near her nipple, it was obvious he was asleep. But how could he take up with some jump off, fall asleep, and leave her up in the room like that?

She could've robbed him, or worse, she could've done what she had already done—robbed me, and showed me just how easy it was to take my man.

"Bitch!"

The pictures continued and I was sick to my stomach.

Her next message read:

I'm gonna send him home with my essence on his lips in case you want a taste too

I wanted to kill the bitch. But the truth was I couldn't do a damn thing. She had my man, my husband, right where she wanted him—naked and vulnerable. I felt like shit, and all I could do was sit and pout.

The knock on my bedroom door brought me back to the present.

"Yes?" I called out.

"Mrs. Nelson, will you be having breakfast today?" the housekeeper asked.

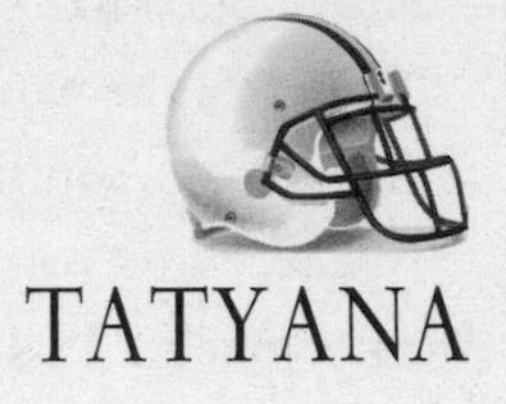

TATYANA

"There's something about her that I don't like," Pamela said.

We walked into the house and the kids came running.

"Auntie Pam! Auntie Pam," Brendon, my five-year-old son, the eternal flirt, squealed.

My other son, eight-year-old Junior, was away at a martial arts camp. My daughter, Bella, the seven-year-old, was glued to her iPod Touch. She barely looked up to mumble hello.

"Grandma called; said she had some questions about our flight," Bella said. Again, her eyes never left the game she was playing on her iPod.

I became irritated. I walked over and snatched the device from her hand.

"Moooom!" she cried.

"Now, hello to you, too," I said. One hand was planted firmly on my hip, and the other held her beloved iPod.

"Hi, Mom." She looked in Pamela's direction. "Hi, Auntie Pam." She pouted.

"You were attempting to give me a message from your grandmother about your trip?" I said.

"Oh, yeah, she um… she said she needs you to call her about our flight information."

"Okay. Now that's better. Did she say anything else?"

"Umm, nu-uh. All she asked was where you was, and I said at a club meeting," she said.

"She asked where you *were*, not *was*," I corrected.

She nodded like she understood.

"Where's the nanny?" I asked.

"I think she's in the laundry room."

"Okay. Now you go find something more constructive to do with yourself," I said.

Her little eyes wandered over to the iPod, and mentally I dared her to ask. She must've known better because she turned and sulked in the direction of her room.

"She's adorable," Pamela said once the kids left us alone.

"Kids are more than a handful these days—that's what she is," I said. "And those brothers of hers!"

"Well, imagine if you had to raise them all by yourself." She frowned.

I thought that was an odd comment, but I told myself to let it ride. I was more interested in what she was saying about Sasha after the meeting.

"I know it's possible, but I guess that's why you plan to let Dax keep doing what he's doing," Pamela added.

That I couldn't ignore. I took a deep breath, then I smiled and said, "Pamela, I have a nanny and a housekeeper. Regardless of whether Dax or any of the help was here, I'd be okay raising my children," I said.

"That makes this even more baffling then," she said. The expression on her face was one of deep confusion.

I knew I should've let that go, but I couldn't.

"What is so baffling?"

By now, we had moved into the family room.

"Why would you allow him to carry on like this if you know you and your kids will be taken care of regardless of whether or not he stays?"

"Pamela," I hissed, "I've told you before; we don't know for sure that Dax is even doing anything. There's no way I'm gonna carry some mess to my husband when I have no evidence that he's even doing anything!"

She was beginning to work my very last nerve with this because it was painfully clear she was not going to let it go.

"Yeah, but I have a problem with the fact that you won't even step to him with any of this. You could be the biggest fool running around this city and not even realize it," she said.

I whipped my head in her direction.

"You mean like you were back in the day?"

Before she could respond, the front door opened and in walked Dax. Dax was every bit the athletic quarterback. He was six-five, two-hundred-forty solid pounds of muscles from head to toe. He had a square jawline with dark features that seemed to pop against his caramel complexion.

Where most men sported a bald style, he kept his jet-black hair in a short, but neatly lined Afro. And to say his smile was perfect would be a gross understatement. Dax took excellent care of himself because he understood that his body and his appearance were valuable commodities. He immediately stopped as he passed the family room.

"Hey, baby." He walked over to me and lowered himself to kiss my lips. "Pam, s'up?" he asked.

His kiss left a minty aftertaste when he pulled away.

Pamela's eyebrows rose on her forehead, and she eyed him up and down before she spoke. The silence before her delayed response made me feel uncomfortable, and I wondered whether Dax would pick up on it.

"What's up with you, Dax?" she asked.

"Ah, you know the drill—navigating the projects for the summer, trying to get it all together for preseason—same ol' same ol'," he said. He didn't skip a beat. Either he missed the delay or he simply didn't give a damn.

I watched the way Pamela looked at my husband and wondered why he couldn't tell she had an attitude. Men were so simple at times. It amazed me how he could memorize all those damn plays, pick up on another player's gesture before he made a move, but couldn't decipher another female's body language.

As Dax rambled on and on about his busy schedule and upcoming agenda, I wanted to scream and tell him she really could care less. But instead, I sat back and watched the scene play out in silence.

"Umph, sounds like you got quite a bit going on," Pamela said.

"Yeah, it is what it is," he said.

"Is it now?" Pamela responded.

I noticed a flicker in his eyes, and he tilted his head slightly. But he smiled and turned his focus back to me.

"Where the kids?" he asked.

"Ah, Bella is in her room, and Brendon is either there with her or in his room," I said.

"Cool. What's up for tonight? Y'all doing some girly stuff?" he asked.

I caught a glimpse of Pamela from the corner of my eye. She had a sour expression on her face, and for the first time since she'd arrived, I wondered whether having her here was a good idea.

"We didn't have any girly things planned. Why? You wanna do something?" I asked.

"Nah, some of the fellas were talking about going out—just trying to decide whether I'm gonna go or hang close to the house, that's all," he said.

"Hmm, you can go if you want. I'm sure Pamela and I can find some trouble to get into tonight," I joked.

Dax gave Pamela a sideways glance and she smirked in his direction.

"Well, let me leave you two alone so you can finish the man-bashing conversation I'm sure y'all were having," he said, then chuckled.

"Man-bashing? Why in the world would we ever?" I feigned, insulted.

"Oh, don't even try to act like I don't know what's up when y'all get together and are alone," he said. He looked at Pamela. "You see your girl over there ain't even tryin' to deny it," he said.

When Pamela rolled her eyes, I was disgusted. It was obvious Dax was in a playful mood, and she stood there completely stone-faced like he had personally offended her.

ELIZA

Meetings with Poppy were so incredibly unproductive. It was as if she needed to spend her time in the office letting the team know she was still the boss. At times, I was certain she simply didn't want to be alone in her office.

"Yes, absolutely. That's the dumbest thing I've ever heard. You need to go back to the drawing board on that one," Poppy said after the first presentation.

My eyes grew wide in horror.

"I'm bored to tears." She yawned and reached for her iPad.

She made me sick.

Hours later, the silence in the room was incredible. You could've heard people blinking as we all held our breaths and waited for Poppy to say something. One by one, each member of the team had stood and given a presentation on pending projects and updates on their files.

It wasn't hard to tell what Poppy thought. At times, her expression indicated severe boredom and sheer disinterest. She'd frown during an explanation and completely throw the presenter for a loop. When she sighed hard and loud, I felt sorry for the person who spoke at the time.

If that outright rudeness and lack of professionalism wasn't enough, we had to stop and wait for Poppy to turn her attention back to us yet again.

She had already taken two calls in the middle of the meeting and basically left us all hanging until she was done arguing with her dry cleaner, her hair stylist, and a popular watchmaker. It was rare to overhear a conversation with her that didn't involve an argument, a disagreement or Poppy being rude.

"Yes, absolutely. I'm serious! You tell him I said we will pull our player and go to Rolex if the shit isn't fixed!" Poppy screamed into her headset.

I tried to calm myself because I knew ultimately I had done my job, and all my files were in order. But I also knew Poppy could find something wrong with perfection. It was simply her nature. Nothing ever satisfied her unless it was something she suggested.

Once she finished that phone call, she turned her focus back to our meeting, but things didn't get any better.

"I don't understand why these meetings drag on for so long. We've been at this for three hours now, and very little, if anything, has impressed me. Perhaps I need a new team!" She stood and gathered her things.

I couldn't believe she was already wrapping up. No decisions had been announced, and Poppy knew we couldn't move forward until she signed off. All eyes remained glued to her. Poppy's slender body towered over most on the team. And I suspected that she used that to her advantage to bully the rest of us. Once she had collected her things, she turned toward the door.

I was perplexed. I couldn't believe she was about to leave.

"Ah, Poppy, there are several press releases that need to go out today. We've got requests for the defensive and offensive coaches to appear on sports radio in the morning, so we kinda need some guidance here," I said.

Poppy stopped and turned back to me in a dramatic fashion.

The look on her face said, "How dare you?" But we had worked hard to make our deadlines. Not that it mattered to her, but it was really the team that kept the office and the players visible in the media. Poppy simply took all of the credit.

"What the hell do I have you for if you can't handle these menial tasks? Yes, absolutely! You took the thought right out of my head! I may as well have a clone because you guys act like you can't get a damn thing done without me!"

I wanted to point out to her quite the contrary. We got most of our tasks done without her. She spent such little time in the office, but because she insisted on being an anal micromanager, she often slowed our progress.

"So, you want me to green-light everything that's due today?"

"What do you mean 'everything'? You act like we haven't been locked in this conference room for nearly four hours!" Poppy exclaimed.

I wanted desperately to point out to her that a great deal of the meeting was spent with her on the phone or shooting down everyone's idea, but I didn't. What stunned me most was the fact that she continued toward the door as if her work was done.

"Poppy," I called out again.

This time when she stopped, she looked at me and rolled her eyes. At that point, the rest of the team looked back and forth between us.

"Take some initiative. I have a hair appointment, and I won't be back until after seven this evening," she said.

"But—"

"Maybe by then you guys can get your crap together, and I'll be in the mood to green-light some of this stuff."

Before I could ask another question, Poppy had pulled the door open and stepped out of the room.

Baffled eyes stared back at me once she was gone.

"What about the sports radio appearances?" someone asked.

"And those press releases," Bill whined. "They shouldn't wait until tomorrow."

"I can't believe her. So, she expects us to work late—to wait for a nod from her? What's the point of having these meetings? She's not gonna do her damn job?" Mary commented. "*Besa mi culo, puto!*" *She can kiss my fucking ass.*

I sighed. I knew she had cursed Poppy, but wasn't going to comment on what she had said.

"Okay. Here's what we're gonna do. Let's send an intern to the radio station with the coaches. Make sure he takes a digital recorder because I don't want any surprises. Someone should also brief them on acceptable topics to discuss and those to avoid. Also, Bill, I've already looked at the releases and made necessary changes. I will take a look at the statement we're sending to the magazine," I said.

Poppy made me sick.

We wrapped up the meeting, and I made my way down the hall toward my office, but stepped into an odd scene in the ladies' room.

"He wants me. He just doesn't know it yet!"

The sound of her voice made me stop cold. I froze and held my breath, trying to determine if she had heard the door open.

"Yes, absolutely! He simply needs more convincing."

I peeked around the corner and saw Poppy talking to her reflection in the mirror above the sink in the far corner. I dropped back against the wall, and quietly eased back out the door.

The last thing I wanted was her to think I was snooping, so I rushed back to my office.

My phone rang almost instantly.

"Eliza Carter," I answered.

"Eliza, McKenzie Fields here. Please hold for Sasha Davenport," she said into my ear.

I rolled my eyes. *Now what?*

SASHA

When I told McKenzie to set up the meeting with Dax and me, she looked at me like I was speaking Arabic.

"You never meet with the guests before the show," she said.

I looked up from my notes and frowned a bit, not too much because doing that caused wrinkles. But still, I needed her to understand my confusion.

"Whose name is on this show?" I asked.

McKenzie sucked her teeth, but jotted down the information I requested. We were holed up in my office, which was a small sitting room off my dressing room. We tried to meet once a week to go over plans for the show and determine what guests we needed to put on reserve for repeat appearances. It was just my luck that the publicity girl was trying to drum up press for the team. I had taken everything Sebastian said to heart. My plan was simple really. I'd meet with Dax and see if he was the missing link.

"So, you're meeting with Dwight and Dax? When and where?" McKenzie asked.

"Is that great Creole restaurant still open on Jefferson?" I asked.

McKenzie was White, but she was still a hood rat. She was always on top of the latest and greatest ghetto finds.

"You always ask about that restaurant, and I keep telling you they shut down, but Tichina Arnold, the actress who played Pam on *Martin*, has a great place called Game Sports Bar Restaurant & Lounge, real discreet, and she performs on Thursdays, I think."

"Hmm, where's that?" I asked. "And Tichina has most recently played the mom on *Everybody Hates Chris*, Chris Rock's sitcom," I added.

"I know that, but she was at her best as Pam," McKenzie said without missing a beat. "And her place is on West Manchester Avenue, I can call ahead and make sure they rope off a section for you and the guys," she offered.

"The last time I went, they had a real nice happy hour, and the place is always dripping with eye candy," she said. Now she was pulling up the restaurant on her iPad. "I'll show you their website."

"You say she performs on Thursdays?" I asked. I was excited about the press Dax and I could get in a place like that.

"Every other Thursday, so I'll set the meeting for a night I know she'll be there. And of course I'll make sure she gives you a shout-out."

"She needs to shout out to Dax and me." I beamed.

McKenzie glanced at me sideways. "What about Dwight?"

"Um, for this meeting it'll only be Dax and me. Make sure you call paparazzi, too." I smiled.

McKenzie put her iPad down and looked at me. She smirked playfully.

"Sasha, what are you up to? You know Dax is very married and besides, Tatyana is in the club."

I had already shared everything Sebastian said with McKenzie, but like many others, she underestimated my drive. Nothing was gonna keep me from getting my own reality TV show. If he said I needed to snag a popular, rich player, and trash it up, then I planned on doing just that, and even more.

"Should I invite Tatyana?" She chuckled.

I shot daggers at her with my eyes.

"You're such a bad girl," she teased. "But here it is. This is the website. It's a really nice place."

I grabbed the iPad and scanned the site. It would be perfect for what I had in mind. "Call and see when she's performing," I urged.

McKenzie picked up her phone and dialed the number from the website. I smiled when she began to talk.

Moments later, she wrapped up the call and smiled at me.

"They're very excited about you two coming. Once I make sure Dax is free, I'll call paparazzi and put in calls to MediaTakeOut, Madame Noire, and a few others."

"Will *TMZ* be on that list?"

"You know we don't need to call them. Who do you think some of the paparazzi work for?" She chuckled.

I laughed a bit at that, too. But what was most funny to me was how simple this takeover was going to be. In the year or so that Tatyana had been in the club, she barely registered on the radar.

Sure, she was pretty, but she was one of those pretty gals who had no clue what pretty needed to do. She rarely dressed in the latest fashions; her hair probably hadn't seen the inside of a shop in years; and there was nothing memorable about her. Tatyana was a nice person, but she was the kind of nice that would be trampled all over because she'd be too busy holding the door open for others to flee.

I almost felt sorry for her. Even if she knew what was on the horizon, there was no way she could adequately prepare for the wrath that was Sasha Davenport on a mission.

"Okay. Call and reach out to him," I said.

She looked at me, then grinned. "Oh, you mean now?"

"Stop playing!" I waited patiently as she looked up a number.

When it appeared it was taking too long, I stepped in. "What's the matter?"

"I'm trying to find his agent," she said.

I rolled my eyes. "You're kidding, right?" She wasn't. "McKenzie, you said it yourself; Tatyana is in the club. We have her home number on file."

Her eyes expanded to the size of oranges, and she pursed her lips.

"You really are a *bad* girl! Are you trying to tell me you want me to call his house?" She balked.

"How else would you reach him to tell him that we are interested in a pre-show meeting?" I asked with a straight face. "This is business, McKenzie," I said.

"Oooh, remind me never to cross you," she joked.

"Just call, will you?"

I eased back in my chair and watched her work. First, she called the club and asked for Tatyana's home number.

"Put it on speaker. I wanna hear," I said.

She dialed the Becalls' residence, and the phone rang three times. I could've been knocked over by a feather when his deep voice filled the room. I felt all giddy like a nervous middle school girl. He sounded delicious and dreamy.

"Hello?" he answered like he was some average Joe.

My eyes widened, and I started grinning.

"Ah, yes, this is McKenzie Fields, Senior Producer with *The Sasha Davenport Show*. I'm trying to reach Mr. Dax Becall," McKenzie said. She sounded so professional I started to feel legit.

"Well, you've reached him," Dax said easily. There was no air about him. He didn't sound uptight and stuffy like the multi-millionaire he was.

"Oh, Mr. Becall, how are you?" McKenzie asked.

"I'd be a lot better if you called me Dax, but otherwise, I'm pretty good. Thanks for asking."

"Oh, great, Dax. Well, the reason I'm calling is because we've received a request from publicity over at the Sea Lions' front office about having you on an upcoming show," McKenzie said.

I didn't like that approach, but I remained quiet.

"Ooookay," Dax said as if this was all news to him.

"Anyway, the reason I'm calling is because the show's host, Sasha Davenport, would like to meet with you personally before that appearance."

"*She* wants to meet with *me*?" he asked. "Wow, I feel special," he said.

I was unable to decipher whether he was being sarcastic or serious, and despite how much it pained me to stay out of it, I kept quiet.

"Well, I'm not sure how familiar you are with the show, but Sasha likes when the chemistry with her guests can transcend through the tube, if you will. So, I'm checking to see if you'll be available this Thursday evening," McKenzie said.

"Uh, here I thought people simply showed up to the studio, then sat and talked. Goes to show how much I know, huh?" he quipped.

I loved his personality already. As I sat and listened to him and McKenzie, it simply drove home to me the idea that I had in fact chosen the right one in Dax Becall. Now all I had to do was convince him that leaving his wife and kids for me and our new life on reality TV would be a major upgrade.

JERRI

I managed to make it through the morning with no drama, but I couldn't say the same for the afternoon and early evening. Morning was easy because I pretty much stayed locked in my bedroom. But I was battling a bad case of cabin fever, and I needed out, fast!

While I couldn't legally venture off the property without written consent from my probation officer, I was able to move around our sprawling estate as much as I wanted as long as I kept my distance from Jason. I was pretty sure he had left.

After breakfast, my plan was to spend a couple of hours poolside underneath one of the cabanas. I started to call the girls over, but after the last time we were together, I decided against that.

Suited in a sexy one-piece, a great book and sunscreen in hand, I headed out to the pool house when I thought I heard strange voices. I was on high alert as I walked quietly toward the sound of women's voices that laughed and talked freely.

When I rounded the corner of the pool house, what I saw stopped me cold in my tracks. I was fuming and ready to commit murder. Laid across the very designer lounge chairs I had handselected were three big, plump, silicone-filled, bare, bodacious booties.

It wasn't until my rage-filled eyes focused that I noticed the barely there strings, buried between one of the glistening mocha-colored cheeks. Otherwise, I would've thought the tramps were naked! Because they were sprawled out on their stomachs, they hadn't seen me, or apparently heard me coming. I preferred the element of surprise anyway.

"Excuse me, but what the hell is going on here?" I snapped.

It gave me great pleasure to know that I had startled them. One at a time, heads popped up, and frowning faces turned in my direction. Bikini tops dangled and fake boobs bounced all about.

"Put on some goddamn clothes! How the hell did you guys even get back here? This is private property!" I screamed.

What pissed me off the most was the lack of movement after the initial surprise. Not only did those skanks not cover themselves, but two of them laid their heads back down as if I was nothing but a mere nuisance. I stepped closer. My attitude increased with every step I took.

"Um, I am not talking to myself out here," I snapped.

The only one who continued to look at me, used her hands, to smooth stray strands of her messy ponytail. But the expression on her face was nowhere near being worried or concerned.

She blew out a breath and said, "Oh, we're friends of Jason. He told us we could come hang by the pool today," she said as if that explained everything.

My eyebrow went up, and before I could control it, my neck had already snaked. "Oh, he did, did he?" I shifted all of my weight to one side and held my stance.

"Kristi," she said, "turn the music back on."

Ms. Fake Ass and Fake Breasts had all but dismissed me. She started digging for her bikini top and was about to lay her head back down.

"You all need to get up and get the hell out! This is my damn house, and I don't care what *Jason* told you!"

I finally had everyone's attention.

"Des, she can't be serious!" Her friend sucked her teeth.

"Don't trip," big-breasted Des said. She pulled a sleek phone from beneath the lounge chair and touched the screen.

As she held the phone to her ear, the other two started to try and pull themselves together. I didn't understand what men saw in fake tits and ass. They looked so incredibly fake. Either the chicks were exhibitionists, or they simply didn't care about being naked in front of me. Either way, I wanted them gone. It wasn't even that hot out there. They were doing entirely too much, and I needed them to do it somewhere else.

"Hey, it's me, Des. That bitch wife of yours is over here blowing a gasket because we're hanging poolside," she whined into her phone.

I stormed over, snatched the phone and tossed it into the pool.

"OHMYGOD!" she cried. Her face morphed into an ugly frown.

"What the fuck!" her friend shrieked.

"Get off my fucking property before I call the cops and have you tramps thrown in jail for trespassing!"

"Who you calling a tramp?!" one of them yelled.

"Bitch, you paying for my phone. Believe that!" Des pointed as she tried to pull herself up from the chair.

"I ain't paying for shit. You guys better hope I don't call the law and have you thrown in the slammer. Get the fuck out! Get out!" I had already dropped my things, so my hands were free. I used my arms to motion in the direction I needed them to go.

The skanks finally began to move like a fire had been lit beneath their fake asses. Weaves flung to and fro, and all kinds of crap was thrown into bright-colored beach bags. When I saw the one who called herself "Des" stumble as she tried to step a leg into a pair of shorts, I moved closer.

"Oh no, you don't. You need to go *now*! Get dressed on the street for all I care. Get the fuck out!"

Startled, she flung the sweatpants into her bag, rolled her eyes at me, and turned toward the back door.

"Let's bounce before somebody gets hurt. Jason is gonna hear about this!" she promised.

"Oh, no, ma'am!" I screamed.

They all stopped and turned.

I pointed toward the gate, "*This* is the way out!" I said.

"But we're damn near naked!" Kristi balked.

"I don't care if you are naked. Maybe next time you'll think twice before trespassing!"

"Ain't nobody trespassing," Des snapped.

"I ain't never laid eyes on you guys before, so in my book, that's trespassing. And I double dog dare you to call me a bitch again!"

Her little nostrils flared as she stormed past me, but her lips remained sealed. The nerve of Jason to tell those hookers they could come and hang out at our pool. That was the kind of crap he pulled on a regular to try and piss me off.

After they left, quiet had returned to the pool area. The sound of the motor humming and the waterfall at the other end of the pool was comforting, but still, something was wrong. I looked around and realized I didn't even want to hang out at the pool anymore. Images of their big butts and breasts had left a bad taste in my mouth.

My mind was busy with thoughts of all the things I should have said to them. I really wanted to go and find Jason's dumb behind, but I knew there was no point. I walked to the pool's edge, leaned over and looked into the water.

The phone lay at the bottom and that made me smile for the first time since the poolside drama went down. Satisfied, I turned and strolled back inside.

I barely caught the phone. When I answered, I wished I hadn't.

"Bitch, you going to jail! That was foul," Jason's voice said.

"Um, let's see. You invite and leave strangers at my house, and I'm going to jail? Think again, and I got your bitch!" I snapped.

"I'm calling my lawyer and getting an injunction to have you tossed out! I don't feel safe with you being here," he said.

"Jason, please stop calling me. I haven't done anything to you. When you want me out of here, let's talk seriously about the money you're trying to hide! Until then, I don't have shit to say to you."

"Bitch, I'm not offering you another red dime! You take what I offered in the agreement, or get nothing at all."

It had been a long time since I'd had one of those phone calls from Jason. His threats meant nothing.

Thinking back now, he was really at the root of everything wrong in my life. That chick in San Diego wasn't the first, and she was far from the last. When he came home, and I all but stopped talking to him, he behaved like my actions were so out of order and so unfounded.

"Some woman is able to take naked pictures of you, send them to me and I'm supposed to welcome you with open arms?"

"I can't talk to you when you're like this," he'd snapped.

He didn't know what he was doing back then, but every little lie, every little misstep, and every whispered phone call chipped away at the love I felt for him.

The next day, I smelled Jason before I saw him, and it dawned on me. I couldn't remember a time he had worn cologne. It was odd, but I didn't mention it for fear of another fight.

We ate a silent breakfast and only talked when one of the kids forced us to speak.

Later, Jason and the kids were gone. I walked into the laundry room and was a bit surprised by what I saw.

"Gina?" I called out to the housekeeper.

She shot around the corner and wiped her hands on a half apron she wore.

"Yes, Mrs. Nelson?" she asked.

"Where are all the clothes?"

"Oh, Mr. Nelson has been doing his own laundry for nearly a month now. I thought you knew," she said.

If I had been a cartoon character that would've been the moment the light bulb would've popped above my head.

"I'm sorry. I did. I must've forgotten," I said. I hurried out of the laundry room. I told myself that I had been putting too much thought into one little indiscretion.

Jason's voice raging in my ear pulled me back from those painful memories of our past. I hated him now more than I ever thought possible.

"You'd better be gone by the time I get back there," he spat. Then just as quickly, he said, "Oh, my bad, your ass can't leave the premises. Bet you think twice before you set fire to something again, huh?"

I heard his menacing laugh long after I ended his abusive call. I got up and walked over to make sure the recording had worked. It had.

TATYANA

"I can't believe this foolishness!" Pamela snapped.

"What's your problem?" I asked.

"You really are gonna let your husband go out with that woman?" She gave me a look of sheer disbelief.

"It's a business meeting! What's the problem? So, now I'm not supposed to allow Dax to conduct business?" I barked back at her.

Pamela was beginning to drive me crazy. I was not about to allow her insecurities to change me or my plan. Suddenly, the three days she had been in town felt more like a month and a half. The really sad part was she still had nearly a week and a half to go!

"And keep your voice down. I don't want him to hear us! You know how he's always talking about man bashing," I said as my eyes darted toward the hallway. "And I meant to tell you about that mess from the other day. The way you were throwing daggers at him with your eyes, that's gotta stop, Pam!"

"I'm sorry, but his bullshit is way too much for me to swallow. I don't see how you do it." Pamela shook her head.

"Pam, I need you to keep it in check. Plain and simple!"

Dax was getting dressed, but Pamela's crazy rant took me back to the moment he got off the phone and came to track me down yesterday.

"Hey, this is kinda odd." He walked all the way into the family room. "That was the producer for Sasha Davenport's talk show.

Says Sasha wants to meet with me before Dwight and I go on," he said.

Pamela's expression changed instantly. She stopped what she was doing and blatantly focused on our conversation.

"Did she say what Sasha wanted?" I asked Dax.

He shrugged. "Not really; said something about a pre-meeting to talk about doing something different," he said.

"Well, if I know Sasha, she probably wants to get you to help out with a prank against Dwight or something," I said.

"Umph," Pamela said.

I tried to ignore her. I wanted her to at least hold off until he left the room.

"I'll keep you posted. But we're meeting tomorrow evening at Tichina Arnold's restaurant or something like that," he said.

"Oh, I didn't know she had a restaurant," I said.

"Me either. They simply told me where I needed to be and what time," he said.

"Girl, you just gonna hand-deliver your man, huh?"

That was the statement that brought me back to the present. I was about to respond when I caught a glimpse of my husband. He was dressed in a pair of dark designer jeans, and a maroon-colored, button-down, short-sleeved shirt with buttoned flaps on each shoulder. He looked good.

"Fix your pant leg," I said.

Dax looked down and pulled his left pant leg over the ankle boots he wore. He walked over and kissed my lips.

"You ladies be good tonight," he said. "Later, Pamela," he added before he jogged out of the room.

Once he left, I turned to Pamela and said, "So, I guess you want to jump in the car, follow him there and find a dark corner in the restaurant so we can spy on them, huh?"

"Damn! I thought you'd never ask. Let me grab my purse," Pamela said.

I burst out in laughter. She couldn't be serious. I was not about to go stalking my husband like some desperate lunatic.

"That Sasha Davenport cannot be trusted around anyone's man. The vibe I get from her is that anything goes. If Dax asks for some head inside the restaurant, I see her dropping to her knees," Pamela said.

"Well, I hope she's good at it because I get tired of sucking on command!" I laughed so hard my stomach ached. But when I looked up, Pamela wasn't even smiling.

"Oh, lighten up, girl. That's what's wrong with you. You're wound too tight. Listen, if that man wants to cheat on me, there's nothing I can do about it. You want me to go throwing accusations around and trying to catch him in the act. That's not my personality. I don't chase men good. I'm a firm believer, whatever is done in the dark will come to light," I said.

She gave me a nasty look, but finally retreated, and I was glad.

"Well, he's gone for the night—um, evening, I mean, and the kids are gone. What are we doing tonight?" she asked.

"Whatever we do, can you drop the comments about Dax? Please trust and believe me when I tell you, I'm gonna be fine regardless of what happens. And despite what you think, I'm not about to sit back and allow anyone to take my husband without a fight."

"But you said—"

"Pamela, I know what I said. What I said was I'm not going to confront him about crap that I have no reason to accuse him of. I'm not gonna start following him around when he has given me no reason to suspect that he's doing anything wrong. You've gotta be able to respect that."

Disappointment was all over her face, but I needed her to understand I didn't need her constantly in my ear with all of the negativity.

"I know I've been riding you since I've been here, but remember, as you pointed out the other day, I know what it's like to be completely blindsided. I will always remember the dull achy pain that sits in the pit of your belly and walking with your head hung low and shoulders slumped. It was such a dark time in my life, and I don't want that to happen to you," she said.

Her words were sincere, and I understood where she was coming from, but it was my hope that this confession would mean an end to the constant Dax bashing she had been doing.

"I didn't mean to say that to you the other day, when I said you knew what it was like to be blindsided," I said.

Pamela shook her head. "You don't have to apologize," she tried to say.

"No, I do. That was completely unnecessary. I'm sorry I said that to you. And I know you're trying to look out for me, Pamela, but remember, I know how to look out for myself, too."

"Okay, okay. I know I can go hard at times, but you know it's only because I love you. And after two divorces I can tell you, it's no fun!"

"Well, it should be for you. After each one, you walked away with hefty cash settlements," I reminded her.

Pamela raised her hand for a high-five. I slapped it, and we laughed.

"Your girl ain't nobody's *complete* fool," she said. "Now let's go find something to do!"

"What about dinner and a movie?" I asked.

Pamela twisted her face. "More excitement, please," she said.

"We can go clubbing," I suggested.

"But not one of those upscale, VIPs only."

"What are you talking about exactly?"

"Let's go slumming. I mean, let's go somewhere no one would expect us to pop up. That means we need to be careful how we look," Pamela said.

"I'm not sure about that. When I go places, it's mostly with Football Widows Social Club members and we go to club events, so I can't even begin to imagine how I would find a place for us to go, and remember, this is L.A. We can't go just anywhere."

"I'm about to get on the computer and see what I can find. Go get ready, and jeans and a cute top are in order—not an after-five cocktail dress," she said.

"I don't need tips on how to dress to go slumming. This is me, remember? I invented the term when we wanted to be treated like goddesses during our cheerleading years."

"Yeah, but we weren't in La-La Land at that time either, remember?" Pamela said.

When I came back downstairs, Pamela looked up from the laptop and said, "Let's go to L.A. Live. That way we can bar hop."

"Sounds good," I said.

"Wow, that's dressing down to you?" Pamela asked.

I wore a pair of white shorts and a natural-colored T-shirt that had a ruffle skirt around my waist. I capped my look off with a pair of nude wedges and a snake-skinned clutch purse. I finger-combed my tresses back into a loose, messy ponytail, left wavy tendrils dangling around my face and had clunky diamond studs in my ears.

"You look hot!" Pamela said.

"Well, what are you gonna do?"

"I'll be back in ten minutes," she said.

Just as Pamela was leaving the room, the doorbell chimed.

"You expecting anyone?" she asked over her shoulder.

"No."

"I'll get it," she said.

I was trying to check the best places to go at L.A. Live, when Pamela said, "A pizza? We didn't order any pizza."

By the time I walked out to the front area, Pamela had already paid the guy and brought the box in.

"I am hungry, but how did this pizza end up here?" she asked.

"I didn't order any pizza. Let me see that box, and what's in the bag?" I asked.

"He said the cheese and pepper we requested."

I took the box and Pamela opened the bag.

"Ain't this a bitch?!" she screamed.

"What?"

"How the hell did *she* get the pizza delivery guy in on this crap?" She waved the small, familiar envelope in the air.

ELIZA

"Did you hear the great news, *Mija*?" Mary asked as I walked into the office.

The moment the elevator doors opened, I could tell Poppy hadn't made it in yet. I smelled fresh coffee in the air, and I heard my co-workers chattering. After I sang a slew of hellos, I walked into my office with Mary hot on my heels.

"So, our department won an award. I'm not sure what's gonna happen, but from what I heard, some of the higher-ups are going to make an in-house presentation." Mary's face looked sour.

"Does Poppy know yet?" I asked.

"*Conyo Sucio*—dirty Conyo. How could she know? We only found out 'cause they were trying to reach her, and her cell kept going to voicemail."

"Hmm, okay, well, I'll see if I can track her down. This is great news. Thanks, Mary," I said.

"You know we have to stick together, *Mija*," Mary said.

I smiled, and she left.

When I dialed Poppy's cell number, her voicemail picked up immediately. That meant her phone was turned off.

Two hours later, Poppy's direct supervisor's name and number popped up on the caller ID on my desk phone.

"Hey, Eliza. I'm trying to find Poppy. Any idea where she is?" he asked.

"Um, I think she's in a meeting, gearing up for Becall and Sampson on Sasha's show. Can I take a message for her?"

"That's right. I forgot about that! That Poppy…she really makes things happen. Okay, well, I wanted to give her a heads-up that the president of the Lions is coming down to make a personal acknowledgment to the team for the award," he said.

"Oh, okay. Can you tell me what time? I know she has another meeting following this one, and I want to make her aware," I lied.

"Yes, four-forty-five," he said.

That meant I had about seven hours to track Poppy down. Of course I had no idea where to start since she wasn't answering her phone. I couldn't think of a time when Poppy didn't have that phone.

I had several calls to make and a few projects to follow up on, so I decided to work and try Poppy later.

When my phone rang, I expected Poppy on the other end. Instead, it was Carlos Trenor, Dax Becall's agent.

"Hey, Eliza. Carlos…got a minute?" he asked. Only his voice didn't sound like it was a question.

"Yes, Mr. Trenor, what can I do for you?"

"Well, I just got off the phone with my client, and he was telling me about a meeting he had with Sasha Davenport last night. Were you aware of that meeting?"

"No, we've already confirmed Dax's and Dwight's appearance on the program. I was not made aware of any meetings related to that appearance, but obviously this is of concern to you and your client?"

"Well, not really to him, but more to me. I've done business with you guys for years over there. And I should tell you that I tried Poppy and couldn't get her, so that's why I'm calling you. If you like, I can wait for her to call me back," he said.

"No, I'm fine. I'd like to see if I can take care of the problem if there is a problem," I said.

"Well, I felt like there was a little pay-to-play action going on with my client. And I know in the past you've cleared an appearance, and that was all there was to it. So, I guess, I'm calling to find out if things have changed around there?"

I had no idea what Carlos was talking about, but I knew we couldn't afford to let it blow up into something bigger.

"Nothing has changed around here. I will call Sasha's producer, Ms. Fields, the minute we hang up and get back to you. But before I let you go, is Dax still on board?" I asked.

"Oh, yeah. Like I said, he didn't really have a problem with it, but when he talked to me, I felt like something wasn't right," Carlos said.

"Give me twenty," I said.

I hung up with Carlos and searched for the number to Sasha's producer. But before that, I dialed Poppy one more time and got her voicemail again.

"McKenzie, this is Eliza with the Sea Lions' publicity," I said the moment she answered.

"Hey, Eliza, what's up?"

"I'm calling for some clarification," I said.

"On?"

"Your pre-show procedures over there. Have you guys made changes?" I asked.

"No, we haven't; why do you ask?"

"One of our players, actually, it's Dax's agent, called, and he said Sasha demanded a pre-meeting before his appearance on the show. We were not made aware of that," I said.

"Oh." She chuckled. "There must've been a misunderstanding. It wasn't a required meeting. Sasha and Tichina Arnold are good friends, and she's a huge fan. The truth is she wanted to meet Dax, but she didn't want to make a big deal out of it."

"So, why didn't Sasha simply tell him that? His agent is over there acting like a surprise is coming down the pike, and he doesn't want to be caught off-guard," I said.

The truth was, I didn't buy McKenzie's story for one second, but I also didn't think it was as bad as Carlos anticipated. I had no clue what Sasha was up to, but I didn't think the Becall camp had much to worry about.

"Okay, well let me let him know he can relax, and we'll see you guys soon over there," I said.

The next series of events unfolded so oddly, I wasn't sure what was going on. I ended the call with McKenzie and picked up the phone to call Carlos back. But before I could dial his number, Mary burst through my office door, without knocking.

"*Mija*, *Mija*, Sweet Jesus!" She spoke in hurried fits and seemed to force her words out. "Turn your TV on!" she screamed.

"What?" I asked. My stomach belly-flopped.

"It's Dax. He's all over the news. Is he dating that talk show lady? What the hell? Where's his wife? *Ai yi yi;* this is a mess! Where's Poppy? What are we gonna do?"

I closed my eyes and took a deep breath as Mary snatched my remote and turned the flat screen on.

The scandal exploded all across the screen. And as Mary surfed the channels, most had video or pictures of a smiling Sasha Davenport with the married star quarterback of the Los Angeles Sea Lions.

When the phone rang, I didn't even need to look to know who it was.

"This is Eliza," I said into the phone.

"What the hell? Yes, absolutely I am pissed! I can't leave you guys alone for a single minute! How the hell did this happen?"

Poppy barked so loudly in my ear, even Mary began to tremble. She fired off a slew of curse words in Spanish, then stormed out of my office.

SASHA

My phone rang off the hook all morning long, and I was so excited by all of the attention. If it wasn't a reporter who wanted a comment, it was someone who wanted to know how long *this* had been going on. And by *this*, they meant Dax and me. I couldn't buy a better brewing scandal. The one call I decided to take was the one I should've avoided.

"Marteen, will you calm down?" I snapped.

Hers had been the only call I had accepted, and I regretted it with every worry word that came out of her mouth. I knew how to play the press if I didn't know anything else. But she was tripping. The last thing I needed was my agent falling apart on me.

"We are on our way to a reality TV show. I need you to keep it together," I said.

"Sasha, this is not the way to go about getting it. We do not need sports fans in L.A., turning against you! Quite surely you can find another player who's as influential, but *single*!"

"It doesn't work like that," I told her.

"He's married. That's a different kind of problem—one we don't need going into the new season for the show you're still contractually obligated to do. Think about it—with weeks away from training camp, we don't want you tied to any sports related or any other scandal as we try to shop you for anything."

She wasn't feeling my vibe. She didn't understand how this

worked, but I couldn't let her bring me down. I knew what I was doing, and I needed her to trust me. I had done my homework. Like many star athletes, Dax was trapped from his college days. Tatyana latched on to his rising star and never let go.

I knew he had a family, but still, I also knew I'd be able to work around that. He needed a real power broker in his corner. What had Tatyana done but ride his coattails? She probably never worked a day in her life. I didn't care what Marteen had spewed. After I spent time with him alone, I knew I was on the right path.

"Isn't his wife in the club, Sasha?" Marteen cried.

"Marteen, it's not like I'm close to her. We have tons of women in the club. She hardly shows up for events anyway," I said.

"This is not good business," Marteen said.

"Oh, that's my other line. I need to run. I'll call later," I told her.

"Sasha, don't do this," Marteen called out as I hung up.

She needed to get with the program. There was no turning back, especially after the way Dax and I connected the night before. He was handsome, looked absolutely delicious without even trying, and I wanted him to realize how much farther he could go with a woman like me by his side. When I saw pictures of us together, images of Beyoncé and Jay-Z flashed through my mind. We were bound to be the next power couple.

I could sense he had been feeling me. Our first date was nothing short of magical. First off, I had my driver wait for him to pull up before I went inside. I wanted us to walk in together. The moment we did, and paparazzi realized we were actually together, bulbs began to flash, lighting up the dark, evening skies. He took it all in stride.

"Are you two a couple?!" one of the photographers shouted, as we glided up the walkway to the club.

I blessed him with a smile. I held it long enough for his flash to go off.

"Sasha, over here!" another photographer called out. I turned to my right and nudged Dax, who did the same.

Right before we walked in, I fell back a little then rushed up and grabbed his arm for the money shot. We strolled in arm-in-arm, and I could only dream about the headlines that would make.

When Tichina did that shout-out, and they put that spotlight on us, it was like heaven! The place roared with applause, and I could tell he was hyped.

"You see how they're responding?" I asked him through my perfect smile.

"Oh, that's all for you, shawty," he said as he looked around and waved to the people we couldn't see because the place was dark.

Tichina's voice was golden. I had no idea she was that talented. As her silky voice filled the air, I locked eyes with Dax. I could tell he was trying to be the perfect gentleman, but I knew that was merely a front. We had bottle service so there was a tall bucket holding a bottle of champagne right near our seat.

"Oooh, I love bubbly," I said.

He reached for the bottle, popped the top, and poured some for me before he poured some for himself.

"So, you wanted to talk about the show?" he asked.

The minute his eyes fixed on me, I ran my fingers slowly through my hair. Then, I reached over and tapped his arm.

"Silly, let's have some fun. There's plenty of time to talk business. Let's listen to the show." I smiled.

His mega-watt smile was gorgeous. Every chance I got, I used my fingers to trace around the mouth of my champagne flute. His eyes watched me, and I was glad. That meant he was interested.

He'd smile graciously before he looked away, and it melted my heart.

A couple of times, I caught him as he checked me out on the sly. I knew he was watching, so I made sure to lick my lips frequently. I understood what that did to men. I knew his mind was probably filled with all of the naughty thoughts about my wet juicy lips. I knew what he had at home paled in comparison to me.

Dax had no clue. He was on my radar, and I needed to do whatever it would take to pull him in.

"Is that Dax Becall?!" a fan yelled.

"Oh, my God, that's Sasha Davenport with him!" another voice said.

"I thought he was married!"

"That's him! It's him. I'd know him anywhere!"

All of the chatter was music to my ears.

He was such a great sport. He posed for some pictures with me, and the fans that couldn't leave us alone. All I could think was hopefully he'd realize that we'd make a much stronger team than what he had.

"You okay?" I asked.

He frowned. And even then, he still looked good. "Yeah, I'm good. Why you ask?"

"Not sure if this is all too much for you, that's all," I cooed. I leaned on his muscular chest as we stood close and posed for yet another picture. He smelled divine. "Your wife is such a lucky woman," I whispered dreamily.

"Oh, I'm the lucky one." He chuckled.

His comment meant nothing to me. It was almost like he felt obligated to say that. I already knew that was the standard response from a married man who was oblivious to being pursued.

When he held me close, and his hand fell toward the small of my back, I wanted to melt right there in the middle of the lounge, and in front of all those people.

"Sasha?" McKenzie called out, snapping me out of my sweet memory.

"What's up?"

"Guess what? Eliza called from publicity with the Sea Lions," she said.

My eyebrows bunched together in confusion, and my heart started to race a little. I didn't need any problems.

"What did she want?"

"Not sure really. She said Dax's agent called concerned about our new prescreening procedures for the show," McKenzie said.

"What?" Alarm had settled in.

"I know, right?" McKenzie said. "Kind of caught me off-guard, too, at first, but I think I fixed it just fine. I told her you were simply taking Dax to meet Tichina who is a huge fan, but she was way shy about meeting him."

"Damn, that was a good one!" I smiled.

"I think publicity, his agent, and even him, they're all probably wondering if we have something up our sleeve," McKenzie said.

They all may have thought that, but I knew for certain that Dax knew for sure what I had in mind for him and all indications from the night before told me he would be down for whatever.

JERRI

"Come on. Meet me over there. Maybe we can sneak off and go to happy hour or something," I said into the phone. "Where's Vanessa?" I asked. I was so excited.

"I haven't talked to her today, but I can try to get in touch with her and see if she can meet us," Natasha said.

"So, you're gonna come meet me then?"

"Yes, girl. This is like your free pass. Of course I'm coming. Here, hold on a sec. Let me try Vanessa on three-way," she offered.

My pulse raced with sheer excitement. I was finally getting a break, and if my girls could meet me, it'd be like the good ol' days.

The next voice I heard on the phone was Vanessa's.

"How the hell is she able to hang anyway?" Vanessa asked.

"Um, don't worry about that. Can you meet us or what?" I asked before Natasha could speak up.

"I guess so, but how are you able to do this? Won't you get in trouble? I can't believe your probation officer is going for this," Vanessa said.

"So, we're meeting you at the office for the Football Widows Social Club; then from there we're gonna go find some place for happy hour?"

"Yeah, you guys can meet me at the club. I need to get my assignment. Then I'll be free for several hours before I have to go home," I said.

"How'd you get this pass again?" Vanessa asked.

"I don't care how she got it. I'm glad she did, so we'll meet you there at six. Is that good?"

"Yeah, should be. I have to be there at five. I'm thinking an hour should be enough. Then I've gotta be back at the house by ten, no ifs, ands, or buts about it," I stressed.

"You know happy hour don't really get happy until around ten," Vanessa whined. "We'll have to leave right when the party starts!"

"Vanessa, when was the last time we all hung out together?" Natasha asked her. She didn't wait for the answer. "I don't care if she only had ten minutes. We need to make it the best time she's had in a while."

"Yeah, I know, but I was just saying," Vanessa said.

"Okay, well, I'm gonna finish getting ready," I said.

I couldn't remember the last time any outing had me so excited. By anyone's standards, my house was the house to be on house arrest in, but there was nothing like bar-hanging with the girls, and I was thrilled.

Once I confirmed the car service, I made sure my outfit, a tank top romper in burnt orange was the right look. I finished with my accessories. The bronze oversized Michael Kors watch and a flirty clutch finished my ensemble, and I was ready to go.

I realized that in my eagerness, I had dressed and gotten ready in less than ten minutes. With extra time on my hands, I decided to enjoy a cocktail while I waited.

Since Jason was still out of town, I had free rein of the house, so I made my way to the kitchen and fixed a simple cocktail of Belvedere, cran-grape juice, pineapple juice and a splash of Sprite.

The drink helped me relax, and I was grateful for that.

My cell rang, and I considered not answering, but it was Baltimore Ed.

"Hey, what's up?"

"You...you know I signed with the Ravens, right?"

I wanted to ask how the hell I would know that, but thought better of it. "Oh, congrats! I'm glad for you."

"Hey, babe, I need to take this call on the other end. I'ma hit you back."

"Okay, cool."

By the time I finished my cocktail, I looked up, and it was time to roll.

Later, when I thought about it in the backseat of the car, I realized the drink was a good thing since I was about to meet Sasha Davenport for the very first time. I didn't need nervousness to impact that meeting.

The social club's office was located off Crenshaw Boulevard near Jefferson. It was a small storefront that was modern and welcoming. I was excited about getting my community service started so I could hurry and finish. There were a few women inside when I walked in and approached a reception area.

"Hi, I'm Jerri Nelson, here to meet with Sasha," I said.

"Hi, Jerri, we were expecting you. Sasha called a few minutes ago. She's running about ten minutes behind. Can I get something for you—a glass of wine, water, ginger ale or anything else?"

I smiled. "No, I'm good, but thanks for asking."

The women all looked like they could grace the cover of high-fashion magazines. I was glad I had selected my wardrobe appropriately. But I watched Sasha's show religiously, and I knew I'd need to come correct.

I followed a different woman to an area reserved for club guests. I already liked the atmosphere in the place and was eager to see where I'd fit in.

"If you need anything, press that button over there." She pointed at a small box on the table. "Oh, and the remote is right there," she said.

Not even five minutes passed before I heard a ruckus going on near the front.

"Today's show was hot," someone said.

"You know how I do it," I heard her say.

Sasha's voice was memorable. She sounded in person like she sounded on her show. I tried to calm myself as I struggled to think I was actually excited about meeting her. Before I could pull it together, a head popped around the corner.

"You must be Jerri. I'm Saaaasha," she said.

I jumped up from the sofa and smiled. I loved the way she pronounced her name. She seemed real cool.

"Oh, hi. I love your show," I said.

She smiled. I had never seen a woman's face look so perfect. There was not a single trace of stress or concern across her face. Her hair was neatly in place, and when she walked completely around the corner, she revealed a bad brown suit. The woman was sharp!

"You wanna come into my office," she said more than asked.

I stumbled a bit as I attempted to follow her and felt like a klutz.

Sasha's office wasn't spectacular as much as it was cute and girly. Her walls were painted purple with soft pink-and-blue ruffles all throughout the room. It was cozy, and I liked it. She had a couple of strategically placed lamps that drowned the room in soft lighting. Her space was so *her*!

She sat behind a small, old-fashioned writing desk and smiled at me.

"Girl, you went and got yourself into some trouble, huh? Well, I ain't mad at you, 'cause I probably would've done the same doggon' thing!"

I wasn't sure how to react. What I had done had cost me dearly. I was arrested, thrown in jail, and eventually placed on house arrest.

"Then, the way you two are living over there? Girl, it's just too much! I'll bet it's all kinda drama going on up in that house!" As she talked, she searched through her desk.

"Well, I'm simply trying to do my time, so I could put this mess behind me," I said.

Sasha smiled. "I know, right?!"

Even my closest girlfriends knew not to question me about what happened with Jason and his then sidepiece. I kept reminding myself that I needed Sasha and her club far more than she needed me. Although she had rubbed me the wrong way by making light of what happened, visions of me picking up trash at a public park forced me to keep my emotions in check.

"So, you'd do your community service here?" she said.

"Yeah, that's what I'm hoping to do. I really appreciate you being willing to help out," I told her.

"Shoot, girl, we gots to stick together. You ain't gotta thank me! I felt your pain when you went through all that drama. I remember thinking, 'Umph, Jason and that trick...what was her name'?"

Was she for real?

"So, what would I do around here?" I asked. It was clear I needed to change the page for her.

"Oh, girl, we'll find something for you. You can file or something. I'm sure Stacy probably has a bunch of stuff she needs help with. I'm glad you're here," she said.

"Wow, so it's a done deal then?" I asked excitedly.

"Yeah, girl. You knew it was gonna be. I'm not even sure why you were even tripping." She eyed me suspiciously.

I got up and prepared to walk out. I did have a date for happy hour, and I couldn't wait to get with my girls, so we could dish on Sasha.

"So, you'll start when?" she asked.

"Oh, once I notify my probation officer that we're all good, she'll give me a start date."

"Okay, well, I'll let Stacy know in case I'm not here," she said.

"Great! Thanks again, Sasha, and I look forward to working with you ladies." I smiled.

"We're happy to have you. Like I said, if your case had gone to court, I can't think of a jury in America that would've convicted you! And besides, maybe one day you'll be willing to pay the favor back by giving me an exclusive," she said timidly.

"Okay, well, thanks, and we'll see about that," I said and ducked out of there before she said anything else.

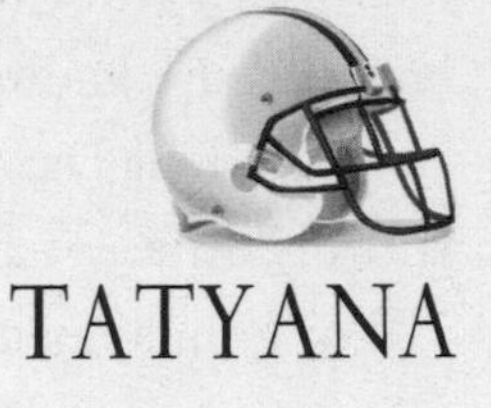

TATYANA

Hours after we were supposed to be gone, Pamela and I sat in the family room and tried to make sense of the newest letter. I had to admit, I was taken aback.

There was no way I was about to crumble and break down in front of her, but it was definitely a struggle. I put up my best game face and held the stoic expression as best I could.

"Sooo, you still don't think you need to say anything to him about all of this?" Pamela asked.

She waved the envelope about. Her voice held a tone of sarcasm, and I didn't have the stamina to check her on it.

"I have a plan, and I need to stay on the course, plain and simple. How this bitch gets close enough to know when a pizza is being delivered is beyond me." I huffed.

My mind was all over the place, and it was obvious I couldn't think straight.

"Tatyana, you haven't figured out by now that *she* ordered the doggon' pizza her damn self!" She blew out a frustrated breath and shook her head.

Warm embarrassment suddenly washed over me. I looked at her but decided not to respond. What would've been the point? It was like she itched for a reaction from me.

I didn't even want to open the damn envelope. The stationery matched the same pale lavender of the previous two. There was something about the fact that Pamela was there to intercept this one. Then it hit me. Even if this chick had ordered the pizza, how did she know when to have it delivered? If that letter had arrived when Dax was still at the house, this could've been an entirely different aftershock.

"I'm gonna open it," Pamela said.

Did it matter? Regardless of whether she read the words first, or heard them from me, I already knew what she would have to say about it. If it was up to her, we'd be upstairs packing my clothes for the great dramatic departure.

I sighed hard and sat on the chaise lounge. I eased back and crooked my elbow over my eyes as if to block out the images dancing through my head. Unfortunately for me, the vision imprinted in my memory was like a stain that wouldn't fade away. The mess had already taken its toll. I couldn't even ask Pamela if I was doing the right thing. Her mind was so clouded with thoughts of what I should be doing and the fact that I wasn't doing enough as far as she was concerned.

With my eyes squeezed tight, I zoned out. Instead of being in my family room being pitied by my best friend, my mind danced back in time. That letter could have been in the works for days, but the day before it arrived, my plan had my full attention. I had wakened early and peeked in on Pamela.

"Hey, you asleep?" I asked, after I quietly pushed the door open.

"Yeah, but why aren't you?"

"I'm about to go for a run. I'll be back in about an hour," I said and eased the door closed.

I didn't need her to bombard me with a bunch of questions and try to get all up in my business anymore than she was already. Instead of taking off on foot, I hopped in the car and drove over to the busy University Village area.

Nearly thirty minutes after I pulled into the parking structure, I finally found a spot and parked. I glanced around to make sure I was alone on that level. When the few people passed and entered the building, I grabbed the dress from the bag and pulled it over my head.

I changed into the sandals I kept in the car, and grabbed a pair of shades and a big floppy hat. Once changed, I got out of the car and walked into the building on the fourth floor.

When the elevator dinged, I hopped on and rode down to the first floor. Not that anyone would recognize me, but I wanted to be extra careful. I strode into the bank and stood in line.

"Yes, I need to make a deposit," I said to the teller once I stepped up to the desk.

"Okay, ma'am, fill out this form and do you have your ID?"

I froze and panic slammed against my heart.

"Since when do I need an ID to make a deposit?" I asked.

The girl shook her head like she was confused. I didn't know if she was new, or stupid.

"Uh, you're right, ma'am. I'm so sorry. All I need is the account number. Will this deposit be a check or cash?" she asked.

"Cash," I said as I slid the form to her that was already filled out.

When Pamela stood over me and ripped the envelope open, I refocused on the present.

"Did the bitch spray perfume?" she questioned aloud.

I rolled my eyes.

I had the good fortune of being able to have my husband's mistress's words read to me.

Pamela cleared her throat, and that was the only indicator that it was time to listen.

"Dear Tatyana," Pamela started. *"I see you want to make this more difficult than it has to be. I really thought you would have been gracious*

and stepped aside by now. He doesn't love you, and if he still says he does, it's only because he's afraid you will try to keep him from his kids! What kind of woman are you? I know you're older and probably think you won't be able to bounce back from this, but I have a good feeling you can if you focus and put your mind to it!"

Pamela did one of those dramatic pauses as if she had to catch her breath. During that intermission, she looked at me with sorrowful eyes.

"On the real—you still don't think we need to talk to him about this?" she asked.

The tone she used with me was one you'd use with a slow middle-schooler. And why would *we* need to talk to *my* husband about a possible mistress?

"Is that the end of the letter?" I asked.

I swallowed the massive boulder in my throat, and fought back tears that burned in the corners of my eyes.

"No, there's more, but I don't know if I should continue. If you're not gonna do anything but file this away with the others, what's the point in me going on?" She shrugged.

Again, she spoke like she was talking to a special needs child who needed extra time to comprehend her words.

I jumped up, snatched the note from her hands and finished reading the letter. By the time I was done, I was good and mad. How did this woman know about him going on Sasha's show? Was my husband sharing pillow talk with this chick? The rest of the letter talked about her excitement over his planned appearance on the show.

When I turned to face Pamela, she shook her head.

"On the real—what are we gonna do?" she asked.

We?

ELIZA

I hung up the phone after a long and frustrating call with Carlos. He was pissed because it took me nearly two days to return his call. But I think I was able to sell him on the idea that Tichina only wanted to meet his client.

I was tired and hadn't even made it through half my day. It seemed as if everyone and everything needed my attention. The rest of the staff looked to me for changes to any periodicals that needed to go out. In addition to outside publicity, I also had to oversee the internal newsletter. Everything fell on my shoulders.

Not only was I frustrated because Poppy was M-I-A, but I felt tugged in every direction. Suddenly, the phone on my desk buzzed. I rolled my eyes at the thought of yet another person or thing that needed my attention.

"Mr. Oliver is coming in forty-five minutes to meet with Poppy. Please find her," the mechanical voice announced.

Our HR director, Charlene Swanson, a fortyish woman with dark eyes, was known for her cold and unfriendly demeanor. I started to tell her that Poppy still wasn't in the office, and that I had been trying to reach her with no success, but she disconnected the line so fast, I didn't get the chance to say anything.

I stared at the phone for a long time after her voice was gone. I had done my job and Poppy's for so long, I probably wouldn't know how to act if I only had my responsibilities to handle. I couldn't think of any other way to reach Poppy. Usually, she'd check in to let me know she'd be out all morning, or she would be checking voicemail, but I hadn't heard a thing out of her, and it seemed everyone was looking for her.

"I'm not going to stress over it. If she's not here, she's not here. I'll tell them she had an offsite meeting that was running long," I mumbled aloud.

I hated to be in the position of having to lie for her, but I'd figure out a way to make it work. I decided to use the time to familiarize myself with our pending and most recent projects in case Mr. Oliver had questions. I didn't want anyone to get the impression that the office couldn't function in Poppy's absence.

Unsure of exactly what Mr. Oliver wanted made me feel like I was stuck cramming for a test I had known about for weeks. I went over things I'd say in my head or talked it out in the mirror.

There were good things to report. Sasha Davenport had confirmed Dax's and Dwight's appearance; several of the players' summer camps were being highlighted in a *Los Angeles Times* story, *Sports Illustrated* was doing a feature on some of the defense, and the coaches' appearance on sports radio was a success. Some of the cheerleaders were being featured in a popular men's magazine. If anyone needed proof that we were productive, I'd have been glad to stand next to our accomplishments.

My head was buried in paperwork, phone calls, and email messages when I heard what sounded like a serious ruckus going on out on the floor. I decided I'd ignore it. I had too much to get done before the meeting. There was only an hour to spare before the meeting with Mr. Oliver.

Mary rushed to my doorway. "Eliza, where's your remote? Turn your TV to *SportsCenter*." She rushed in and turned on the flat screen.

By the time she found the channel, the sportscaster was talking with a picture of Terrance Kyle, our linebacker, over his right shoulder. I closed my eyes when I realized the picture was a mug shot.

"After spending the night in jail for allegedly assaulting his newlywed wife Saturday night, Sea Lions wide linebacker, Terrance Kyle, was released from jail this morning. Kyle appeared before a judge at eight-thirty A.M. and his bond was set at twenty-five hundred dollars. He was ordered to have no contact with his wife, bathing suit model, Tara Menlo. Kyle's attorney, Greg Smith, told the *Los Angeles Times* that Menlo was not present for the bail hearing. Kyle's agent, Drew Hollen, declined to comment. Police say the argument started when Menlo confronted Kyle about a receipt she had found for a box of condoms. According to an arrest affidavit, Kyle's wife said she was taking groceries into their home when she found the receipt in the car's trunk. When the two were seated back in the car, they began talking about the receipt and their marriage.

"That's when Kyle got upset and allegedly assaulted his wife, the report says. Menlo ran to a neighbor's house and called police. A responding officer said he saw a three-inch cut beneath Menlo's right eye, according to the affidavit. Kyle did not have any visible marks or bruises. When questioned by police, he confirmed there was an argument over the receipt, but said his wife had struck him. Now released, Kyle will still face other judges—Lions General Manager Jason Redland, Head Coach Taylor Almond, and NFL Commissioner Roger Goodell.

"Kyle had been arrested for domestic violence previously. While in college, he got into an altercation with his then-girlfriend, Susan Carson. He was placed on probation for the offense and required to take anger-management classes."

I was sick.

"Has anyone called for a comment?" I asked Mary.

"No, not yet," she said.

"Okay, go call his agent. Find out everything so we can try and get ahead of this."

"Got it," Mary said as she headed out.

This was the last thing I needed.

SASHA

SLAP! SLAP!

"Oh, shit!" he cried, but he grabbed my hips tighter, and that made me wiggle harder. Our bodies rocked in sync. Sticky sweat dripped from my body on to his. I felt electricity in the air. Our skin made loud slapping noises and the room smelled rank and muggy.

"Ssssss, ugh."

He was harder than steel and so deep; it felt like he was touching my tonsils from the bottom up. I was in paradise.

"Damn, girl!"

I could tell he felt it, too.

We were so intense, I rode him hard.

SLAP!

He frowned, but that could've been his sex face.

SLAP! SLAP!

"Damn, Sasha, watch that shit! That hurt!"

That was music to my ears. I slapped him again—this time harder.

SLAP!

He snatched both my hands and held them tightly in front of me. But his hips never stopped moving.

The whole time, I moved my hips and wiggled harder.

"Violent and shit," he muttered.

But we were still in ecstasy.

After a few minutes, I pulled away from his grip and slapped him again.

"That shit ain't cool!"

He held on to my hips like he didn't want to let me go. But I was in the zone. I closed my eyes. I still rode him hard and fast. The sounds grew louder, more sweat dripped. Suddenly, I felt myself letting go.

"Grab my hair!"

He held on to my hips.

"My hair! Grab it!"

"Look, you not running this show," he said. He grabbed my breasts and pulled me closer to his face.

"Oh, shit!" I cried.

He suckled my nipple like he was brought here solely for that purpose. My body was on fire.

"Damn, Sasha!"

"Oh, Dax! Dax! Right there, baby, right there!"

Suddenly, he stopped.

This time, there was no mistaking the frown on his face. It was a menacing glare.

"You just called me some other fool's name!"

"Whoa! Hold up," I said.

My brain wouldn't rewind. The sensational feeling vanished instantly.

Tim shoved me off his body with such force, I nearly tumbled from the sofa and on to the floor.

"Dax? Yo, so you still chasing them ballers, I see," Tim said. "I thought you told me those pictures were a publicity stunt!"

Tim was a celebrity trainer with a body that was out of control. He had a mean six-pack, bulging pecs and all, but his face was worthy of a brown paper bag and nothing less. He was good to fuck in private, but I would never be seen in public with his ratchet-looking face.

He got up and started looking for his clothes. He cursed and fussed the entire time he got dressed.

I thought we were clear on our relationship. He was *fugly*, but he was a magnificent fuck, and he made me feel beautiful. I didn't mind when he kept me company because if nothing else, my toes curled, and he helped me to take the edge off.

"Can't believe you called me some other sucka's name! You real foul for that, Sasha. Yo, lose my number!" Tim said as he slammed my door on his way out. Pictures on the wall shook because he had slammed the door so hard.

"Damn, Dax on the brain for real!"

At first I was pissed about the missed orgasm, but then I grabbed the remote and grinned when I saw a familiar picture on one of the tabloid shows.

I could not be more excited, happy and proud, or any other adjective one would use to describe how I felt. I was so proud of what I had already accomplished. Every time I turned around, I saw pictures of my and Dax's smiling faces. *Star* and *People* and *US Weekly* all ran the photos on their websites, and I could only imagine they'd be plastered all over their magazines, too.

If you didn't know any better, you'd think we were a bona fide couple. My plan was already off to a great start, and we still had an entire week and a half to their appearance on the show. But still, as far as I was concerned, he and I spent lots of time together.

The next plan would require more creativity, but being Sasha Davenport meant it would get done. I pulled on my robe and moved to the desk. I sat and drummed my fingers on the desk as I held the phone between my head and shoulder. This call should've been made from the office for legitimacy purposes, but what I saw on TV had me hyped and excited. I waited for someone in the Sea Lions' publicity to pick up.

"Hello, Publicity," a voice greeted.

"Hi, this is Saaaasha Davenport, and I'm calling because I wanted to see if there was any way you guys could assist us with something I think would be a great photo op for one of your players. Who am I speaking with?"

"Sasha, this is Mary. I'm the administrative assistant for publicity. I love your show!"

"Oh, thank you so much, Mary. I appreciate you watching my show."

Once I heard that, I knew for certain my plan would work out perfectly fine. Since Mary was already a fan, I knew she'd be willing to assist with the project.

"Mary, I'm not sure if you're aware, but in addition to the show, I also run a very successful social club here in L.A. It's called the Football Widows Social Club. Our primary objective is serving the community, but we also offer lots of classes and workshops designed to empower women, so I'm wondering if you'd be willing to help convince Dax Becall to come over and teach a Football 101 course. We could get tons of press before, during, and even after the class," I said.

"OHMYGOD! Love it! Love it!" Mary screamed.

"Great!" I said.

As Mary went all ballistic over my great idea, I was already ahead of her. I had calculated how many meetings Dax and I would need to have to prepare for the workshop. This would ensure more one-on-one time with him.

"This is brilliant!" Mary cheered. "But here's what I need to do. I have to speak with one of the higher ups—you know, to get the ball rolling. Don't get me wrong, I think it's a no-brainer, but it's just technicalities," she assured.

"Okay, so when can I expect to hear back? I mean, someone from the Rams inquired," I said.

"The Rams! No, no, listen when I tell you; we want to do this, I need to take it through um, how do you say—the proper channels. I know just the right person who is going to green-light this," Mary squealed.

"Oh, great. Who is it?"

"Eliza Carter," said Mary.

"Oh, Eliza! Yes, she's working with my producer for the guys' upcoming appearance on the show. It's Dax and Dwight," I said.

"Yes, we're so excited about that, too. And I want you to know we're running billboard ads, doing e-blasts to our one-point-five-million fan base, and working on a contest for his fan page all surrounding that show."

"Oh, that's great!" I said. "Then why don't we count this as one of the many events you're planning in the media blitz," I said.

"That's great."

"You know, Mary, I'm thinking, maybe I should have my producer McKenzie reach out to Eliza. They already work together, so I'll bring her up to speed."

"Sure, you can do that, but I'm telling you there's no doubt we're interested in this project. It's a great idea and precisely the kind of thing we like to be a part of in publicity. If you feel more comfortable, I can tell McKenzie to call Eliza. I can give Eliza a heads-up, so she knows to expect her call."

"Mary, thank you so much. I really appreciate your support. I look forward to working with you ladies," I said, then hung up. I eased back, grinning like a Cheshire cat.

Moments after the phone call with Mary, I buzzed McKenzie.

"Hey, Sasha, what's going on?" she asked through the intercom.

"Hey, do you have a second? I want to discuss something with you. Can you come over or are you busy?"

"No, I need about five minutes," McKenzie said.

"Great. I'll see you soon."

While I waited on McKenzie, I went over all of the reasons why this workshop would be great. I also decided that it would require at least two meetings to work out everything we needed. We'd have to meet as quickly as possible, then at least a few days before the actual workshop. All of these thoughts swarmed in my head until a knock at the door interrupted my thoughts.

"Come in," I sang.

McKenzie stuck her head in and asked, "Is this going to be a quick meeting or do I need—"

"No, no, no, this is gonna be quick," I told her.

She walked in and took a seat on the small loveseat.

"What's up, Sasha?" She smiled.

"Well, I have come up with what I think is a great idea. You know to help promote Dax's upcoming appearance on the show," I said.

McKenzie twisted her lips to the side as curiosity etched its way into her features. I didn't care. She worked for me!

"So, here's what I'm planning to do. Dax and I are going to do a workshop at the club. The workshop, Football 101, will be an exclusive event, and we'll do a press conference to announce it."

"In exclusive you mean for members only? Or is this open to the public?"

"Eeeewww, not. We do not want this opened to the public," I squealed. "This is a private, exclusive affair, and it's only open to a select clientele."

"Oooh, I see. Then why have a press conference about it?" McKenzie asked.

I rolled my eyes at the silliness in her question. "A press conference means cameras, videos and pictures. What better way to plaster my and Dax's faces all over everything?" I asked. "It's like preparing the world for the inevitable, us being together," I announced.

"Man! You are good. You are really good," McKenzie said. "So, what do you need me to do to help?" she asked.

That was the thing I liked most about McKenzie. She knew how to play her position really well. Once she got on board with an idea, she wasted no time in rolling up her sleeves to see what needed to be done to make it happen. Unlike Marteen who sat and nervously thought about why a plan wouldn't work. She even sent weekly emails reminding me about the many single players I should be going after.

"Well, here's what I need from you. If you can contact publicity at the front office and let Eliza know what we're planning to do, that would be most helpful," I said.

"Okay, sure. I'll call her up and ask her—"

"No, no, no, no," I cut her off. "I didn't say *ask* her anything. Make it appear as if Dax has already agreed, and let Eliza know that out of courtesy we are offering them the chance to contact the press first," I said.

"Oooooh, okay. I like it. I like it," McKenzie said. "But how do we get Dax on board?" she asked.

"You let me worry about Mr. Dax, but trust and believe it will not be a problem. Think about it. What man do you know that would not want to be in a room filled with women hanging on his every word? I know Dax, and trust and believe when I tell him about this, he'll be good and ready," I said.

JERRI

I made it to the restaurant earlier than expected, so I decided there'd be no harm in enjoying a cocktail before Vanessa and Natasha arrived. I needed to take the edge off.

Still a bit rattled after that awkward meeting with Sasha, I wasn't sure what to make of the things she had said. All of her innuendos about what went down with Jason and me, made me wonder if working there would be the best thing for me. Sure our pictures were splashed all over the tabloids, and the gossip blogs and TV programs ran our story until I felt like it had gone out of style, but that had all been in the past. The last thing I wanted was to be reminded of what had gotten me caught up in the first place.

I told myself it was Sasha's job to try and get me to talk about it. Then there was the part of me that also prayed she may have simply been struggling to make small talk.

"Hi," said the waitress who bounced her way over to my table. She reached into the apron around her waist, pulled out a paper drink coaster and slid it in front of me.

"What can I bring you to drink?" she asked.

I looked into the waitress's face. Her big, brown eyes were bright against her dark skin. They made her look like she was barely old enough to serve alcohol.

"Hi," I said and picked up the drink menu. "Sure, let me—" I glanced at her over the top of the menu. "I'm meeting friends," I told her, then focused back on the menu.

"Oh, well, would you like to wait before you order?" she asked.

"No, no, I need something to drink while I wait," I said. "And, um, I think I'd like a Washington Apple."

"Okay, one Washington Apple coming up. Would you like to nibble on an appetizer while you wait?"

"No, just the drink should be fine."

The after-work crowd poured in, and the restaurant began to bustle with noises as people talked, laughed and drank. I soaked up the atmosphere as much as I could. I felt goose bumps form on my skin. I missed being out and was thrilled to be around people other than the staff at the house.

As the waitress walked away, my mind drifted back to my marriage, when the shit had started falling apart.

"So, who you texting?"

Jason nearly jumped out of his skin. I hadn't meant to sneak up on him like that. But we had been tiptoeing around each other in the house. We barely spoke unless it was about the kids, and I found him skinning and grinning while he texted on his phone. He was dressed in workout gear, but I had caught him before he made it to the gym.

His startled expression confirmed that it was that tramp.

"Here we go with this same ol' bullshit again!" he screamed. "I told you that chick does that shit to mess with y'alls heads. She knows the wives and girlfriends hate her. I'm not the only one she did that with!"

He was right. It was the same ol' bullshit, but only because he really expected me to believe that those pictures were old. That was how he had tried to explain that shit away.

"It was way before your time!" he screamed.

I hated him. I wasn't sure if I hated him more because he cheated or the fact that he blatantly lied about it.

I snatched the phone from his hand.

"Why are you still talking to this bitch! I am dumbfounded!"

I shook the phone in his direction after I saw the skeezer's name. He rolled his eyes dramatically. His nonchalant reaction pissed me off even more.

"Look, I ain't gonna keep repeating myself. I told you; Missy cool with all the players. She just be fuckin' with y'all!"

He looked like *he* was disgusted with *me*.

"You too damn jealous, man! I told you those pictures were way before your time. She done been around the entire offense and defense!"

Since that incident, our marriage became nothing more than conversations about the kids and occasional plans for dinner. I didn't understand how he could still be friends with the very bitch who caused problems in our marriage? How he couldn't see the blatant disrespect!

The writing was on the wall. He had already started washing his own clothes, which told me something was up. He shook his head like he was so over the conversation, then he took off down the hall.

I knew he was headed to the weight room to work out. So I crept into his section of the closet and saw a pile of his dirty clothes. I knew once he started working out, I'd have some time. I grabbed some of his jeans and checked the pockets. I found a couple of valet ticket stubs and some change. There was nothing there, but when I picked up his shirt, I sniffed and the scent of another woman damn near slapped me in the face.

"Damn, so now we've resorted to that type of shit, huh?"

I jumped so hard, I squealed a bit.

"What you so deep in thought about?" Vanessa's voice shattered the memory.

My gloom instantly changed. I jumped up from my seat and threw my arms around her, then I reached for Natasha.

"Hey, what's going on?" I asked.

Just then the waitress walked over with my drink.

"Oh, two more," she said.

"I didn't know how long you guys were gonna be, so I tried to get a head start," I admitted.

"What is that?" Vanessa asked.

"It's a Washington Apple," I said.

"Would you like one?" the waitress asked.

"What's in it?"

"Sour apple pucker and Crown Royal, with cranberry juice," the waitress said.

"Nah, let me see—," Vanessa said.

"I'm gonna have a Bellini," Natasha said.

Once their drinks arrived, it started to feel like the good ol' days, before my life was turned upside down.

"So wait 'til I tell you guys about the strange-ass meeting I had with Sasha Davenport," I said.

"She seems so fake to me," Vanessa said.

"I like her show," Natasha added.

"Well, I used to like it, too, but how about she kept wanting to talk about what happened with me and Jason and that super groupie, Missy!"

Vanessa's mouth dropped. "I knew that bitch was messy!" she said.

"What do you mean she wanted to talk about it?" Natasha asked. "What about why you were there?"

"Yeah, that's the trip part. She was cool about me doing my

community service there and all, but she spent more time asking about the incident. Then she had the nerve to tell me that she basically expects me to come on the show and talk about it!"

"What kind of hot mess is that? I think you should find something else to do." Vanessa smacked her lips. "She wouldn't be making no fool outta me!"

We both looked at Vanessa.

"Anyway, I said I was glad when other scandals knocked mine into the past. The last thing I wanna do is go stirring shit up again."

"I feel you on that," Natasha said. "People make mistakes. You're human. You're paying your debt to society. I say leave well enough alone."

"Yeah, 'cause the last thing you wanna do is give Missy and her family the idea that she could try to sue you," Vanessa added.

"Sue me?"

"Yeah, girl, like in civil court, to help pay for all of her medical bills and shit," Vanessa said.

After I was arrested and thrown in jail, it never dawned on me that Missy had that option. As far as I was concerned, the bitch should be glad she escaped with her life!

TATYANA

Pamela, the letters and my growing doubt had started to take a toll on my relationship with Dax.

"You okay, babe?" he asked a few days after the last letter.

"Why you ask?"

He stuffed his mouth with pancakes and began to chew. I waited for him to finish his mouthful.

"I dunno. You been acting strange lately. I know I came in late last night, but you actually slapped my hand away, and all I was trying to do was pull you close," he said.

"I was probably real tired. You yourself said you came in real late," I said.

"Yeah, I did. That Sasha is wild," he said and shook his head.

My eyebrow dipped a little, and I frowned. But I figured he was too focused on his food to notice the subtle change.

"What's that supposed to mean?" I asked. I couldn't help my tone at that point. How was I supposed to know he had been with Sasha the entire night? And what kind of meeting needs to happen at night in the first damn place. I made a personal note to remember to chat with Sasha the next time I saw her.

"What's *what* supposed to mean?" he asked. He was looking up at me and confusion was all over his features.

"You said Sasha is wild. I was asking what you meant by that," I said.

"Oh, nothing really. I was talking about us being at that club. She had a bunch of photographers snapping pictures and shit. Then when Tichina did a shout-out, it really got crazy in there," he said.

"So, you guys stayed there the whole time?" I asked.

His brows furrowed, and he looked up at me. "Uh, where else would we go? I ain't cool with her like that," he said. Dax put his fork down. "Actually, now that I think about it, we didn't even really get the chance to talk about the stupid show."

"Isn't that why you all were meeting in the first place?" I asked.

"Yeah, but I'm telling you, things got crazy and as loud as that place was, there was no way we could conduct any kind of business."

"But you guys were there the whole time?" I said again.

He frowned. "What's really going on, Tatyana?" he asked.

"Nothing," I said. "Why you ask that? I can't talk to my husband about his date?" I giggled.

"Date my ass. That chick is wild. She got all drunk and shit!" He laughed. "But seriously. I think she's worried about us being on the show or something. I've never had to meet with somebody to talk about being on TV, but I guess she don't want to leave anything to chance."

"Umph."

"It was supposed to be business. I would hardly call that a date," he said. "Besides, my wife won't let me date other women, will she?" He snickered.

I balled up my napkin and threw it at his head. He ducked and laughed.

"Hey, I was only checking—making sure the rules haven't changed." He laughed.

We were both laughing when Pamela strolled into the kitchen.

"What's so funny up in here?" she asked as she walked over to the cabinet and opened it. "I could hear the two of you all the way upstairs."

"Oh, you had to be here," Dax said. He finished up his food, then kissed my forehead.

"I'll see you ladies later," he said.

Once he was gone, Pamela looked over her shoulder as if she was about to discuss top secret plans.

"So, I take it you never said anything to him," she whispered.

"I told you already, Pamela, Dax hasn't given me any reason to think he's doing anything wrong. I don't know who this woman is, but I'm not about to let her get inside my head."

"Umph, well, I guess we'll have to sit back and wait until this thing blows over," she said. She jabbed at her pancakes as she cut them into small pieces.

"I don't feel like talking about those stupid letters. What are we doing today? That's what we need to talk about," I said. I used the most cheerful voice I could muster up. It had only been one week, but I felt like Pamela had been here a lifetime.

"I don't care what we do. Surprise me," she said.

"Do you want to go shopping or to the spa? Help me out here."

"You decide. I really don't care."

"You're in L.A. There's nothing you want to do?"

"Nope, not like this is my first rodeo. We can do whatever you want to do." She continued eating.

"You wanna go on skid row and help feed the homeless?" I asked in jest.

Pamela shrugged her shoulders. "If that's what you want to do."

"Really, Pamela?"

She looked up at me like she was confused.

"What?" she whined.

"So, you really can't think of anything to do? You'd agree to go on Skid Row?" I admonished.

"Well, it could be part of your community project or whatever the hell you guys do over at that Football Widows club house," she said.

"Hmm, okay. I'll give you that then."

"Dang, thanks. You act like it's a crime. I don't live here. What I look like having a long list of things to do?"

"Okay, Pamela. Let's go to the Grove. We can do some shopping, then we can have lunch and kind of play it by ear."

"Sounds good to me," she said.

I got up from the table. "Okay, I'm gonna go get dressed. I'll meet you back down here in about an hour," I said.

"Okay. Cool."

An hour and a half later, Pamela came downstairs.

"You ready?" I asked. "That's a real cute dress."

"Oh, thanks, girl," she said.

"I like the Grove." The phone rang. "Can you get that please?" I said.

I grabbed my hobo and started to pull items out of it.

"Becall residence," Pamela said into the phone. "Ah, Missus or Mister?"

I looked over at her.

"Well, Mrs. Becall is here. Hold a second, please," she said.

Pamela covered the mouthpiece of the phone and looked at me with a worried expression on her face.

"This is Gigi with La Perla, Rodeo Drive," Pamela said. She spoke like she was trying to imitate a bad British accent.

I was about to burst out laughing until I realized she was dead serious.

"They want to talk to you," she said and angled the phone in my direction.

"Ah, La Perla, like the very expensive lingerie store? What are they calling me for?"

Pamela shrugged and shoved the cordless phone to me.

I was still confused as I pulled it up to my ear. "Hi, this is Gigi at La Perla on Rodeo Drive," the woman announced.

"Oookay," I said, still unclear about why anyone from La Perla would call me.

"We're wondering if we should return the items on hold to the sales floor," the woman said.

"Items on hold?"

"Yes, we are only allowed to hold for twenty-four hours, but for our exclusive clients we will hold longer. I'm looking, and we're quickly approaching day five, so this is a courtesy call before the items are returned to the sales floor," she said.

Pamela was standing so close I could almost smell her breath. "What is going on?" she asked.

"Gigi says they're returning items on hold to the sales floor," I told her and shrugged. Hell if I knew.

"Nuh-uh, tell her to hold them. Let her know we are on our way," Pamela said.

I frowned. She snatched the phone. "Hi, yes, we'll be there in thirty minutes," Pamela said. "Keep the items on hold," she barked into the phone.

I looked at her, baffled. I didn't have anything on hold at La Perla. This had to be a mistake.

Once she ended the call, she turned to me and said, "Don't you see what's going on here?" Pamela asked.

Her eyes twinkled, and she was hyped.

"We finally have some doggon' proof. We need to go to that store and get to the bottom of this. He must've been buying shit for his jump off! This is how we'll find his little twenty-three-year-old!"

I had no idea we were looking for her. Fear gripped my heart and squeezed tightly.

ELIZA

Nobody had seen nor heard from Poppy all morning and most of the afternoon, yet ten minutes before the meeting with Mr. Oliver, like an unwelcomed storm, she blew into my office and started with the complaints.

"Yes, absolutely. This place is falling apart. I work off-site for a few days, and it's like you guys don't know what to do!" she shouted. "Why didn't someone say something about this shit with Dwight?" she snarled.

"We are on top of it," I said.

"On top of it?" she growled.

It was just like her to come coasting in with complaints and demands at the eleventh hour.

"I tried to call you for a while," I said.

"Yeah, and at what point were you gonna add you were calling because one of our star wide receivers, Terrance Kyle, had been thrown in jail?" she asked nastily.

"Well, I was trying to call you before this news broke. Mr. Oliver called a meeting, and I wanted to give you a heads-up."

The color drained from her face. Seemingly unable to speak, she muttered, "Mr. Oliver?"

"Yes," I said. I flicked my wrist and said, "It's in about ten minutes, actually."

Poppy looked mortified. She took a few breaths as if she was trying to contain herself. Suddenly she glanced around the room.

"Any idea what he wants to meet about?" she asked. She couldn't hide the nervousness in her voice.

"Nope, was just put on alert. I figured he might want an update on everything in the works," I said.

Poppy blew out a breath. "Hmm, yes, absolutely that's completely possible. Do I need to be briefed on anything?" she asked.

"Like what?"

"Anything. I don't want to be blindsided. I can't believe you didn't get a hold of me. This is crazy. I can't go in unprepared," she said.

I wanted to say, "If you were worried about being prepared, you would've been in contact with the office." She had to have seen one of the dozens of text messages or missed calls from me. I wasn't sure what was going on with Poppy lately, but it was obvious she realized how much she had slipped.

I sat and stared at her blankly.

"There's no way I can download all we're working on in the five minutes we have before this meeting," I said, agitated.

I looked up and noticed the herd of people who had moved toward the conference room.

"Hey, *Mija*, you want me to hold a—" Mary stopped mid-sentence at the sight of Poppy. She clamped her mouth shut. "Oh, thought you were in here alone," Mary said.

Poppy frowned at her.

Mary eased out of the doorway and moved down the hallway.

"We need to figure out a way to get rid of her," Poppy said. "Absolutely!"

I kept my thoughts on what needed to be done.

"Earlier, I caught her on the phone, and it sounded like she was having phone sex with someone," Poppy accused. "That's so inappropriate at work. There's no telling which player she's screwing now."

The nerve of her. I never bothered to respond.

By the time we made it to the conference room, it was packed. I knew no one from management was present because the chatter and small talk spilled all the way down the hall.

Once the meeting began, I sat, anxious to see how this would all play out.

Mr. Oliver's secretary addressed the body and gave him a brief introduction. Mr. Oliver was a man whose athletic build had slipped years ago. He sported a well-developed beer belly. His skin looked like worn leather, and his sandy-brown hair sported an old-fashioned high top.

"I won't take much of your time." He glanced around the room. He breathed so hard like he had just finished a marathon. "A sign of a good and effective department is one that operates just as well if not better independently as it does under direct supervision. That's why I'm so proud to announce that publicity has been nominated for the Silver Anvil Award," he said.

The room burst into a loud enthusiastic applause.

"Poppy McDaniel, get on up here," Mr. Oliver said.

She stumbled and took center stage.

"We wanted to first acknowledge our own before you're recognized on a national level," he said as he slipped an envelope to Poppy.

"Mr. Oliver, I know how busy you are, so it means quite a bit that you would recognize me in such a public way. I'm glad to know all of my hard work is appreciated." She smiled.

They posed for a picture, and I felt sick. I wondered if I was the only person who had those traitorous thoughts.

"Keep up the good work," Mr. Oliver said. They shook hands, the photographer snapped a few more pictures and Mr. Oliver edged past her and out of the meeting.

I waited for Poppy to mention her team, but she never did.

SASHA

"I'm gonna have to tell my wife she needs to watch out for you!" Dax joked as I greeted him with a social kiss. We were cool like that now.

"Muwah!" I exclaimed.

When it was over, and he pulled his head back after the single right cheek to right cheek kiss, I wanted to melt. He smelled so damn good and had offered no resistance whatsoever. I wanted to warn him that no truer words had been spoken, but decided against it. Some of the most pleasant surprises were completely unexpected.

"So, are we finally gonna have that meeting you talked about the first time we hooked up?" His smile was nothing short of dazzling.

Was it me, or had he thrown around a lot of sex-laden phrases? It must've been his subconscious peeking out. First, there was the warning Tatyana comment, and then the one about us hooking up. They confirmed for me that he felt it, too. The chemistry between us couldn't be ignored for long.

We turned heads as we were led through the restaurant.

"Is this okay?" the hostess asked.

"Perfect," I said.

She left, and we took our seats at the Cannon Sidewalk Café in Beverly Hills, and I couldn't be more thrilled. We were out in the open where we could soak up the wonderful sunshine. But more importantly, we had become sitting ducks for the paparazzi that were scheduled to arrive within minutes.

"Yes, we can talk about that and the workshop." I smiled.

"Oh, yeah, the workshop, I actually think that's a great idea," he said. His eyes darted to my left. "Damn, you're like a magnet, huh?" he said.

"What are you talking about?" I asked as I turned my head in the direction of his stare.

"Do they just show up everywhere you go?" he asked, referring to the paparazzi. Even with a frown on his face, the man still looked good.

"I'm sorry," I said bashfully.

"Oh, not your fault," he said as he angled his body in his chair to look at the photographers.

"You wanna go somewhere else? Somewhere more private?" I asked, then waited and licked my lips sexily.

My question pulled his attention back to me. First his eyes connected with mine, then they fell to my lips where they lingered. I licked my glossy lips, and he glanced away as if he suddenly realized what he was doing.

Passion ravished me from head to toe and I prayed my face didn't reveal how badly I wanted him.

"Nah, no biggie to me as long as you good," he said.

I turned to look at the bank of photographers gathered across the street again. I was certain they knew their boundaries. Their flashes began to flicker like crazy. It had been a gamble, but I had to work my plan to the fullest. One can never be sure whether they'd show up after being tipped off.

I grabbed Dax's hand and brought it up close to my face. From their angle, I was certain it would look like a kiss to his hand. When he didn't jerk away, I felt good.

"I've wondered about the hands of quarterbacks," I said.

Dax chuckled. "Uh, what about them, and why would you be wondering about that of all things?"

"Just curious about whether clutching that ball gives you calluses," I lied.

"Nah, nothing like that," he said.

When he bit the left corner of his lip, I wondered if I had gone too far. His eyes squinted slightly. We were at just the right angle, so I hoped the photographers caught what had to be the money shot of the day. Images of the headlines danced through my head and made me so happy, I was ready to wrap things up.

Gently, Dax eased his hand away from me and used it to pick up the menu.

"So, let's see what we've got here," he announced.

We placed our orders and fell into easy conversation. He seemed like the perfect man. He was down-to-earth and easy to be around.

"So this is like one of your show topics?" he asked.

"Yeah, my audience is predominantly female, but I try to make sure I inform them enough that they want to pull their partners in to watch, too," I said.

His expression was so intense as he clung to my every word.

"So, do you get dudes on there to talk about this stuff, too?" he asked, like he was really interested.

"Of course! What, you think it's just a bunch of women talking? We get the male perspective, too," I boasted.

"Oh, nah, I mean, that's cool. But on the real though, I kinda find it hard to imagine what man in his right mind would go on a national talk show and confess that he wishes his wife would get a job."

"What about you?" I asked.

He laughed so hard, he nearly upchucked his lemonade. When

the laughter that nearly did him in subsided, he cleared his throat.

"Ahhhh, what about me?" He frowned. "I'm not going on national TV spewing no BS like that!" he exclaimed.

I laughed at his reaction.

"No, silly. I was asking what you thought about the fact that your wife contributes nothing to your bottom line," I said.

"Ooouch! That's harsh," he said. But his smile never faded. "I wouldn't say she doesn't add *anything* to my bottom line," he said.

But his words seemed strained. It was obvious I had touched a sore, or at least a soft spot.

"Oh, so Tatyana does work. I'm sorry. I thought she stayed at home," I said innocently.

"Nah, she does. I mean, she doesn't work outside the home, but she raises our kids and does stuff around the house," he said.

"Oh, my bad, so she's different than most of these NFL wives. She does it all on her own. Let me guess: No nanny, no housekeeper?" I feigned surprise, eyes widened and all. "Then I stand corrected," I added.

Dax laughed.

"Guilty as charged. We have all of the above." He chuckled. "But I guess what I'm saying is as long as she keeps everything working at home so I can take care of business on the field, it works for us." He shrugged.

I heard what he said. But I also understood that he only *thought* it worked because he didn't know anything different. If he knew what it was like to have a real woman in his life, somebody who was more than just a wife, he'd understand. I would help him in the board meetings, compliment potential deals and look out for his best interests. Sure, I'd play my part, all the while allowing him to take the lead, but make no mistake about it: We *will* make a magnificent team.

JERRI

"You remember that night?" Vanessa asked.

Snap! Snap!

I heard when she snapped her fingers in front of my eyes, but it was too late. In my mind, I was already back there. I was back at that night, after the deed had been done.

"As far as I was concerned, he brought that shit on himself and her!"

"What did you do? Why are you wearing a negligee?" Vanessa asked the moment she opened her front door. First, she looked over my shoulder, then she walked out of the house and looked around. "Jesus! You're like soaking wet. What is going on? What happened?" she asked. "Come in here before you get sick! What have you done, Jerri?" she asked. She walked me into the house and led me to the sofa. "Sit right here." She ran toward the back then came back with a pair of sweats and a T-shirt. "Put this on before you get pneumonia."

I pulled the nightgown off and slipped the shirt over my head.

"Whoa. Didn't mean right here, but okay. We'll go with that," Vanessa said. She had already gotten Natasha on speakerphone.

"What's going on over there?" Natasha's voice asked.

"I don't know. The girl showed up on my doorstep wearing lingerie and soaking wet," Vanessa reported.

"Should I come over there?" Natasha asked.

"It's four in the morning!" exclaimed Vanessa. "I was stunned to find her here," she said.

Vanessa looked at me.

"What the hell happened?" Natasha asked.

"I did it," I said. "I did it!" I exhaled.

"You did *what*?" Natasha asked over the speakerphone.

"Start at the beginning," Vanessa said.

"After we had dinner, I went home, showered and changed into something nice. I took a picture with my phone and sent it to him. I knew for sure he'd respond—damn an argument," I said. Telling the story only took me back to that place. Instead of being on the couch with Vanessa, I was in bed waiting for him to respond.

I looked at the clock. It was still early. The green numbers on the digital clock flickered 10:30. I took another picture—more provocative than the first. By midnight, I knew exactly where to find him, and I was determined to make sure he never ignored me again.

A wave of raw hurt gushed over me. I felt my blood as it boiled. I had something like an out-of-body experience because one minute I was in my high-heeled slippers and the next I had the can of gasoline. I even had some in the beer bottle.

"The bastard thinks parking down the street and around the corner is gonna cut it?" I muttered as I passed his car.

I was sick and tired of being sick and tired. I turned into a nearby driveway and drove back by his car. The street was dark and empty. I glanced around, and when I didn't see anyone, I got out and doused his car with some of the gas. I pulled out one of the books of matches I had brought and rushed back to my car.

I pulled alongside his car again, lit the entire book of matches and flung it onto the hood of his car.

A dark orange and blue plume of flame danced up inches into

the sky, lit up the dark night, and I smiled. By the time I got to the corner and looked into the rearview mirror, the entire vehicle was fully engulfed in flames. When I rounded the corner, I heard what sounded like an explosion.

Back in front of Missy's house I looked around to make sure no one was outside on her street. I crept around to the side of the house, and poured gasoline as I did. When I had surrounded her entire house, I poured what little was left onto her car, then I struck a match and lit the book of matches. It ignited a trail of gasoline, that danced so fast along the path I had created that I had to move quickly. Before I got to the walkway, I lit and tossed the Molotov cocktail. It landed on the ground between the car and the garage door.

Flames lit up my eyes. I took off down the street and climbed into my car.

"Are you crazy!" Vanessa screamed. "What if you killed them? He's not worth it!"

As the sun came up, we sat on Vanessa's couch and watched the news, listening to them talk about me like I was a fugitive. What I had done suddenly hit home.

"The wife of a prominent sports figure is wanted for questioning in connection with trying to burn down another woman's house in what police are calling a love triangle gone wrong. The suspect, thirty-one-year-old Jerri Nelson, wife of Sea Lions star wide receiver Jason Nelson, faces felony arson charges.

"An eyewitness tells police he saw Mrs. Nelson, who was wearing a nightgown in the early-morning hours, douse her rival's house with liquid, start the fire and run. That eyewitness, a man who happened to be riding down the street around two A.M., says he saw Mrs. Nelson standing in front of one of his neighbor's houses. He says at the time, she was wearing a white teddie nightgown with polka dots. The witness said he then saw Nelson pour liquid along the front of the house, ignite it with matches, then stand there and throw a Molotov cocktail toward the car and run away. The witness then rushed to wake up the homeowner.

"He told police that Mrs. Nelson had set the fire. He recognized her because he had seen her in tabloid magazines and on TV cheering on her husband at football games. In addition to the homeowner, Sea Lions' wide receiver, Jason Nelson, was also inside when the fire was set.

"Thanks to the witness, no one died, but the homeowner did suffer burns over twenty percent of her body. Arson investigators determined that the fire had been intentionally set with the aid of some sort of flammable and combustible liquid. The on-scene investigator said the liquid, which smelled similar to gasoline, had not only been poured along the rear and the front exterior of the residence, but also on the vehicle parked in the driveway. In what police are investigating as a possible related matter, residents around the corner called police to say a vehicle was on fire.

"The witness was provided a photo lineup and was able to positively identify Mrs. Nelson."

"Wow!" was all Vanessa said.

TATYANA

"Why are you sitting over there looking like you're so lost in deep thought?"

Pamela's voice mocked me as I made a right turn onto Rodeo Drive. I scanned the addresses with my eyes and searched for the address number 433 North Rodeo Drive.

"You see that spot right there?" Pamela asked and pointed a few cars ahead.

"Yeah, I got it," I said.

I guided the car closest to the car ahead of the empty spot and parallel parked with ease. The parking spot was a few doors down from the address where we were going.

"Good! We finally got the goods on this nucca," Pamela said.

Her voice was chipper and even borderline excited. I wasn't sure exactly how I felt, but I knew that what I felt was nothing close to the excitement I heard in her voice.

Once I had parked the car, I pulled in a deep breath before I pressed the button to shut the engine off.

"Girl, what's wrong with you? Chill out. This is a damn good thing," Pamela said.

I turned to her and sighed. I didn't understand what she could've possibly thought was a damn good thing. A few people walked by. I wanted to be one of them. I wanted to be anyone but me.

"Come on," Pamela urged.

We got out of the car and strolled up the sidewalk as if we were simply shopping. When I saw the elegant, black block letters that spelled La Perla next to the glass double doors, my heart sank to the bottom of my feet. I wanted to go anywhere but through those double doors. I wasn't ready for what this would mean.

Pamela paused for a second to frown at me.

"Girl, you'll be fine." She reached for the door, and stepped inside. I was right behind her.

The air inside the exclusive boutique felt different than the air we'd just left. It wasn't the obvious change in temperature, but everything seemed different. The florescent lighting had a blue hue to it and that seemed to add to the ambiance of the room. The area was as quiet as a library, but with soft music that drifted faintly throughout the space.

My nostrils were met with a combination of lavender and chamomile. It was pleasant and calming, at least for me. Pamela had charged full speed ahead like the Energizer Bunny.

My eyes lingered on one of the sales tables that held beautiful dainty, lacy bras. Everything looked exquisite and expensive.

"Welcome to La Perla Rodeo Drive," a thin brunette greeted us. The greeting was more for me than it was for Pamela who had simply swooshed by and headed straight to the counter.

"Thank you," I said.

"Is there something specific I can help you find?" the woman asked. Even her voice was soothing. I wanted to tell her not to waste her time and energy on me, but I smiled instead.

I kept an eye on Pamela as she talked to someone at the counter.

I glanced at one of the headless mannequins. It wore an eye-catching white lingerie set with a garter belt and matching white stockings.

"It's our featured bridal selection for the week," the sales clerk's voice whispered. She startled me. But I smiled at her and eased away from the display.

Suddenly, Pamela motioned for me to join her at the counter.

"Tat, come here. Listen to this shit!" she said.

I took heavy steps toward Pamela. But she didn't wait for me to arrive.

"Okay, this is Tatyana Becall," Pamela said. "And we really need to see the items you have on hold."

The sales clerk's eyebrows bunched together, and she looked nervous. She eyed Pamela suspiciously then glanced at me as if she was waiting for another option.

"I'm confused," the sales clerk began. "I thought you were here to purchase the items."

"We need to *see* the items," Pamela said. It was clear to me that Pamela was angry. She stammered as she spoke, and her eyes did this odd, quick blinking thing.

I wanted the tension and anxiety to leave the room. I didn't even want to be there. This had all been *her* idea. My plan needed time. I needed time. Finding this mystery person who I wasn't supposed to know about was nowhere near being high on my priority list.

"Okay, let's start over," Pamela said. She used her hands to try and deflate the situation. "You called the house saying the items needed to be paid for, or they were going back to the sales floor. I'm saying before we pay for them, I need to see what they are," Pamela tried to explain.

"So, you did not put the items on hold is what you're telling me?" the clerk challenged.

"What difference does it make *who* put the items on hold? I was actually going to ask you whether you remember who put the items on hold."

The woman's frown deepened even more.

"Here at La Perla Rodeo Drive, we are very protective of our clients' privacy," she said.

Her eyes glanced between Pamela and me.

"But you called *us*," Pamela said. Her finger emphasized her words and pointed at her chest.

"It was the number attached to the hold," the woman said.

"I'm Mrs. Becall," I finally announced.

Pamela turned to me and gave an approving smirk. The sales clerk instantly turned her attention to me. It was as if she'd suddenly dismissed Pamela.

"Mrs. Becall, we have the items right in the back. I'll bring them out for you." She smiled.

"That's all you had to do in the first damn place," Pamela snarled.

The sales clerk's face tightened. She spun on her heels, then turned and left us.

"All she had to do was go get the shit in the first place," Pamela said to me as if she expected me to co-sign. She stood and tapped her foot like she had a nervous tick.

The sales clerk returned with a stack of hangers that seemed to dangle from her fingers.

"This is a very nice array of items here," the sales clerk said. Her entire demeanor had changed. She began to flip through the hangers with ease.

"Uh, how much are these items?" Pamela asked.

When the sales clerk looked at Pamela, she did so with a nasty scowl on her face. Her mouth was now a thin, twisted line. She didn't answer Pamela right away. As if the interruption might not have happened, she continued her detailed description of the items.

Pamela gave me a knowing glance, then looked down at the

hold tag attached to one of the hangers. My eyes focused in on my last name and phone number, and I wondered what the hell was going on.

"What's the total for all of this?" I asked the clerk.

"Oh, it's only thirteen thousand dollars." She smiled.

Thirteen thousand dollars? I wanted to scream. Instead, I held my poker face and waited for her to finish her presentation. When the words tumbled from my mouth, her smile vanished, and her pleasant demeanor changed.

"I've changed my mind, so you can return the items to the sales floor," I said.

ELIZA

At first, I didn't want to take McKenzie's call. I needed to talk with Poppy in private, but I also knew I needed to stay on top of Dax's and Dwight's appearance on Sasha's show. I couldn't think of a time when any player required so much pre-planning just to be on a show, but I had to roll with Sasha and McKenzie until the guys were on that couch. I didn't need to give Poppy anything else to flip out about.

"This is Eliza," I greeted.

"Eliza, it's McKenzie Fields with the *Sasha Davenport Show*," she said.

Each time McKenzie called, she introduced herself as if we'd never spoken before, and it was her very first call to me.

"Yes, McKenzie, what can I do for you? The guys are still doing the show," I said, more than asked.

"Oh, yes, of course, of course, but that's not the reason I'm calling today," she said.

My eyes shifted toward Poppy. She seemed so disconnected.

"Oh, well, what's up?" I asked.

Poppy never looked in my direction.

I listened as McKenzie detailed the latest plan for our star quarterback.

"Of course we want to handle press for that. No, no, it's a great idea. Well, my boss is right here," I said as my eyes glanced over to Poppy again. Still, she seemed to be in her own little world.

I wanted to force her to actually do some work, the very work she had been credited with doing, but hadn't done. When Poppy spent time in the office, she seemed to be preoccupied and rushed. Mary told me she had heard her arguing on the phone with a man and someone else walked in on her during an awkward meltdown. It took me back to the moment I walked into the ladies' room, and she was talking to her reflection.

Back in the day, Poppy wore all of the latest designers and her hair stayed freshly done. She often looked like she was about to grace the cover of any top fashion magazine.

I wrapped up my call with Sasha's producer, then got up and closed my office door. Drastic times called for something drastic.

Poppy hadn't moved an inch.

"Did you hear any of my phone conversation?" I asked.

She didn't respond.

I walked back to my desk and took my seat. I stared at her for a moment to see if she'd speak, but she didn't.

"Poppy, I hope I'm not overstepping, but if I may speak frankly," I began.

She barely looked up at me. Poppy sat and picked at her cuticles. In all the years I had worked with her, I'd never seen her nails look so horrible, and I couldn't recall a time I'd ever seen her look so disheveled and unkempt.

When I noticed her dark roots, I figured I'd try to intervene. It wasn't that I liked her, but her stability, or lack thereof, could've been detrimental to my career.

"It's none of my business, but you're slipping here at work. You don't look like yourself lately, and when you *are* here, we never know what will make you snap," I commented softly.

Poppy jerked her head sideways and finally glanced up at me.

Her red puffy eyes looked hollow and distant. "Yes, absolutely! You're right, Eliza," she said dryly. "It is *none* of your business," she snarled.

I was a bit taken aback. Heat quickly rushed up my neck and face.

"I have an award and a nomination that says I'm holding things down just fine around here. Now if you want to keep your job, I suggest you do what you were hired to do, which is support me, and not question me about things that," she smiled, "like you said are none of your business."

I burned with fury. Then the anger began to boil. I wanted to tell the meth-mama that she needed someone to mind her business because she was going downhill faster than the speed of light.

But when she turned her focus back to her cuticles, I decided I'd take her advice. I logged on to my email and reviewed a few player request forms and searched for the email McKenzie promised about the Football 101 workshop.

It was a little hard to work while Poppy simply sat, but I decided to ignore her. I didn't understand why she got all of the credit for all of the work when she barely lifted a finger.

"Why aren't I good enough for him?" Poppy asked.

I couldn't hide the startled expression on my face. My eyeballs danced from side to side. She had to be on the phone.

"Do you have a man? Or are you a lesbian?" Poppy asked me.

I was stunned. We had never discussed our personal lives, and I wasn't comfortable with the discussion.

"You know what—it's not important. But, one damn day, everyone is gonna know my friggin' name!" she screamed.

The next thing I knew, she burst into tears. Tears spilled from her red eyes and ran down her puffy cheeks. I couldn't pick my mouth up off the desk. What the hell was going on with Poppy, and why had she chosen my office as the place to have a meltdown?

SASHA

What hot-blooded man in his right mind would choose Plain Jane, Tatyana Becall over me—Sasha Davenport? It made no sense. I was every man's dream even when he didn't realize it. I commanded attention when I entered a room; I received endless compliments on my appearance because of my keen fashion sense. I didn't dress merely for my body type—I dressed for men's viewing pleasure. I understood the difference and importance of dressing to please the opposite sex.

Men were visual creatures by nature. Their eyes gravitated toward a woman's breasts, so mine were always prominently and tastefully displayed. They enjoyed a woman's lips, so mine always looked glossy and wet. And my long legs stayed soft and smooth to the touch.

I glanced at my reflection in the mirror and marveled at how far I had come. I wasn't always as polished as I appeared. I had learned some tough lessons. My first marriage taught me a valuable lesson: No woman in her right mind should ever marry for love. Marriage was and should always be a business arrangement. By marriage number two, I had the right idea, but again, the wrong man.

He was a third-string player who had a little change, but he thought he could turn me into what *he* wanted. That didn't last long. If I had to admit it, I'd say my thirst for Mr. Right might have been too aggressive, but when he left the league, I knew I had to find a replacement. I had no idea it would take as long as it had. I had been single for more than five years and that was not a good look—not with all I was trying to do.

But now, I knew exactly what I wanted. I wanted a man like Dax. I wanted to be on the arm of a bona-fide superstar player.

"But this time, I know I'm gonna get it right," I said as I turned to look at my ass in the mirror. I couldn't leave anything to chance. If Dax was gonna be at the event, I had to be on point. Brown was his favorite color, so I worked the hell out of a satin, brown pencil skirt and a matching lace halter top. I knew for sure I'd catch his eye and hold his attention. I had done everything in my power to make sure he'd be there; I knew he'd bring Tatyana, but I couldn't do anything about that. Besides, her presence wouldn't stop me from working my jelly, so it was all good. I pressed a button on my cell phone and listened as the phone rang loudly.

"McKenzie, it's Saaasha. Call me right away," I said the moment her voicemail clicked on. Then I ended the call.

Because Tatyana was in the club, I'd have to be subtle, but it was time I made my intentions known. I fussed with my hair a little more, then added more MAC lip gloss.

When the phone rang, I reached for it. It was McKenzie.

"Hey, is everything in order?" I asked.

"Yes. The photographer has his marching orders. Everyone is in their position, including that new chick, and from what I hear, Tatyana and Dax have RSVP'd, so we know they'll be there," she reported.

"Okay, good. And we have the kids confirmed, right?"

McKenzie sucked her teeth. "Sasha, what's up?" she asked.

"Whaaat?"

I wasn't really irritated, but I hated when she made it seem like

I was doing and being too much. She had been with me long enough to know when I had my mind set on something, I'd do whatever was necessary to get it done. Dax was no exception. I had a meeting with Sebastian set for the following week, and I wanted to be able to report some substantial progress.

Dax and I had already been photographed in what had to be considered questionable positions, and I wanted to capitalize as much as possible on the hard work I had already done.

I didn't spend much time at the club, so I didn't really know whether Tatyana suspected anything or whether she even had a clue, but I knew for sure we'd find out after the event.

"You act like I'm new at this," she huffed.

"It's not that," I said.

"Well, you already know I've got this all under control. Not only do I have plans for you to be photographed *with* him, but I've also set up for you to have a few private moments alone with him and Dwight," she said. "You know, to talk about the show," she added.

The way she said show, made me know she was fully on board. She knew what was up, and she was going to do whatever she needed to help me accomplish my goal.

"So, I'm mixing business with pleasure?"

"Lots of business is done in pleasurable settings," McKenzie said.

I had to admit: I was impressed, but not enough to tell her.

"Oh, okay. Well, I see you are on top of things, huh?"

"Yes, so please don't keep the car waiting too long," she said.

"Well, you know I'm not trying to get there too early," I said.

"That's why I've arranged for you to come in about an hour and a half late," she said. "Fashionably late is always best."

"Yeah, but damn, that's *really* late."

"Late enough for you to walk right in to be photographed with the girls. Then you'll be ushered into a meeting with Dwight and Dax. You don't want to mingle too much. If you do, then you'll blend in, and if I know you like we know I do, the last thing you want to do is blend in," she said.

I could picture the way she frowned as she said this. I had to give it to her though because she was right. Sasha Davenport didn't blend well.

"Okay. I'll be ready when the car arrives," I said.

"Good. I'll hold it down until you get here, and I'll keep you posted on the happenings via text," she said.

"Umph, what would I do without you?"

"We won't ever have to find out because I plan to be right by your side as producer of *Simply Sasha*. I have to be on my game," she said.

"Producer, huh?"

"Producer. Just like I am for the current show," she said.

"The way you've been handling the business, I'd say that's a real possibility," I said.

"Possibility?" McKenzie balked. "Well, if that's all it is, that tells me I'm not doing my job," she added.

"No, no, McKenzie, you know doggon' well if the decision is mine, it's yours," I said.

"Sasha, I feel like you can get anything you want. In all the years we've been together, I can't think of a time when you were denied something you wanted. But we're getting ahead of ourselves. We've gotta focus on lining up all of the pieces so that everything falls into place," she said.

"You know I got you, right?" I asked.

"Yeah, I know, but I also need you to know that I don't expect anything to be given to me. I'm willing to work for it," she said.

"Then I think we're gonna be fine," I said, and I meant that.

When we ended the call, I slipped off my mountain-high heels and eased on the couch to relax with the latest issue of *Essence* magazine. If I had an entire hour and a half, there was no reason for me to rush over to the club.

After flipping through the glossy pages, I began to imagine my life with Dax. We'd open our home to *Essence*, *Ebony*, and *Jet* magazines. I wanted to make sure everyone recognized how fabulous our life together was going to be.

JERRI

We could laugh about the mess now, but back then, when I didn't know if I'd ever see the light of day again, it was no laughing matter.

I knew he'd tell the law exactly where to find me, and he did. It wasn't that I tried to kill them, but the audacity! He had no shame, and neither did she. I needed them to pay for what they had done to me, to our marriage. It might not have prevented another affair, but I felt good and vindicated as I walked away and felt the heat of the flames burning behind me.

"What time you gotta be home?" Natasha asked.

Her question pulled me away from thoughts of the past drama with Jason.

"I wanna get there before nine," I told her.

"Hmm. Okay." She twisted her mouth.

"Why you ask?"

"Was thinking that maybe we could go someplace else when we done eating," she said.

"Dang, girl, you know I really want to, but seriously, on my first night out?" I rolled my eyes dramatically. "I don't wanna take any chances. The ol' hag is probably gonna get a turn-by-turn, detailed report of every place I've visited as it is," I said.

"Yeah, that's a good point. Umph," Vanessa grunted. She pursed her lips and frowned a little. "I'll be glad when you get your freedom back. This hanging close to home and checking in before every move is so not the look," she said.

She looked away.

"Hot at two o'clock," Vanessa muttered.

Natasha's head and mine turned in the same direction, at the same time, to take in the vision.

We were silent as we watched the good-looking man walk by. His swagger was undeniably sexy. He had an athlete's build, broad shoulders that had muscles discreetly protruding near his neck, but he wasn't so buffed that he grossed you out. His angular face had a perfectly lined goatee that darkened his features. He looked good. When we had taken in his handsome face and near-perfect body parts, we returned to our conversation.

"Imagine how I feel." I shrugged and drained my glass. "It's been so long since I've been out, I barely know how to act."

"Okay, so when do you get another pass?" Natasha asked.

"Actually, if the hag confirms she got the paperwork, I may be able to make it for an event that's happening at the club," I said.

"Uh, will there be any players there?" Vanessa asked.

"Girl, yes. It's something about a show Sasha is doing, so knowing her, the place will be wall-to-wall with sports celebs," I said. The truth was I didn't really know if that was the case, but if I had to spend time at the Football Widows Social Club, I might as well be able to invite my girls to hang, too.

"And it's cool if we come by?" Natasha asked.

"I don't see why not," I said.

"Okay, well, text and let us know the details."

We wrapped up happy hour, which really had been *happy*, and I agreed to text everyone to confirm that I'd be able to go back to the club for the event.

When I arrived at the house and saw several cars parked outside, I was instantly curious. I couldn't pull around to the back fast enough.

"So, Jason is having a party. I should crash it," I muttered as I listened to laughter, voices, and music pouring from the main house.

That was the kind of stuff that really pissed me off about him. He had wasted no time in calling the police when it was just me and my two girls. Then, he had the nerve to organize a party and not even check with me!

Suddenly, I decided my night had finally gotten a much-needed shot in the arm since I had to end at happy hour. My mind raced with the many ways I could embarrass him in front of his party guests. I rushed to my part of the house and went up to my room to change clothes.

What I wore would've been fine for a crash, but I needed to make sure I added a whole lot of extra just for him. I went into my bathroom and snatched my silk robe from the hook on the back of the bathroom door. I undressed down to my underwear and slipped on the robe. I wanted the officers to know that my estranged husband didn't care about anything but himself, and his party guests, of course. Here I was trying to get some sleep, and this mo-fo was throwing a party? Oh, but no!

Once I had the robe on, I used a makeup remover pad to clean my face and tousled my hair. I didn't walk through the long hallway that connected several rooms in our house. That would've been too easy. And besides, if I went that way, someone could've seen me coming. I figured I'd go through the front door, so I could take them all by surprise. If I was worried about his reaction, I would've called the police anonymously, but I was something far better than worried. I was mad, and bitter, so because of those two feelings, I wasn't interested in doing anything that might make his struggle a little easier.

I strolled alongside the house and up around to the front. I nearly salivated at the thought of the shock he'd experience. I quietly rounded the bushes and crept up to the front porch. Before I got to the door, I pulled out my cell and called the police.

"Yes, my name is Jerri Nelson." I rattled off my address, informed the officer that I was in the midst of a divorce with my estranged husband, and I heard a loud ruckus on part of the property we shared.

"Are you in danger?" the female dispatcher asked.

"No, but I walked over here because I'm concerned about who is in here. I was not informed about any kind of party, and well, I know you've heard about those rave parties that go on when people think houses are empty," I said.

"Ma'am, I'm sending a cruiser right over. It may take about fifteen minutes," she said.

"Okay. Thank you," I said and hung up as I approached the door.

Unsure of whether to knock or ring the bell, I looked around as I stood in front of the huge wooden double doors. The noise had been taunting me as I walked around the side of the property and made my way to the front. Even when I talked to the dispatcher on the phone, I heard sounds of a party underway.

As I was about to knock, one of the massive doors swung open and a short Hispanic man wearing scrubs smiled at me. He was petite with very pretty features. His dark features were a dramatic contrast against his olive skin. He was man-pretty in an awkward kind of way. His eyebrows were waxed, and his skin was so flawless, it looked like he had never grown any facial hair.

"Oh, good. Did you find it okay?" he asked. "Yes, yes, you did!" he answered himself.

"Uh," I was confused.

But he wasn't the least bit deterred by my confusion.

"Oh, c'mon in here. See, I like that you dressed the part, too. Not like the rest of these divas. Who shows up for a pumping party fully made up and dressed to the nines, right?!" he exclaimed. He used his palm to slap his forehead playfully. "Sshheeesh!"

His shiny fingernails were perfectly manicured.

Before I could protest any further, he ushered me into the foyer that boasted volume ceilings. From where I stood, I was closest to the spiral stairway that was offset with custom ironwork. I had a clear view of the living and entertaining areas and all that was going on. The man slammed the door shut behind me. The music had been playing. It didn't sound as loud as I first thought because I could hear voices, chatter, and laughter that overpowered it once I was completely inside.

An odd smell invaded my nostrils and made me twist up my nose.

"What are you getting done?" the man asked. "Let me see," He pinched my cheeks and tugged at my skin. "No Botox for you just yet."

I didn't get the chance to ask what he meant because a couple of women rushed in our direction.

"Hector, I told you I want a bah-dong-a-dong booty like those vixens on the rap videos," a petite woman pouted.

Hector rolled his eyes better than I had seen most women do.

"Jeness, I told you these things take time. Turn around. Here, lemme look at you. Sheesh! I know I don't have to remind you of what you started with, do I?" He gave me a knowing look as if we were in cahoots together and used one arm to twirl Jeness around.

I frowned and looked around. The place was crawling with women. Some looked like they were dressed for the club. Others looked like they were attending yoga. In addition to the women, a couple of men in scrubs milled around the room.

When I saw one man with a hypodermic needle, my eyes focused on what he was about to do. I eased away from Hector as he fussed with Jeness and her friend. My mouth dropped to the floor when I noticed that man as he injected something into a woman's breast. My eyes nearly popped out when I recognized his patient. I saw the tricks I had kicked out of my swimming pool.

"What the hell is going on here?" I asked no one in particular.

"It's a pumping party," someone answered. "Duh."

If the chicks from the pool were there, I knew this pumping party couldn't be anything good!

I turned to see two different women on my heels.

"You tryin' to act like that ass is real?" one of the women snarled in my direction.

"Excuse me?" I said.

"Girl, please. You ain't gotta front for us. Who hooked you up? I like your booty because it's not too big and not too small. Even in your robe I can tell you got some fierce curves."

"Deon, Deon," the speaker tugged the other woman's arm. "See this is the kind of booty I want. Hector be trippin.' I told him I don't want nobody else working on me, but still he act like he hard of hearing or something like that."

Deon sucked her teeth as they both eyed me up.

"Um, a pumping what? What's—" I looked around the room in baffled amazement.

"Who you work with?" the first woman asked.

"I don't work with anyone! I don't even know what the hell a pumping party is. What is going on here?"

Suddenly, everyone stopped what they were doing and all eyes focused on me.

TATYANA

"All I know is y'all better figure that shit out, and I mean real fast-like. The shit don't make no damn sense!" I heard my husband scream before I saw him.

Immediately my heart thudded hard in my chest. I felt my ears warm up, and I didn't know what to do. Did he not know I was still in the house? Was he on the phone with *her*? Instinctively, my head whipped to the left, and then to the right. I needed to know where Pamela was. I did not want her to hear him on the phone with whomever it was he had been talking to.

He didn't even have the decency to wait until I or he left the house? What had we come to? Part of me felt stupid because I didn't think our marriage was *that* bad. I figured we were simply like any other couple married for more than a few years.

"Who the fuck should I ask if you don't know? What the hell do I pay you for then?"

I finally released a breath that had been trapped deep in my chest. He wasn't on the phone with *her*. He wouldn't be paying his *jump off*, would he? It wasn't that I had tried to eavesdrop, but if I wanted to be honest with myself, I'd admit, we'd been disconnected for some time. There hadn't been any major issues between us, but the letters made me think about the fact that our marriage had been vulnerable for a long while.

I peeked around the corner. I saw Dax's broad, muscled back

flex and watched as he grabbed at his forehead with his left hand. He faced the large bay window in his office and talked on the phone.

"Yeah, well, you need to have Mitch call me immediately. I don't give a damn about the golf course. I would think this constitutes as a maw-fuckin' emergency!" he yelled.

I eased into the office, but I didn't say a word. When Dax got hot, he reverted back to his street lingo. I remembered when that was such an incredible turn-on for me. As I listened, it simply sounded odd and out of place.

"This shit ain't been adding up for more than a minute, and you expect me to be some kinda sucka? You got me all messed up in the head. Get Mitch on the phone 'cause I ain't even tryin' to hear much more of this weak shit you spewing right now," he said.

It was obvious this could not have been the woman or woman-child on the side. My husband was angry, and his tone and lingo had me more than a bit curious.

When Dax spun around, I looked into the face of a man I didn't recognize. His eyebrows were scrunched together like they were being tugged by a string. He held up a finger and that silenced me.

"Yeah, get on that shit!" he screamed. "I need to hear from somebody in the next sixty minutes. Otherwise, I'm rolling through," he threatened.

I watched as he pressed a button on his Bluetooth and ended the call. He sighed hard and shook his head as he opened his arms and motioned for me to move close to him.

"Hey, babe. How much of that did you hear?" he asked when I fell into his strong, muscled arms. His embrace still felt good. I used to enjoy the way I felt in his arms. His body had always been hard and strong.

"Ah, yeah. What's going on?" I asked.

His heart raced against my chest, and I smelled his scent like he had been on fire.

"Strangest thing," he said.

I eased back and looked at my husband's face as his frown deepened. He looked both pissed and confused, but mostly pissed.

"Honey, I have been trying to avoid this discussion for a real long time now." He sighed.

My spine tightened and my heart dropped to the soles of my feet. Was this the moment? I suddenly wanted to bolt from the room and never come back. The plan was nowhere near complete.

"Ah, you wanna talk?" I asked.

"Yeah, but I'm not quite sure how to put this. I didn't mean for any of this shit to happen," he said.

It was as if he needed to convince me.

I stared into my husband's eyes and wondered if I needed to bring up the letters. Pam's voice rang loudly in my head, and it told me in no uncertain terms that I should have absolutely brought up the letters long ago. Had I played my hand wrong? Had he been two steps ahead of me all along? I swallowed hard.

Are you really gonna give him a free pass? You need to check his ass!

Pam had gone to take a nap, but her words made me feel like she stood right next to me.

"Here. I need you to take a seat," he said.

He ushered me into the leather chair behind his desk. But I bounced back up.

"I don't need a seat. I can take it standing. Actually, that's what I want to do. Just tell me and get it over with," I said.

My nostrils flared and my throat felt drier than the Mojave Desert. I clenched and unclenched my fists. Everything about his body language had me concerned. He seemed nervous, and I didn't know what to make of it. My eyes scanned the desk for anything I could throw if needed.

"Just sit. This is gonna take more than a minute," he stammered.

I eased back onto the chair, but only because his body seemed to force me back down. I glanced up at him through lowered lashes and tried to brace myself for the bombshell I was certain he was about to drop. My hands tightened around the arms of his chair. I pulled in a few ragged breaths to try and calm myself. He stood over me and that didn't give me much room to move.

"Like I said, there's no easy way to for me to break this to you," he repeated. His jaw seemed to tense.

"Yeah, you've said that already," I told him.

"Yeah, babe." He shook his head. "I was trying to get some more information before I came to you with this madness, but the shit still stinks, and it's gonna be a long while before it starts getting better," he said.

I couldn't take it anymore. The more he procrastinated, the more he made me anxious and even madder. I needed him to spit the shit out, and I needed it done fast.

When he dropped down and kneeled in front of me, I felt a sense of relief. He wouldn't dare get that close if he was about to leave me for a younger woman, would he?

"Baby, I dunno...we are um...we're broke," he blurted out. His head dropped, and I could've sworn I heard him crying.

I felt the air leave my lungs, and although the word didn't come from my lips, it still flew across the room.

"What!?" Pamela screamed from the doorway.

We both looked up and in her direction.

Her thinly plucked eyebrows twisted into a frown. "Oh, I know damn well you're not buying that shit," Pamela spat.

ELIZA

"OHMYGOD! Did you just try to make a pass at me?!" Poppy's scream was so loud it felt as if the sound pierced my eardrums. My wide, panic-stricken eyes couldn't focus.

Before I figured out what had happened and how we took such a drastic wrong turn, a group of people burst through my office door.

"What's going on in here?" a male voice boomed.

I knew I was too close to her. Her screams for help had caught me completely off guard. My hands flew up as if I had been caught red-handed. A whirlwind of adrenaline rushed through my veins.

Two security guards, Bruce and Kent, rushed to her side. I could see how the scene must've looked to them. They walked in and found me hovering over a damsel-in-distress-looking white girl who sat and cried uncontrollably.

"I'm…I don't know…I don't understand—," she grumbled under her breath.

Charlene, the HR director, approached me as if she had to be careful. I expected the worst.

"We can talk about what happened here," she said easily.

I shook my head. "N-n-n-nothing happened," I stammered.

My breath caught in my throat. My stomach twisted into a ball of fear.

"S-s-she just…" I couldn't find the right words.

Charlene glanced over at Poppy, who was putting on what could've rivaled an Academy Award-worthy performance. She had nearly everyone in the room eating out of the palm of her hand. I couldn't believe what was happening.

"I understand that this is your office, but until we figure out what happened, we're going to have to ask that you leave and come with us," Charlene said to me.

They tried to talk to Poppy, who snorted a few times, but she didn't respond.

The frown lines in my forehead must've deepened because I couldn't figure out why *I* had to be the one to leave *my* office. It was Poppy who was out of place. I had been coming into work every single day. I had been doing not only my job, but hers, too, and suddenly because she screamed and cried, they needed me to leave?

"Where am I going?" I asked.

"We simply need to figure things out. We need to talk to the two of you separately," she said.

This woman's voice had never elevated. She spoke to me like she was speaking to a child, but what she had suggested, offended me to no end.

"This is *my* office. Poppy here was having an emotional breakdown, and I moved over to try and comfort her," I tried to explain.

"I am not a lesbian!" Poppy started again.

I rolled my eyes dramatically.

She had finally broken out of her trance as a dawning recognition crossed her face. But her words brought sheer horror to mine.

"I tried to tell her I'm not a lesbian."

Why did she insist on saying that? I didn't know where she was coming from with that.

Most of the eyes in the room turned and looked at me as if I had done something so incredibly hideous.

"I tried to tell her. I have a man. I am in a committed relationship, but she kept moving into my personal space, and I didn't know what to do," Poppy sobbed. "I-I-I just felt threatened."

"Here, let's go and talk in my office," Charlene suggested to me.

"No! I don't want to leave. I want to hear what she's going to say about me. I haven't done anything wrong, but she's accusing me of—actually, I don't know what she's accusing me of, but I don't want to leave until this is all cleared up!"

"What I'm trying to tell you is that the best way for us to clear things up is to separate the two of you, so we can figure this whole thing out."

"But this is *my* office! I was conducting business, doing what I was supposed to do and she sat here staring off into space and throwing out incoherent statements. Then, I looked up, and she had completely fallen apart. I walked over there and attempted to console her," I said.

"W-w-we talked about you being gay, then all of a sudden you moved in to try and kiss me!" Poppy yelled.

"What?!" I screamed. "That's not true. That's not what happened!"

Charlene looked at me with pity in her eyes.

"Eliza, honey, sometimes, two people can look at the same picture and see something totally different," she said. She spoke to me like I was some special kind of head case.

I looked at Poppy with disbelief in my eyes.

"C'mon, dear," the woman said. This time she reached out to touch my arm. "Let's go and have a sit-down in my office. I think the time apart will help you remember the situation better."

I didn't want to leave. I wanted to confront Poppy. I needed to know what she was thinking.

Reluctantly, I allowed the HR lady to steer me out of the office. As we walked down the hall, all eyes were on me. I had never felt so embarrassed. It was like being a criminal on a perp walk. For what it was worth, the HR lady tried her best to make me feel like this was all normal.

"We'll get to the bottom of this. Sometimes a little time apart does a world of wonder," she said.

In my mind, I had strangled Poppy with my bare hands. I couldn't believe that she was that much of a loose cannon. By the time we arrived on the fifth floor where HR was located, I had calmed down a bit.

Inside Charlene Swanson's office, I took a seat and glanced around. There were pictures of people all over her desk, the walls and on her storage cabinets. She was in most of the pictures, smiling with the other smiling faces.

"Can I get you anything—water, a Coke or coffee?" she asked.

"Oh, no. I'm fine, but thank you for asking," I said.

The walk had given me enough time to clear my head of the craziness between Poppy and me. I felt better being away from her, but wondered how far she'd go with her bogus claim.

"Ms. Swanson, I'm sorry about what happened back there. I can't believe Poppy. I don't know what's been happening with her lately. Before she started yelling and screaming and carrying on, I was pointing out to her how much she had changed recently."

"We've noticed some issues, too," she said.

My eyebrows shot up.

"So, you guys know something is wrong?" I asked.

I was surprised because for all of these months I wondered how she had been so successful at flying beneath the radar. It wasn't that I expected her to be in the trenches with us, elbow deep in the work, but she was hardly ever at work. And so many times I wondered whether any of the higher-ups cared or noticed.

"Poppy is on everyone's radar," she said, "but I don't want to spend all of our time together talking about her. I want to know more about you. What happened back there that you didn't see that the two of you were headed for disaster?"

I thought about her question. In all the years I had worked for the Sea Lions' front office, never once had I really brought my personal life to work, and I tried not to take work home too often. My only issue with Poppy was the fact that she was so comfortable taking credit for work she never did. But, otherwise, she and I adhered to the idea of keeping personal and professional lives separate.

Something told me that this was bound to be the beginning of the end, and this was going to result in even more ridicule for me. But as I tried to tell my version of what had gone down in my office, I couldn't shake the feeling that life in our office would never be the same again.

SASHA

"Sasha, we need you to do that again. You said bayer instead of player," the director said in my ear.

I rolled my eyes. I was tired. I didn't have an attitude because I said something wrong. I had an attitude because I couldn't figure out what else to do to get closer to Dax. It simply was not fair that he and I were not together. When we spent any amount of time together, we had so much chemistry it was maddening.

Maybe I should try to have a heart-to-heart with Tatyana. Lord knows everything else I had tried was simply ignored. What woman ignores the writing on the wall?

"Let us know when you're ready," the director said into my ear.

I sighed hard.

"Okay. I'm ready," I said.

We went through and recorded the segment without any additional screw ups on my part. Although I was there and working, my mind was where it seemed to want to stay these days.

"Am I cleared?" I asked.

"Just a sec," he answered.

I still had to go by the club to take care of a few things, and I didn't need to be sitting around the studio.

"That's a wrap. You're cleared," he announced.

I jumped up so fast, I nearly forgot I was still connected by a few wires. Once the floor assistants came and removed the mics and cords, I rushed to my dressing room.

I took care of what I needed in there and headed over to the club. Had I known what was awaiting, I would've found something else to do.

The moment I walked in, I could sense something was off. Danielle and Josie both tossed me icy glares and that slowed me instantly.

"Hey," I said. My eyes traveled from one to the other, but both behaved as if it literally hurt them to speak to me.

"Sasha, we need to have a quick talk," Danielle said.

I looked around and wondered how I had walked into this brewing mess.

"What's up?" I asked. They didn't even let me drop my bag or purse off at the office.

"I'm speaking on behalf of several members of the Football Widows Social Club," she began. "And, well, a few of us have a real issue with what's going on with you and one of our member's husband," she said.

"Um, what exactly is going on?" I asked.

They looked at each other before she answered me.

"Tatyana is a loyal member of this club. How could you be parading all around town with her husband like that and not think anything of it?"

I had to admit to myself that this had caught me completely off guard. I had been so focused on getting closer to Dax that it never crossed my mind that I would be confronted.

"We are supposed to be a team that sticks together and helps each other out. It's bad enough we have to fight against groupies and gold diggers, but now to have to worry about one of our own?" Her face twisted, and she shook her head.

"What's Tatyana saying about all of this?" I asked.

The moment the question fell from my lips, I realized it wasn't the best question to ask, but to hell with it. What was done was done.

"So, how long have you guys been talking about me behind my back?" I asked.

They looked like I had obviously insulted their mamas. In actuality, I didn't have to explain a damn thing to any one of them.

"So, you haven't said what Tatyana is saying about any of this," I said.

"What difference does that make? Where's your shame? He is a married man, and do you think it's okay for you to be out in public with him like that? I mean, you're sharing romantic lunches, leaving hotels together. It's all just too damn much!"

I rolled my eyes. I wanted to tell them if they were really concerned, they'd tell Tatyana to fall back! They had no idea that nothing they could say to me would make me abandon this mission. I had gazed into Dax's eyes. I saw what the cameras couldn't capture, and I knew in my heart of hearts that we had a future together. I also knew that I could do more for his career than some plain Jane who wanted him to retire when his best years were still ahead of him.

"So, you have nothing to say?" Josie asked.

"What do you want me to say? I really don't see how this is anyone's business but mine and Dax's," I said.

Danielle's eyes became saucers. "So, you're basically admitting that you're sleeping with her husband! What the fuck, Sasha?!" she hissed. "You could have any damn man you want. Why do you have to go after someone else's husband? And not just anyone else, a member of our own club? That shit is foul!"

By now I had put my bag and purse down. I stood ready for battle.

"I haven't admitted anything! If you guys want to know what's going on with Dax and me, ask him, because I'm not confirming or denying a damn thing. And if Tatyana put you all up to this—"

"She didn't have to put us up to a damn thing!" Josie yelled. She had cut me off, but I wasn't pressed. This unexpected little confrontation wasn't that bad after all. I needed people to get used to the idea of us being a couple and being together, so it only made sense that we start close to home.

"I am not about to stand by and let you ruin this woman's family. It's just that plain and simple," Josie said.

My hands flew to my hips because it sounded to me like those were fighting words.

"So, you basically saying you gonna take an ass whooping over someone else's man?" I asked.

Their expressions told me my words stung. But that was exactly what I was going for. If these heifers thought I was about to abandon my plans simply because their feelings were hurt, they had another damn thing coming.

I began to remove my big silver hoop earrings when Danielle and Josie frowned at me.

"I knew you was nothing more than some ghetto-assed hood rat," Danielle spat. A spray of saliva flew from her mouth. "Bitch! We don't fight. We press charges!" Danielle reached down and opened a drawer. She dug in and pulled out her purse.

"I'm not for any drama. This shit is out of order." Danielle snatched a few framed pictures from the desk. "And as God is my witness, Karma is a bitch. The same way you got his ass, trust, is the same way you'll lose him!"

"Whatever," I said. I dismissed her warning with the wave of a hand.

"We're outta here. I don't want to be associated with you or this club if you could do some low-down shit like that to someone you call a friend. Shit is out of order," Josie said.

They grabbed their things and left me standing there alone. The problem with that was, they pretty much ran the club because most of the members worked or had other things to do. I quickly dialed McKenzie's number.

"You will not guess what just happened to me!" I yelled into the phone the minute she answered.

JERRI

"So, explain to me again: What exactly tipped you off?" the detective asked.

I pondered the question and felt awkward. Sure, I wanted to get Jason into some kind of trouble. That was why I had called the police in the first damn place, but who knew it would lead to all of this?

My probation officer, who stood off to the side with a fierce scowl on her face, eyed me suspiciously. I wondered whether she remembered what the detective had said. I was praised for busting up this illegal and dangerous ring. I was *not* the criminal here, nor had I done anything to break the law, yet the way she looked at me, you couldn't tell.

It wasn't my fault they called her up out of her bed during the wee hours of the morning. When the two officers arrived, and quickly called for backup, I simply needed to let someone know I was on probation and was only at the house because I feared someone had invited themselves in to have a party while my soon-to-be ex was away.

"I can't say it was any one thing," I said. The officer looked at me like he was studying me.

I knew I had to choose my words carefully. They didn't need to know that I called the police because I thought I was about to see Jason be hauled off in handcuffs. If I had known he wasn't even at the house, I'm not sure I would've wasted my time. On second thought, if I knew his pool-crashing friends were there, I would've slapped the cuffs on those cows myself.

"I guess that story on the news about the kids who had taken over a stranger's house to throw a massive party." I shrugged.

As I talked, the officer jotted things down on his little notepad, and that made me a little uneasy. But I wanted to make sure I didn't appear suspicious in anyway whatsoever. I was, of course, making it up as I talked, but he didn't seem to notice.

"Yeah, we're seeing so much of that now," the officer said.

"Well, honestly, at first, I thought that was what may have been going on. True enough I don't talk to Jason, but the other day I overheard him say something about a business trip. So, it was confusing to me when I arrived home to find all of these cars and people inside the house. He hadn't left word for me that he would be entertaining," I said.

My face was as straight and serious as I could maintain. When the front door opened and two plain-clothes officers strolled in, I noticed the bank of news trucks lined up outside. My pulse began to race. It seemed I couldn't stay out of the headlines no matter how hard I tried.

"Detective Anderson, over here," the cop who spoke to me said. He waved one of the new lawmen over to where we stood. "This here is Jerri Nelson. She's the one who made the call."

"Mrs. Nelson, I'm Detective Anderson. I've been on these guys' trail for nearly two years now," he said.

Detective Anderson was a short man who looked more like a banker than a cop. His look was clean-cut but straight out of the '70s. He wore a polyester suit with cowboy boots. The knot in his tie was fat, and his shirt even had a butterfly collar.

"Let me tell you a little something about these pumping parties," he said. "They continue to increase in popularity despite the inherent risks." He was sharp and very knowledgeable, despite his throwback appearance.

"I had never heard of a pumping party before. I'm still not one hundred percent clear on what they are," I admitted.

"Well, it's simple. A pumping party is when you're invited to a host's home and everyone is injected with silicone in the parts of the body they want increased. They pay hundreds of dollars to the injectee, who has no medical training, versus the sometimes costly price of plastic surgery and Botox. Unfortunately, many young women see this as an easier and less costly way to obtain pseudo plastic surgery results."

I watched as Deon and her friend were escorted past us in handcuffs. "Are they going to jail?" I asked.

The officer looked at the women.

"In most cases, they'll take them in and try to get more information for the case. You'd be surprised by the number of women who won't cooperate. They don't want to rat out the fake docs. It's really sad," the detective said.

"Is this like a new fad or something?" I asked. My eyes stayed on Deon and her friend until they were escorted out the door.

"Oh, no, pumping parties have been around for a while. They're illegal, but as the demand for physical perfection continues, the popularity of these parties increases. What many people attending these parties don't understand is that silicone being injected into their body is not medical grade or done by a board certified plastic surgeon. It's just plain deadly. When silicone is injected improperly, it travels through the bloodstream and causes the blood to form masses in the lungs. That creates obstructions that can be immediately life-threatening, especially if it's not identified and treated quickly."

The officers questioned the women in different parts of the house. The place was abuzz with activity. I couldn't believe the kind of people Jason was now associating with. For the first time since the drama unfolded, I began to wonder what would have happened if our kids were here.

"So, we've got your statement. And you say you only heard the women refer to him as Hector?"

"Yeah, no one really used last names, but they all seemed to know each other pretty well."

"What the hell is going on here, and what is *she* doing in here?"

I didn't need to turn toward the angry growl to know Jason was home.

He approached us like he was pissed off at the world, but stunned me when he opened his mouth.

"Officer, my wife didn't have anything to do with this. Why is she here?" Jason asked.

I stood stunned by his comment. Since when did he start referring to me as his wife?

"Sir, who are you?" the detective asked.

"I'm Jason Nelson. I own this house," he replied.

"*We* own this house," I corrected.

"Yes, we do, Jerri. And, well, I wanted to talk to you about that." I tried hard to read his body language, but couldn't.

"I don't have anything to say to you," I spat.

"You should reconsider. Aren't you tired of all of this?"

"All of what exactly?" the detective asked.

I was confused. I wasn't sure if he was trying to drag me into the mess, but I wasn't about to fall for his tactic.

The detective looked at him, then back at me. Who knew what thoughts must've run through his mind.

At first I was outdone by the thought of Jason coming in and stealing the spotlight, but the way the detective looked at him made me fall back a bit. Maybe the detective saw through his façade, too.

"Mr. Nelson, were you aware a party was going on here tonight?" the detective asked.

"Yeah. Didn't I just say it's my house?" Jason asked.

I wanted the fool to dig a deep hole for himself, and he looked like he was doing a pretty good job of it.

"Okay, then. What you're telling me is you were aware that a pumping party was scheduled to take place here, and that didn't bother you?"

Jason's eyebrows went up and the look on his face told me he suddenly regretted speaking up so boldly and loudly.

"A what party?" he stammered and glanced around the room.

"You said you were aware that a party was taking place. Does that mean you gave your permission to the people who assembled here tonight?"

Jason looked at the detective, then he looked at the officer and glanced at me. He suddenly seemed baffled as if he wasn't so sure whether saying anything else would be a good idea.

"Uh, a friend of mine said something about having a few friends over," he stammered.

His eyes danced all over as if he was looking for someone. I folded my arms across my chest and listened as he stammered and stuttered his way through the explanation.

"And, this friend of yours," the detective began. Jason looked petrified. He grabbed his cell phone and dialed. "What's her name, and is this the same person you gave permission to use your house to execute an illegal activity?"

Jason pulled the phone up to his ear.

"David, I need you to come over. Yeah, now. The police are

here, and I don't think I should say anything else until you get over here. Yeah. Okay, in ten."

When he hung up, he had a triumphant smirk across his face.

"Again, this friend you were talking about," the detective tried once more.

But it was too late. Jason had completely shut down.

TATYANA

I stood with a blank stare plastered across my face.

My brain couldn't even absorb Dax's shocking words, much less process them, because what Pamela had said stopped the show before it could begin. Both Dax and I turned our attention to her. The girl looked like she was about to explode, with rage.

"Pamela, this is not a good time," I said easily.

Silly me because I thought she'd recognize this moment screamed for two instead of three. When she didn't attempt to retreat, I was stunned. I shook my head for good measure, and again, tried to communicate with her silently. My voice was calm and soft because I was still trying to process what my husband had said. I didn't understand how we could be broke. We didn't live lavishly, and we didn't spend out of control. There had to be a mistake.

"What the hell?" Pamela barked. "If it was up to you, there would never be a good doggon' time!"

Her outburst had rubbed me the wrong way. The look in her eyes told me she had already passed the point of reason or return. She looked like she was more upset than me! I tried to widen my eyes to tell her this was so not a good look. I needed her to retreat, pivot, leave the room, and ignore the conversation. I needed this private time alone with my husband, but she didn't get it.

When her hands flew to her hips, and she began to snake her neck, I flinched. This was *not* how I wanted to confront Dax. Sure, he had thrown me for a loop, but I wasn't ready. My plan was nowhere near completion. He had dropped the mother of all bombshells, and instead of dealing with that, I had to handle my BFF first! She had burst like an overheated gasket. Her reaction—the outburst—it was all preposterous to me.

I stepped toward her. I figured if I could get to her before Dax composed himself, I could redirect her before she moved even further out of bounds. But when I moved in her direction, Pamela sidestepped me and rushed in closer to where Dax sat. At first, he sat slumped forward and cupped his chin in his hands. I didn't know if he was pissed or in deep thought, until she went in.

"So, now you expect us to believe you're broke? You the damn starting quarterback for one of the NFL's most successful franchises. How the hell are you gonna be broke?" When Pamela threw her hands up, my husband popped up from the sofa like a startled Jack-in-the-Box. His wide eyes looked wild and crazed.

"Pamela!" I screamed. But she ignored me.

The expression on Dax's face was one mixed with fury, confusion, and something else I couldn't read. When he jerked his head sideways and looked in my direction, I rushed to try and contain Pamela. I needed her to calm down—to stop and let *me* handle the situation. But she was on a roll.

"You are out of line," I hissed. I grabbed her by the arms and held her firmly. "I got this!"

I heard my heart thumping loudly in my ears. It raced like a speeding bullet, and my skin was moist with a thin layer of nervous perspiration. I needed to take control of the situation and force calmness.

But Pamela's eyes were filled with so much rage, the area beneath her right eye began to twitch. She was wild with what had to be pent-up frustration. The more I held on to her, the more she resisted until she finally squirmed and wiggled free. But before she turned away, she looked me in the eyes and said, "I'm doing this, not just for you, but for my godchildren. You cannot let this man get over on you like this!" Her lips trembled, and she waved me off like she was disgusted with me.

"Pamela…let…me…handle…this," I said through clenched teeth.

Pamela jumped beyond my reach as if she was frustrated with my lack of action.

When she was gone, I squeezed my eyes shut and braced myself for the beginning of the end. I turned slowly at her words.

"You lowdown, cheating bastard! Now you wanna cry broke? After all you've been doing to her? Isn't it convenient that you're all of a sudden broke?" Pamela hissed.

She turned to me as if she expected me to jump in and pick up where she had left off. But my voice was gone. I was stunned silent—literally.

"You wasn't broke when you ran up a thirteen-thousand-dollar bill in La Perla, were you?" She snickered.

"Pamela, what in the hell is your problem? What are you talking about?" Dax asked.

Spittle gathered at the corners of his mouth as he yelled at her. His once tear-filled voice had vanished. Suddenly, his sorrowful eyes focused in on me. And if looks could kill, I would've been as stiff as a board.

"You need to get her," he warned.

His long index finger jabbed in her direction, and I feared he might reach out and smack the shit out of her. But Pamela didn't even flinch. She didn't cower, and she didn't back down. She was all up in his personal space.

"Tatyana, has given you the best years of her life, and this is how you repay her? Men! How fuckin' typical!" she exclaimed.

Then she did it.

The world may as well have stopped on its axis. I felt like I had an out-of-body experience and was watching a movie in slow motion.

When she used the palms of her hands to shove my husband in his chest, I nearly passed out.

"Pamela! That's enough! I need you to leave!" I screamed and rushed to jump between her and Dax who had stumbled back slightly. He looked bewildered.

I wasn't sure what stunned him most—the fact that Pamela had gone and lost her ever-loving mind, or the fact that I had been unable to prevent this from happening.

"I'm confused here, Tat. Why would your girl think it's okay to talk to me all out the side of her neck like this?!" he suddenly screamed at me.

My voice was gone. I stammered, but incoherent thoughts tumbled from my mouth and sounded like gibberish.

"Are *you* gonna tell him or am I?" Pamela asked.

She looked at me with a stone-faced glare like she was now pissed at me. I felt like I was the only person who had a legitimate beef, but yet I was in the hot seat. I was stunned.

Dax threw his hands up, tossed me a disappointed glare, shook his head in disgust, and walked out.

ELIZA

"I can't believe I'm having to sit this out over some bogus-ass claims from that bitch!" I said to Mary.

The moment Mary found out it was strongly *suggested* that I take some time off, she'd been calling me secretly from the office. I was glad someone wanted to keep me updated on what was going on.

"Everyone thinks what she did to you was the worst!" Mary said. "*Sucio Cono…dirty cunt* you should see how she's floating around here, all happy and looking like a million friggin' dollars."

"Wait a sec. So you trying to say she finally pulled herself together?" I asked, stunned.

"It's the craziest thing," Mary whispered. "When the she-devil strolled back in here on Monday, we could hardly believe our eyes. She looked a lot like the old Poppy. You know, fresh designer suit, expensive shoes, and her hair looked like she'd just walked out of the rich people shop."

"So, all of a sudden she snaps out of it like nothing happened," I said.

"Yeah, everybody is still talking about it around here. The day she flipped out on you, Karen down the hall told me she was next to her in the bathroom, and she couldn't believe the stench," Mary said.

"Stench from Poppy?"

"Yeah. It was wild. I mean, if you would've told me that Poppy of all people would've fallen off like that, I'd be like, take me to the man who caused this because he must be like some Greek god or something," said Mary. That's when it hit me. Poppy was having man trouble and it had impacted everything from her appearance, to work and anything in-between.

Visions of that day in my office were still imprinted on my brain. In my mind I combed over every detail that happened that day. One minute she was in her own world. I couldn't even get her to weigh in on the call from McKenzie. The next, she was crying like a big baby, and then she accused me of hitting on her. She was all over the place. If I didn't know any better, I'd think she was a real head case, either that, or she was stoned.

"What are you gonna do? We heard they *suspended* you," Mary whispered.

"*God!* Is that's what's going around the office? I'm not suspended! You know how it is. They strongly suggested I take some time off."

"I knew it! I knew you were not suspended. Between me and you, the reason it's going around the office is because that's what Poppy keeps slipping and saying. I swear I can't stand her! *Conyo Sucio*!"

"Mary!"

"Yeah? It's what she is!"

"Well, I don't understand why she suddenly turned on me," I said.

"*Mija*, since you've been gone, she's been in every single day, early. And what's so funny is the way she's taking over everything *you* were doing. If I hear one more comment about the show with Dax and Dwight, I think I may scream out loud for real. You should see how we look at her when she strolls down the hall. It's like, lady, are you for real? We have known from day one that you've been doing absolutely nothing at all!"

"Well, you guys try to keep it together until I come back next week," I said.

"You'll be back for sure?" Mary asked.

The surprise in her voice made me concerned, but I wasn't about to share that with her. What if she knew something I didn't know?

"Yeah, I'll be back. Like I said, I'm only taking some time off to try and de-stress, that's all."

"Okay, cool. I'll be right here taking in everything she's doing and telling everything. I think it's way screwed up that she gets all the credit for the big show with the guys when we all know she didn't lift a finger to do a damn thing," Mary said.

I agreed with her, but I knew I needed to remain politically correct.

"As long as it goes off without a hitch, I guess I can't really complain. I mean, think about all that work we did, and then she waltzed in to accept the award. It is what it is, right?"

"You got that right," Mary said. "All I know is she can't be trusted."

I didn't want to co-sign on that aloud, but I couldn't agree more.

By the time I wrapped up my call with Mary, I started wondering why Poppy wanted to come back all of a sudden. For months, she wouldn't so much as call the office to check in. There were times when I had to all but force information and updates on her. She hated work like healthy people hated the flu. But something made her want to come back. I needed to figure out what it was. Then it hit me. The season was about to start again.

Poppy wanted to be back in the limelight again. Maybe her man was a player. She left all of the cleanup work for us during the off-season, but now, it was show time, and everyone knew it.

If I wasn't so pissed at her, I'd pat her on the back. But she was about to learn that she had messed with the wrong one. For years

I had worked my ass off in her shadow, and now that I knew what she was up to, I decided I'd spend my time off trying to figure out how to make her regret the way she tried to play me. Maybe I'd start with the man who had her walking around looking like a zombie.

"No, I need to hit her where it really counts. She could get another man with no problem, but the prestige of her job would have more impact, especially if things suddenly started falling apart for her!"

SASHA

The process wasn't moving fast enough for me! Less than two weeks away from the start of training camp, and I still felt like I had a very long way to go. I needed my man, and I needed him now—not later. I wasn't sure what those tricks from the club were gonna do after the confrontation, but since I hadn't heard anything, I figured they realized they couldn't stand in the way of true destiny.

If things worked the way I had envisioned, by the time the season rolled around, I'd be a welcomed fixture among the Sea Lions players, coaches and their close friends and families. I didn't want to play my hand too soon, but maybe I needed to get some pictures photo-shopped and leak them to the rags. I needed to do something to jumpstart the multimillion-dollar union.

I picked up the phone and called McKenzie.

"Hey," I said the moment she answered.

"What's up?"

"You got some information for me?" I asked.

I scrutinized my reflection in the mirror. It was nothing less than flawless, and that was how I liked it. So many times I considered being upfront with Dax about my plans, but because he had a wife and kids, I needed to make him think that this was the best way. If I pushed him, I'd go down as a home-wrecker, and I didn't want that.

Besides, in addition to being sexy and handsome, Dax was a great guy. There was no way he'd be willing to walk out on his family just like that. And of course, I wouldn't want him to do that, but how long would I have to wait?

"I told you my cousin would get the goods." McKenzie giggled.

"W-w-w-what?!" I screamed into the phone.

She had suggested that I give her cousin a chance to help out. He had done some online course to become a private investigator and was really hungry for work. At first I thought it was the craziest thing I had ever heard. Who took an online course like that? But then the more I thought about it, what did I have to lose? At worst, he'd tell me that Dax already had a side piece. Either way, I told McKenzie I'd be willing to spend two to three hundred max with her cousin. After all, he had absolutely no experience.

I decided I'd work with whatever he could do with that amount. When he agreed to take the job, I was psyched.

"You at the studio still?" she asked.

"Yeah, girl. We've been taping promos," I said.

"Okay, well, I'm like fifteen minutes away," she said.

"Let's go have a drink, and then you can tell me all about it over cocktails and dinner," I said.

Suddenly, my adrenaline was racing, and I was excited. There was no way in hell McKenzie would tease me if she didn't have something substantial to tell me. I didn't think it was time to run out and start selecting China patterns or anything like that just yet, but I had a gut feeling that I'd be so much closer to getting my man.

I considered changing, but quickly decided against it. I knew we'd probably go to the Grove or somewhere close because that's what McKenzie liked, so my professional gear would have to do.

I looked over some notes for the big show, grabbed my purse, then headed out.

By the time I made it to my car, I had already received two text messages from McKenzie. One read: Cheesecake Factory with several question marks, and the other one read: or The Fat Cow?

I rolled my eyes and sighed. It wasn't bad enough that we had to go to the Grove, but I'd be damned if I wouldn't have a good meal. I was starved. Before I got in the car I responded to her text messages: Let's meet at Maggiano's or Morel's steakhouse. I wasn't going to wait for her to respond. After I buckled up, I texted one word back and took off toward the Grove.

The inside of Maggiano's was as amazing as I expected, bustling and busy. The atmosphere was great, and that was the mood I was in.

"Table for two, and I'll be at the bar," I told the hostess.

She ran a finger down a sheet of paper and looked up at me.

"What's your—oh, wait. You're Saaaaasha," she mocked me. "I love your show!" she squealed.

I grinned. "Thank you."

She leaned in closer to me. "I'll make sure you get a great table."

"I'd appreciate that," I said sincerely.

"Okay, so table for two, and you'll be waiting at the bar. Who's in your party?"

"Oh, her name is McKenzie. She should be here shortly," I said.

"Cool. I'll let her know where to find you." She smiled.

I was sipping on my drink when the hostess walked over and tapped me on the shoulder. I turned and smiled.

"Ms. Davenport, your party is here," she said.

McKenzie looked at her like she was crazy, but I didn't mind.

"Oh, thank you. Is our table ready?" I asked.

"Let me check," she said and rushed away.

"Um, what's up with this place?" McKenzie asked as she eased onto a barstool. She looked around. "I've never been to Maggiano's."

"Oh, you'll love the food. I love it here," I said.

"What are you drinking?" she asked.

"My signature—the lemon drop," I said.

The bartender stopped in front of us. "What can I get for you?" he asked.

McKenzie looked at my drink again and said, "I think I'd like a martini."

"Lemon drop?" he asked.

"Oh, no, I ain't got time for nothing sweet like that. Give me a dirty martini," she said.

"Okay. One dirty coming up," he said.

"Make it really dirty—like porn-star dirty," she said.

He winked and went to make her drink.

The second we were alone, I leaned in and said, "I can wait on the details, but give me the lead now. What's up? What did he find out?"

McKenzie grinned and started squirming on her barstool like she was listening to something other than the boring elevator music that played through the restaurant's speakers.

"Girl, don't play with me," I warned.

She pursed her lips and started to snap her fingers. All the while she snaked her body and wiggled on the barstool.

"W-w-w-what?!" I said.

"I'm not sure if I'm ready to spill just yet," she said.

My eyes grew wide. "McKenzie, if you don't start dishing, and I mean like right now!"

"What? What you gon' do? You can't kill me 'cause then you'd never find out why Dax Becall and his wife are separated."

Time stood still.

JERRI

"I've tried to talk to her. I need this shit cleared up before the season starts," Jason had the nerve to say. "You need to take your ass on *The View* or *The Today Show* or something!"

His smart comments were far from funny. I shifted in my chair and tried to remember my attorney's words of advice before we agreed to the meeting.

This is a chance to meet them halfway. Let's see what they're talking about. You can't enjoy sharing a house with him. I think it's time we see this thing through to the end.

Sure, my attorney's words were front and center on my brain, but I absolutely refused to be low-balled. I think the bust at the pumping party made Jason's head coach say enough is enough. And in my opinion that was really the only reason Jason and his lawyer wanted to suddenly talk about a settlement. Ever since then, Jason had been trying to be more cordial toward me.

But I knew that coach didn't tell him to send me on the talk show circuit. He probably told his ass to clean up the mess in his personal life off the field or ride the bench. I knew Jason, and I also knew that nothing talked to him like the thought of losing money or his position on the team.

I leaned over to whisper into my attorney's ear. "Until they meet us close to halfway, I don't want to entertain anything he has to say," I said.

She nodded.

"We want the family house, the vacation house in Belize, and your monetary offer needs to increase by at least twenty-five percent before we'll think about settling," my attorney said.

I watched as Jason leaned in and whispered into his lawyer's ear.

"If we reach an agreement today, are you prepared to sign the decree?" his attorney asked.

"I don't know that we are any closer to an agreement than we were the last time we all met," my lawyer said.

"Why you trippin'?" Jason asked me.

All eyes shifted in my direction.

"You expect me to go quietly. I have your children. I refuse to struggle as a single mother," I said.

"Our offer is more than generous. Mr. Nelson is and will always be committed to the well-being of his children. Besides, I can't imagine you are comfortable with the current living arrangements," his attorney said.

Not that I would admit it, but he had a point there. The whole pumping party bust and all of the media coverage around it was a huge mess. I thought I'd get the pleasure of seeing Jason harassed by the police. I had no clue what was really going on over there.

The more I thought about it, the more I realized how lucky I was. If my probation officer hadn't been there, that could've turned into a violation for me, and that was the very last thing I needed.

I didn't intend to spend my entire day dealing with the meeting either. I was expected at the club by four, and I couldn't be late.

"So, we're clear: The family house, vacation house in Belize and at least twenty-five percent more than the original offer," my attorney said.

"Can we deduct the amount set aside for the kids' trusts?" Jason asked.

He made me so sick. I didn't respond. I gawked at him in hopes that his simple behind would realize what an ass he sounded like, but he never cleaned it up.

I scooted my chair from the table and grabbed my purse.

"That's all I have for today," I announced. Once again, all eyes shifted to me, but I didn't allow that to stop me this time. "I will call you later so we can discuss our counteroffer," I said to my attorney as I walked out of the conference room.

"Ain't this a bitch?!" Jason huffed. "You won't hear me out, and now you're done for the day?"

I heard a loud noise that sounded as if something was slammed onto the desk, but it was no longer my concern. As I left the room, Jason continued to yell and throw a fit. I laughed to myself as I made my way to the elevator, where I pressed the DOWN button and waited patiently.

The nerve of him. He thought it was gonna be that simple. Well, he'd soon learn that the drama was just beginning as far as I was concerned.

When the elevator doors finally opened, I waited for a few people to step off, then I walked inside and released the trapped breath I'd held for the past two hours. Emotionally, I was tired of the living arrangements. I didn't feel comfortable trying to move on with my life. But I didn't want him to feel like he could get over on me either.

Just as the doors prepared to close, a hand slid between them. I rolled my eyes because I'd know that hand anywhere.

He walked in and stood next to me. We stood mere inches from each other and both looked up in silence as the doors closed.

"Real talk?" Jason said.

I didn't respond.

"What happened with us?" he finally asked after moments in silence.

I chuckled at his question.

"Your jump offs—that's what happened to us," I said.

"But when did you start hating me so much? When did this thing get so far out of control?"

"Let's see...you tossed your vows away for any piece of ass you could pull on the road, then expected me to fall in line and accept your bullshit. I'd say that just about did it," I said.

"It was never like that. You were always paranoid. I kept telling you things weren't nowhere near where you thought they were."

I wondered what was taking the damn elevator so long. Being so close to him made me uneasy.

As if my question was answered, the doors opened, and I moved to step out, until that same hand touched me. I looked down at his hand then up at him. We stepped off the elevator, and he invaded my personal space.

"Is there anything we can do to fix this?" he asked.

"Fix what?"

"This, Jerri, *us*. I told you: There ain't nobody else," he insisted.

"Perhaps not now, but what happens when you hit the road again? The season is right around the corner. We've been at war for so long, Jason, I can't even remember a time when we were friends," I said.

"Just think about it. You don't have to say anything now. Just give it some thought. You already told the lawyers you wanted some time to think, so add this to the list of things you're thinking about," he said.

I looked at him a long time.

"What exactly am I supposed to add to the list, Jason?" I rolled my eyes.

"*Us*. Think about us giving it another go," he said. Then, he turned and walked away. As he swaggered down the hallway, I couldn't get his words out of my mind.

TATYANA

It was the best thing to do. It was the best thing to do. Those were the words that rolled around in my head as I drove around near LAX. I slowed my car and stopped for a red light. I sat there and replayed the nightmare in my head over and over again. I couldn't stop thinking about all of the things I should've said or what I should've done.

I needed to slap the shit out of Pamela. I needed to do anything that might've shut her the hell up. But I had done nothing at all.

When Dax stormed out of our front door, my heart literally deflated. It felt like someone had released the air out of a massive balloon. He had left Pamela and me in the room alone. And that room had never felt so small and so suffocating.

"You were so out of order," I said to her.

"Someone needed to put him on notice!" she said.

"Why? For what? This is *my* marriage. He's *my* husband. I don't need you to speak up for me. I can handle him, this!"

"Your husband is creeping around with some woman child and you expect me to believe you've got things under control?" She twisted her mouth.

The sound of a horn blaring behind me made me jump. I glanced up at my rear-view mirror.

"I'm sorry," I said and did a little three-finger wave, then took off.

As I left the airport I couldn't stop thinking about the fact that I had all but sent Pamela packing and still had no clue about my husband's whereabouts. So many thoughts crowded my mind. If we really were broke, what would I say or do? This would definitely change my plan. Maybe Pamela was on to something. Maybe I should have said something to him about the letters. But I wasn't ready. I drove around longer than I needed to and took the scenic route so that I could think. Pamela and I had fought many times before, but there was something that felt so final about this last fight.

"Who cares about him leaving? It's probably for the best anyway—to save you the embarrassment. Imagine when the press finds out about him and his mistress who's barely legal," she hissed.

My eyes narrowed as I glared at her. But that did nothing to quiet her rampage.

"He's got some nerve. So now he wants to claim he's broke. I know what he's trying to do." She paused. When my glassy gaze didn't change, she continued. "You see, Tatyana, if he can convince you that the money is all gone, maybe you'll take it easy on him when he and his jump off decide to go public. Then, you'll be left humiliated and holding the bag with three kids to feed and clothe while he gets to start his new life with his newer, much younger wife!"

"Is that how it's gonna happen?" I asked.

She looked at me with surprise in her eyes. Her face twisted slightly.

"Pamela, this is not you and every man who has ever done you wrong. This is *my* life. This is *my* husband we're talking about, and he stormed out of here because you couldn't shut the hell up!"

Pamela frowned.

"Oh, my dear, you've got bigger problems if you think that's the reason he stormed out of here. The reason he left is because someone finally had the balls to call his ass to the carpet, and he was caught completely off-guard by it."

"So, you had the balls, huh?"

"Someone had to say something," she said.

"I want you gone," I spat.

"Well, I'm not in the mood to go anywhere," she said and turned her attention away from me.

My next words stopped her in her tracks.

"No, I mean, it's time for you to pack and go back home," I said.

When her head whipped around in my direction, she looked stunned. I wondered if she felt half of what I felt when she spewed off at the mouth with Dax or when she raised her hand to him. The scowl on her face told me she wasn't happy. When she turned to face me, I nodded to confirm it.

"You not only disrespected my husband, but you disrespected me. I can't have that kind of confusion here in my house," I said.

Pamela put her hands on her hips and shifted her weight to one side of her body. She tapped her right foot. The scowl now turned into a defiant smirk.

"Ain't that a bitch," she snarled. "You pick a fine-ass time with me to grow some balls, but you let him walk all over you—talking about he ain't got no damn money!"

"It's my business, Pamela. I told you, I wasn't tripping off the damn letters, but you wouldn't listen. All you wanted to do was confront him about issues that have absolutely nothing at all to do with you! You were out of order. You should've kept your thoughts to your damn self and let me deal with him!"

"Oh, you were gonna deal with him? *When*, Tatyana? When? When he told you he was leaving you to be with his new younger wife? Or, maybe you were gonna deal with him when he was moving that new wife into your house?"

I turned and walked away.

"Hey, where are you going!?" she shouted after me.

"I'm going upstairs to toss your shit into a suitcase because I mean it's time for you to go!"

"Tatyana!"

She called after me, but I kept it moving. There was no way I was about to stand in my house and have a debate with her about how I should handle my husband.

After I threw her things into her bags, I went back downstairs and found her right where I had left her.

"I'm pulling the car around," I said.

"I can't believe you're doing this. He's cheating on you, Tatyana. This is not gonna end well for you. I was only saying the things you felt but couldn't bring yourself to say," she said.

"Well, you said too damn much. You went too far," I said.

ELIZA

"Where the hell is she going?"

I sped up then slowed down when the two cars in front of me changed lanes. I wanted to stay behind Poppy, not too far, but not too close either.

She exited off the freeway, then made a left and a quick right. If I didn't know any better, I'd think she knew someone was following her.

When she turned her car into an exclusive neighborhood, I was the only one behind her, so I turned, too. I was stunned when she suddenly pulled over and parked. At first, I thought she was going to visit someone, but she didn't get out of the car. I drove right past her and parked several vehicles behind hers, but on the opposite side of the street.

We sat for the longest time, or at least what felt like the longest time. But the strangest thing happened after nearly an hour. When one of the front doors opened, she quickly ducked down in her car like she was trying to hide.

"Is she spying on someone?" I asked aloud.

We sat for another hour before she started her car and pulled out into the street. I jotted down the address and made a mental note to see if I could figure out who lived at that address. I had no clue whether the door that opened was the target of her stake-out, but to be on the safe side, I made note of several addresses.

Later, when she pulled into the post office parking lot, I wondered if I should get out or simply fall back and wait for her to come back outside. When she walked in, I didn't notice a package in her hand, so I figured she might have been going to pick something up.

After about ten minutes, when she still hadn't come out, I decided to go inside and look around a bit. I grabbed my keys and got out of the car. I locked the door and strolled along the parking lot until I made it to the main entrance. That put me at somewhat of a disadvantage because you could see out of the smoky glass windows of the post office, but I couldn't see in from the outside.

"Thank you," I said to the man who stood and held the door open for me. "I appreciate it."

Once inside, I looked at the long line that snaked around toward the entrance. There were two postal workers at the counter, and I could only imagine how pissed the people in line must've been.

I didn't see her in line, although I couldn't really look the way I wanted to.

"She must have a P.O. box here," I said, and rushed out of the line. I walked past the automated machines and as I rounded the corner I nearly bumped right into her.

"Ah, watch where the hell—," Poppy said.

It was obvious her eyes made the connection before her brain. Suddenly, she frowned and tossed her hand to a hip. She did look better. Gone were the dark roots and the luggage that had made their home beneath her eyes. The polished and spectacular-looking Poppy was back in full effect.

"Why are you following me? Oh, yes, absolutely, of course, you're following me," she snarled. "Well, this madness needs to stop!"

"Poppy, why in the world would I be following *you* of all people?"

"If you're not following me, why are you here? You don't live in this neighborhood."

"Neither do you."

"Well, I have business here. You'd better not be following me. And whatever you had in mind, you can forget about it. If I catch you following me again, I'm calling the cops."

"You still haven't said why I'd be following you in the first place," I said. She didn't have anything in her hands, so I figured she wasn't there for a pickup.

"You're probably looking for the right moment to fall on your sword and beg for your job back," she hissed.

"Why would I need to beg you for anything, and besides, I didn't lose my job, so there's no need for me to beg for something that's already mine."

When the smirk made its way to her face, I wanted to smack it away, but I knew I couldn't.

"You won't have that job much longer."

Poppy stepped around me and strolled away. I glanced around to see her toss me a nasty look before she slipped through the door.

The shock of Poppy's words numbed me from head to toe. I had no idea there were plans to get rid of me. It must've been a well-kept secret around the office. The thought weakened my knees. But if it was true, I was grateful that Poppy wouldn't be there to witness my fall.

My instinct told me to call Mary and find out if she had heard anything, but I knew the answer to that. She had been doing a good job of keeping me in the know. There was no way Mary would've kept that to herself, if she had known.

I watched through the smoky glass window as Poppy sat in her car and talked on the phone. She never looked up, which made me think thoughts of me had already been erased from her mind.

I watched as she used her left hand to rub her brow like she was frustrated. I wondered who she was talking to and whether there was someone I could call to verify her threat about my job.

The idea to follow Poppy had come four days prior. I had been following her ever since. She went to work and after a couple of hours she'd leave and go to lunch. Then she'd go to the mall, a couple of boutiques and back to the office. Once she left the office for the day, she'd go to a couple of restaurants, but she'd never go inside. I thought that was strange, but she was a strange bird, so there was no telling what she was up to.

The trip to that house was the first since I decided to follow her. Initially, I wanted to corner her somewhere so we could talk and try to work things out. But the encounter at the post office told me that would be a waste of time.

I abandoned the tail on her and called it an evening. I had two things on my mind, I needed to call Mary to find out more about whether my job really was in jeopardy and I needed to look up the address I had jotted down.

SASHA

"You tell your cousin I said he's getting a huge bonus!" I screamed into the phone. The moment McKenzie and I had finished our face-to-face, I headed to the house. Her only assignment before I left was to tell her cousin I needed an address, and I needed it before sundown.

It was less than an hour after our meeting when my cell rang. I had just arrived home, but was still in the car.

"Hello?"

The butterflies in my stomach were going wild. Ever since my prayer had been answered, I could hardly think straight. I needed to calm down and play this out just the way I had over and over again in my dreams.

"He's staying at the Ritz—the one closest to the stadium, and he's under the name Ty Goldberg. I've already talked to him, and I told him you needed to meet with him immediately to discuss saving the show," McKenzie said.

"Oh, that's a real good one, girl. You are something else," I said.

"Okay, seriously though, Sasha, you haven't heard. Dwight has pulled out and the team is concerned about the class."

I frowned. This was not how this was supposed to go down. I stretched one leg out of the car, but I waited before getting completely out.

"What do you mean he's pulled out? Pulled out of what?"

"The reason it took so long for me to get back to you is because something has happened with Dwight and his wife, Roxie. Now she's campaigning for the team to disassociate itself and its money from the club. Why didn't you tell me something had gone down? What happened?"

"McKenzie! You have got to be shitting me! Are you trying to tell me that everything I've been working my ass off for is now in jeopardy because these heifers are mad at me?"

"No. I'm telling you I don't know what happened at the club but whatever *that* was, it's now causing conflict to the point that Dwight has backed out, and Dax is saying he's out, too."

"Okay, okay." I stepped all the way out of the car. I pressed the button on my remote and hightailed it to my apartment. Multiple thoughts rushed through my mind. The show with Dax and Dwight was going to kick off the season, and then we were going to follow up with the workshop. My bosses, my agent and my future producer were all salivating and waiting for this to go off without a hitch.

"Okay, McKenzie, slow it down and repeat. I'm lost."

Unfortunately, even after she slowly explained the situation and where we were, nothing had changed. As far as I was concerned, my career was at risk.

"Now that I've filled you in, I need to know what I'm dealing with. What happened all between you, Danielle and Josie at the club because it's clear they said something to Roxie."

I started at the beginning and reminded her how the two basically attacked me then walked out and left me hanging. I had to cancel a tour of the club and everything; it was a complete mess.

"So, they found out that you're after Dax and got mad?" she hissed. "And let's not forget: Those are Roxie's girls."

"I really don't have time to analyze what they're mad about, and who is whose BFF. I need to get in here, change, pull my stuff together and get over to the Ritz. Can we discuss this tomorrow? I have a star quarterback to seduce."

"Well, go get your seduction on. Don't let me stand in the way of progress," McKenzie said.

I promised to check in with her later and hung up.

Once inside, I grabbed the basket, a bottle of wine, some crackers, dried salami, cheese and a container of chicken salad I grabbed from Whole Foods the day before. I slid two wineglasses from the rack and gave the stuff in the basket a once-over before I closed the lid.

"Okay, that's done. Now what to wear? I need something simple, but sexy, yet not too overstated."

I rushed to the closet and settled on a long, fitted but flowing maxi that showed off all my curves. It was sexy, but not dressy and what I liked most was how daring it was.

After I changed, brushed my teeth, and grabbed the basket, I headed over to the Ritz to get my man.

I connected my iPhone to the console and jammed my favorite playlist as I cruised over to the Ritz. As the sexy lyrics from the songs worked like an aphrodisiac, I couldn't wait to finally be alone with him.

When I pulled up to valet, I grabbed my basket, and my phone then nearly skipped all the way to the elevator. Thanks to McKenzie, I already had the room number and he was expecting me. I was not the least bit surprised to see a few photographers snapping pictures. While I would normally sashay specifically for their lenses, I had other pressing matters that needed my full attention. Besides, I was sure that they knew he was staying at the hotel, and I also knew a few pictures of me added with that fact meant I didn't need to utter a word or pose for a single shot.

Inside the elevator, I refreshed my perfume and my lipstick.

I knocked softly on his room door and waited for him to answer.

After a few minutes, I started to get nervous, until I heard his voice.

"Sasha, that you?"

Yes, daddy, it's me! I thought.

"Yes, and I'm alone."

I heard heavy steps move toward the door and the excitement rushed through my veins once again. When the locks sounded and he pulled the door open, I wanted to melt right where I stood. He looked so rugged and distressed, but as handsome as ever. I wanted to kiss all of his misery away.

"Awww, are you okay?" I pouted.

He cracked a half-smile, and then blushed. I couldn't remember a time when he looked better.

"Hey, girl. S'up?"

When he did that slight nod of his head, it turned me on. I wanted to strip him naked right there, but I had to pull it together.

"Can I come in?" I asked.

We stood there grinning and admiring each other. There was simply no denying the chemistry that existed between us. I felt it, and I knew for sure he had to have felt it, too.

"Yeah, yeah. Come on in. Where's my head, damn!"

Dax moved aside and I allowed my hips to sway a little harder.

"Damn, you smell all good and shit. What's in that little bag you got there?"

I turned and smiled.

"Well, I heard about the, um, *challenge* you're going through, so I wanted to bring some stuff to help lift your spirits," I said.

Once I made it all the way into the room I saw the bottle on the table and turned around with my mouth hanging open.

"Oh, no! I'm too late. You've already started hitting the bottle," I joked. "Wow, you're worse off than I suspected, and here I thought some wine and crackers might help."

He started laughing. And that was a great sign. I didn't want to walk in being all pushy and aggressive. I knew I needed to make him feel like he was in complete control.

"Wine!" He balked.

"Yes, wine, with crackers and cheese!"

"Uh, what did you think I was gonna do with some wine and cheese? That's that ol' girly stuff." He chuckled.

"Well, compared to that, yes, it most definitely is girly," I said as I eyed his bottle of aged Patron.

"So, that mean I gotta keep drinking by myself?" He shrugged.

"No, not at all! I'll have a drink with you. You can enjoy your Patron, and I'm gonna enjoy my wine." I smiled.

Dax was so clueless it was cute. If a few shots of Patron was all it would take, I'd do that and then some.

His eyes were glassy, but he looked genuinely happy to see me.

"Okay, so I know you didn't come all the way here to keep me company while I get drunk off my ass, so what's up, Sasha?"

JERRI

Imagine the sheer panic that washed over me when my eyes focused in on the words plastered on the paper sign taped to the front door of the Football Widows Social Club. I didn't want to believe my eyes. My heart began to race as I prayed this was all a huge mistake. I moved in closer and with each step I took, my heart felt like it was dropping from my chest. This could not be real!

"What do you mean *closed*? I need to get my friggin' hours in," I muttered. I glanced around in both directions. This couldn't be happening.

I walked up to the window and brought my hands up to cup around my eyes, so I could get a better look. The inside was completely dark, so I couldn't make out a thing inside except a tiny red light that blinked near the back of the room. Not only was the place closed, but it looked as if it had been closed for a while. My pulse continued to race like we were in competition at a NASCAR event.

This was too much. Between Jason's offer, my shot at easy street during my community service, and the start of the season looming, I was teetering on the edge. I turned around and leaned my back against the locked door. I didn't understand. Why hadn't someone called to warn me?

"What the hell am I going to do?"

As my eyes filled with tears, visions of me in an orange jumpsuit, picking up trash on the side of the Harbor highway flashed through my mind and nearly took my breath away. What little dignity I had left would surely be gone by the time this was all over. Then, if I decided to get back with Jason, I'd surely look like the biggest fool alive.

I wallowed in self-pity and couldn't decide what I should do. If I called to report this, I was certain my probation officer, "Big Bertha," would try to find a way to make this my fault. What if I didn't call her, but still reported in like everything was okay? Would that be so bad?

"All I need to do is take a couple of days to figure out what's going on."

That was it! That was the solution here. There was no way Sasha would let her club fail, so this had to be temporary. Maybe someone had a death in the family.

"Something had to have happened," I decided.

"Yeah, like you must really be going nuts. You out here talking to yourself and answering your own damn questions?"

Vanessa's voice startled me. I looked up to see her and Natasha as they approached me.

"What's wrong with you? And what happened to the party you *said* was supposed to be popping right about now?" Vanessa asked.

She mocked me by looking around as if the crowd might have been hiding. Natasha looked at me and then through the window at the darkened office behind me.

"You okay?" Natasha asked.

I blew out a heavy breath.

"I don't know what happened. One minute I thought I had all this shit under control; the next thing I know, I come to report in and the place is locked down like I imagined it all."

"So what are you saying?" Vanessa asked. "Maybe the party was never gonna be here in the first place. You know, like it was always gonna be somewhere else. Can't you call somebody and find out?"

I noticed Natasha's hand as she tried discreetly to tap Vanessa's arm.

Vanessa frowned and looked down at Natasha's hand.

"Whhhaaaat?!" she screamed. "She was the one bragging about how this party was gonna be the shit—players and ballers galore. So now I'm just supposed to act like it's no big deal?"

Natasha moved closer to me.

"Looks like the place has been shut down. What does this mean for your community service?" she asked.

"That's exactly what I was *talking* to myself about," I said as I mocked Vanessa and rolled my eyes at her.

She crossed her arms over her chest and rolled her eyes right back at me.

"You had no idea they had closed up shop?" Natasha asked.

"I would not have told you guys it was all good if I had any inkling this would happen. And let's not forget, this is more than just a canceled party for me. Now I may need to find a different type of community service," I said.

"Eeewww. I sure hope you don't have to be picking up trash like out at the park," Vanessa interjected.

She shook her arms like the mere mention gave her the heebie-jeebies.

I turned my attention to Natasha.

"Think about it: That would mean I no longer have a place to perform my community service," I said to Natasha.

"Damn! What are you gonna do?" she asked.

"I wish she would call somebody and figure out where the party's at!" Vanessa said.

"Let's hold off until tomorrow. We can find out what happened before we start to panic," Natasha suggested.

"So, lemme guess: No party, right?" Vanessa rolled her eyes. "Can we at least go grab something to eat somewhere? I mean, you thought you were gonna be at a party anyway, right? So, technically, you have a pass for tonight."

For the first time since she appeared, I was glad to hear words coming from Vanessa's mouth. She had a point. It wasn't like Big Bertha would know that I was not performing my community service. I basically had a pass for a few hours, and there was no point in allowing that to go to waste.

Before Natasha dismissed Vanessa, I spoke up.

"She's got a point," I said.

Natasha's head whipped in my direction. "What do you mean?"

"I mean, if nothing had happened, I would've been out until at least eleven or midnight even."

My friends' eyes lit up as I talked.

"So, we can technically go somewhere, and you would not be in violation?" Natasha asked cautiously.

I nodded. "Well, I guess, technically."

Then reality began to sink in. I could go and hang out for a few hours, pretend like these were the good ol' days.

"Why are we still here then?" Vanessa snarled.

The way I felt made me unsure about what to do next. I wanted to go and hang, but I also wanted to know what was up with the club. Then there was the situation with Jason. The minute that thought flashed into my head, I realized there was no better time to be with my girls.

"Oh, snap! I totally forgot to tell you guys about Jason," I said.

There was no mistaking the spike in both my voice and my sudden change of attitude. I knew I had a real dilemma on my hands. Living the way we had been living for nearly two years was nothing short of frustrating. But now, Jason wanted to give me the ability to reclaim my old life. Sure, I would've been fine without him, but there was no mistaking what being with him would mean.

People loved to give free things to important people. Together, we received VIP tickets to exclusive events, star-studded events, and the best perfumes, purses, shoes, and even clothes. Yes, membership definitely had its privileges.

"You know what: On second thought, we do need to find a bar. I didn't tell you guys I'm getting back with Jason, so drinks are on me," I said as I started to walk toward the parking lot.

I stopped when I realized, I had made the few steps alone. When I turned to look at my girls, I noticed they stood frozen with their mouths hung low to the ground.

It was clear they were more stunned than me over the news I had just dropped.

TATYANA

I felt like the sick and shut-in country pastors always talked about. I had been locked in my house for three days and had no clue about my husband's whereabouts. I hadn't washed my ass, barely brushed my teeth and swore I felt crustaceans in the corners of my eyes. But I didn't care. My exit plan was no longer important. I had all but abandoned the plan when Dax said we were broke anyway.

Calls to his cell phone went straight to voicemail. So, imagine how sick and disgusted I was when I ventured outside and found yet another damn letter in the mailbox. I was fit to be tied!

I snatched the envelope like I was angry at it and wished I had the strength to trash it without reading it, but I didn't. There was no way to tell how long it had been in there. I glanced around as if I might be able to see something or someone who could offer a clue.

"What the hell?"

I inspected the envelope closely. It was the same stationary that had haunted my dreams from the day the very first one arrived. Who was this bitch, and how the hell was she able to get so close to me? I flipped through the rest of the bills, bypassed the junk mail and sighed.

"Tat!"

My mind must've really been far away because it took some

time before it finally registered that someone had called my name. I was stunned when I turned to see Roxie and Danielle making their way up the walkway that led to my house.

I frowned more because I knew I looked a hot, funky mess than because I was more than a little surprised to see them. I prided myself on being friendly with everyone at the club, but I didn't socialize or mingle as much as I knew I should've. So, seeing club members at my house was really a stunning sight.

"Hey," I said faintly.

The two of them looked like they'd just stepped out of the latest fashion magazine and that made me feel even more self-conscious. The sweats I wore had been on my body since I'd returned from the airport days ago. My dingy T-shirt should've been trashed, but it was saved because it was comfortable.

Not that it did any good, but as they got closer, I tried to fuss with my hair that was all over my head. I smiled awkwardly and tried to look like company dropping in unexpectedly was okay.

"Girl, glad we found you," Josie said.

She sounded like she was struggling to catch her breath. I glanced around and wondered how the hell they knew my man had left me. Quite surely that was the reason for the unexpected visit. I didn't move because I wanted them to say what they had come for, then turn around and leave. I was not in the mood for company, and pity company was even worse.

Two hours later, my mouth was on the floor as the four of us sat around my kitchen table with a bottle of wine and several glasses.

"So you trying to tell me that bitch was smiling in my face and all along she was plotting to take my man?"

Danielle's face was fixed with a menacing frown. She nodded as Josie spoke. I was fired up.

"Not only was she smiling in your face, but when we confronted her about it, she acted like her shit didn't stank!" Josie said.

"I was too through," Danielle said.

"So, this was going on all this time?" I was stunned.

Now everything made sense. I was so tempted to tell them about the letters, but now I was even more unsure of whom I could trust. The bottom line was they were *Sasha's* friends, and they had no real ties to me. For all I knew, this could've been part of the plot to get Dax with their girl.

"Tat, it didn't bother you in the least—the tabloid pictures, the headlines? I mean, she went after him pretty hard and strong, and it was like she didn't care who knew," Josie said.

"I had a lot going on," I said.

"Yeah, but pictures of them sharing intimate dinners, holding hands, it was more than we could stand. So, we told her about how trifling she was, told her it was wrong for her to be parading around, not just with a married man, but the husband of one of our members," Josie said.

"What did she say when you guys confronted her?"

"Baby, she started taking off her damn earrings!" Danielle said.

My eyes grew wide.

"She did what? What do you mean?" I asked.

"Instead of denying any of what we threw at her, the bitch was ready to go to blows! Now it's not our business, but do you think Dax could be having an affair with her?"

Their words made so much so clear for me. Of course he was having an affair with her. Pamela's warning rang loudly in my ears. What if he really was trying to keep his money for his new life with Sasha Davenport? How could I have been so stupid? I all but handed my husband over to her.

"Well, she'd call the house—"

"Hold up!" Josie screamed. Her bony index finger moved from side to side. She sprang up from her seat. "What do you mean she'd call the house, like your house? Oh, that bitch is bold for real! You mean she had the audacity to call him *here*?" Her finger pointed toward the floor.

I shrugged. "I didn't think anything of it. She was talking to him about doing a show and helping with some football workshop she wanted to do. I really thought it was all legit!"

Danielle and Josie exchanged knowing glances and shook their heads in disgust.

"Bitches like her—"

Josie cut Danielle off. "It's a damn shame!"

I appreciated them filling me in on this, but I wanted them gone. Now that I knew Sasha was the one behind the letter-writing campaign, I wanted to take another look at the letters.

There were so many questions floating around in my head. Why pretend to be someone else? She wanted me to think my husband was gonna leave me for a much younger chick. I wanted to slap the taste out of Sasha's mouth!

I buried my face in my hands and tried to rub some misery away. Suddenly, an arm eased around my shoulder.

"It's okay," Josie's voice said. She pulled me closer. "You know, it's one thing to have groupies chasing our men, but one of our own? This shit is such a violation. I really wish I was a fighter. I'd whoop her ass for you!"

I struggled to hold it together. Why did they feel the need to bring this to me? I wasn't sure how much longer I could go without falling apart. I was already on the edge because Dax had left, but now knowing he had run into the arms of a woman who basically sat and plotted and calculated my demise then taunted me along the way? It was enough to push me over the edge.

"We simply thought you should know the funky shit she was trying to pull," Danielle said.

"It's wrong on so many levels." Josie said.

"I appreciate y'all letting me know what's up. If you don't mind though," I said.

"Oh, yeah. I know. I understand," Josie said and stood.

Danielle stood, too.

I took a deep breath and stood along with them. I needed time alone. I needed to think about my next move. Did I want to go and confront Dax and Sasha? Did I want to sit and wait to see what would happen?

"If you need anything, seriously, I know we haven't been particularly close, but the moment we found out what she was doing, we wanted to reach out," Josie said. "The truth is, she latched on to Dax for whatever reason, but the bitch could've picked any of our men."

Ten minutes after they left me alone, I closed the door, locked it, and allowed myself to finally fall apart.

ELIZA

Mary agreed to meet me for lunch. I still had no clue what Poppy was up to, but I wanted to know what I was dealing with before I went back to work and stumbled into the unknown.

How did they decide I was the one who needed to go? Had Poppy still been attacking me in my absence? How had she been able to turn things around so quickly?

I didn't like lunching with Mary because her favorite restaurant was the Hard Rock Café. But since I needed her information more than she needed my company, I had agreed to meet her there. I found a parking space in the Hollywood and Highland Center and made my way toward the restaurant.

Before I hopped onto the elevator, I jotted down the floor number where I had parked in the garage. I could never remember where to find my car when it was time to leave, and I had a feeling today would be no different. I wasn't sure what to expect from Mary, but because she was the office busybody, I suspected she'd know what was going on. Even if she didn't know for sure, over the years, I had found that most rumors around our office often pointed toward the truth.

Mary sat on a bench near the hostess podium as I walked in from the back of the restaurant. From a distance, it looked like she was in deep thought, but I knew better. She was studying the podium that housed memorabilia from a famous or infamous rock 'n' roll band.

"Heeey, *Mija*," she greeted me.

"You two ready?" a hostess asked.

"Yes," I said.

Mary glanced back at the display one last time before she moved.

"Right this way." The hostess gestured her hand in the direction she wanted us to go. Mary went first, and I followed.

The Hard Rock Café in Hollywood was close to empty at 11:30 on a Wednesday morning. I was disturbed by how dark it was inside, but Mary marveled at everything she saw as we were led to our table. She behaved as if it was her first time inside the restaurant. We sat next to the display of Elvis's jumpsuit and a flashy guitar.

"I love this place," she said as she gazed dreamingly at the glass display. "Those guys were on to something when they came up with the idea for this place!"

She looked around at some of the other displays.

My right eyebrow went up. Not only did I not like the restaurant, but I hoped she wasn't about to get into a long drawn-out discussion about the history of the Hard Rock Café. I had lunched with her and some other coworkers on several occasions at this very location.

We got comfortable at our table and started to look at the menus.

"Ladies, what can I get you to drink?" the waiter asked.

I never even saw him approach.

"I'll start with water and a lemon wedge, please," I said.

"Yeah, me, too. I'll take the same," Mary said.

"Coming right up," he said and darted away from our table.

"So, what's the latest?" I asked immediately. I felt like she'd be able to stay focused if I got straight to the point.

Suddenly, her expression changed. "Is that the dress Tina Turner wore for 'Proud Mary'?" Mary asked in astonishment.

I turned my head to the right to see what had caught her attention.

"That's new," she said.

And before I knew it, she had gotten up from her chair and rushed over to the display. She stood in front of it like she was in a trance. I sighed hard as I swung around in my seat and looked back at her. How did I get attached to all the damn crazy people? My job was my life and just because my boss had lost her damn mind, I had to plot in order to find out what was going on in the office I had dedicated a good part of my life to. I was frustrated.

"Ma'am?" The waiter's voice pulled my attention from the freak standing in front of the display.

When I looked at him, I could see confusion on his face. "Are you guys ready to—"

"Maaary!" I yelled before he could finish.

She spun around and looked at the waiter and me. We were still the only people inside the main dining space.

"Oh." Mary rushed back to the table. She snatched her menu from the table and started to look at it like she was suddenly in a hurry.

"I can come back if you guys need a few extra minutes," the waiter said.

"No need. I'm gonna have the California chicken club with onion rings instead of fries," Mary said.

The waiter looked at me.

"I'll take the Hard Rock nachos," I said.

"Is that an appetizer for the table or your meal?"

"My meal," I said.

We gave him the menus, and the minute he turned the corner, I started the conversation.

"Mary, I saw Poppy recently, and she said I am being fired—that when my time off is over, I'm not coming back. Do you know anything about that?"

Mary's eyebrows furrowed as she stared at me. She frowned, then shook her head. "If there's anybody who is on thin ice, I think it may be Poppy," Mary said.

My eyes grew wide at that. "Why do you say that?"

Mary leaned in as if someone might hear what she was about to say. I wanted to remind her that we were damn near alone in the restaurant, but decided she didn't need any other distractions.

"Well, you remember that show with Dax and Dwight, and the workshop? Well, upstairs has been monitoring our work closer than we thought, and once you left and both those high-profile projects fell apart, Poppy's been skating on thin ice," Mary said.

Her words flew around in my brain.

"How could Poppy have screwed that up? Those were already set in stone."

"I think that's what's got her on shaky ground. Upstairs was fully aware that those things were done deals, so they began planning national ad campaigns around the two events. Leading into the season, the plan was to take the press overseas ahead of the NFL game in London. Now it looks like that entire plan will have to be scrapped." Mary twisted her nose. "And so close to the start of the season, I think she's scrambling to try and fix this."

"Do you think she knows she's fucked up?"

"Oh yeah, but most of us are trying to figure out why she had it in for you. Trust me, if she said you're not coming back, it's because she's got something up her sleeve. I told you, you can't trust that skank."

I leaned back in my chair. As our food arrived, I decided I might need to stop by the Football Widows Social Club.

SASHA

I felt like someone who suffered with some kind of mental problem. The voices in my head had been going nonstop, and it felt like nothing I could do would stop the chatter.

After I spent the last two days avoiding my agent's calls, I finally decided it was time to face the truth. And the truth was, I had failed. I was no closer to snagging Dax than the day I started on my plan. I felt like such a complete loser, having wasted so much time and energy only to wind up empty-handed.

I was lucky and found a parking spot right in front of the little Mexican restaurant on Pico Boulevard. It was a hot spot, mostly for police officers that had a great happy hour. For once, I had arrived before Marteen, so I walked into the little storefront and stepped down into the restaurant. A crowd had already begun to form.

The TV monitor in the bar was on a sports channel and a group of women were partying it up in a corner. I walked up and claimed the two barstools that were left.

"What'er you drinking?" the bartender asked.

"I want a large peach margarita with salt," I said.

I eased onto the stool and started to think about how things took a turn between Dax and me. I felt like I had put in the work with him. We would've made such a great team. My mind went back to that awful experience at his hotel.

Sure, he was already drunk when he opened his room door, but I figured that simply meant my work was halfway done.

"What do I want?" I repeated his question.

We were cozy and comfortable. My shoes were off, and I was on drink number two. He had thrown back a few shots in the time since I had arrived.

"Are you serious?" I asked him.

"About what?"

"You don't know what I want?" I asked sweetly.

By that time, I felt good. The setting was just right. He had left his wife and kids, and I had him right where I needed him. All I had to do was get him naked so we could seal the deal.

"Nah, you women are something else. You being like Tat now. Y'all expect us to be able to read your minds and shit, and it don't work like that."

I didn't want to talk about his wife, and I didn't want him to either.

"Can you believe what she did, man?"

His question made me change my approach. He had been married for a while. Even though I suspected he had gotten his fair share of ass on the side, I figured I needed to hear him out. After all, I wanted to show him the difference between her and me.

"You never said," I told him.

He jumped back and frowned.

"I ain't told you what that bitch did to me?" he asked.

My heart began to flutter. Maybe things were a lot worse than I suspected. Had he just called his *wife* a bitch? The liquor had made him raw, and I liked it. I wanted to fuck more than ever before.

"Damn, I don't believe she did me like that." He sobbed.

I couldn't tell if he was actually crying, but I knew what he said didn't make any sense.

"What did the bitch do?" I pressed.

"She started telling Tat that I was lying and shit! She straight dissed me in my own damn house. She had been all up in our crib and shit, and she gon' tell my wife I had some jump off or some shit."

I was so lost. He wasn't making any sense.

Instead of taking another sip, I put my glass down. So, the 'bitch' wasn't his wife? I had no clue what or who he was talking about. I decided to try a different approach. I eased closer to him on the sofa. When I did, I could've sworn he backed up a bit. It was a subtle move, but I noticed. How did he not realize I was giving him the green light? I was about to loosen the straps on my top when his next statement stopped me cold.

"Pam ain't nothing but a lonely, bitter, old bitch," he spat.

"Who?"

So he *had* been seeing someone else? How did McKenzie's private eye of a cousin miss a mistress?

I pulled back and looked at him. He was past pissy drunk, but I was confused.

"That bitch! Pam!" he stated.

I felt foolish. All this time I thought Plain Jane was my only competition, and here he was with another chick on the side. So from what I was able to gather, his side chick showed up at the house, and there was some kind of confession. Apparently, that was what led him to being tossed out of the house. When he reached for his bottle again, I wasn't sure what to do. Flashes of our life together seemed to fade from my mind.

I readjusted myself on the sofa and wondered if knowing about a side chick was enough to deter me. The bottom line was I needed Dax to get what I wanted. Sure I wanted him, but I had been married enough times to know that sometimes a man wants more than one woman, and I was cool with that. But I needed to see this Pam. I needed to know whether what they had was real, or whether she would be okay remaining in the wings.

"Just 'cause I messed up and shit," Dax mumbled.

I nearly didn't want to ask. I stood to undress when he had started back up again.

"I lost all my damn money," he confessed.

That time I was certain he was crying.

"What do you mean you lost all your money?"

"You ever heard of R. Allen Stanford out of Houston?" he asked.

"What about him, and what does he have to do with you and your money?"

I thought Dax was rich. He was one of the highest paid in the league. Quite surely it was the alcohol talking.

"This dude, we invested in his business, heavily. All the money is gone. What was left was seized by the FBI," he said.

"Oh, shit! So you trying to say you *broke*?"

The sound of the door opening brought me back from the horrible thoughts of my last night with Dax.

"Hey, sorry to keep you waiting," Marteen said. "You sitting here daydreaming?" She chuckled.

"Something like that," I said.

The bartender came back as she sat down.

"I'll have a margarita on the rocks—top shelf," she said.

"I'll take another frozen. This time lime," I added.

Before Marteen could catch her breath, I dropped my dilemma on her.

"What are my chances of getting the show by myself, without a man, or the drama we talked about before?"

"Slim to none, I'd say." That stung, but I knew she was right. "Look at the climate you'd be competing in. *Real Housewives of*

Atlanta is blazing up the ratings with their antics. *Love and Hip Hop Atlanta*, *Mob Wives*, and I could go on and on. But the truth of the matter is you alone simply aren't enough to carry an entire reality TV show."

Her words didn't shock me because I had known all along what was on the line. I knew all too well what was on the line—my show, my professional future, and my love life. All of it hinged on my ability to get a man who wasn't what I thought.

"What happened with the show?" Marteen finally asked.

I shrugged. I thought the show was the least of my concern. My focus had been on getting Dax.

"Sea Lions' publicity called, and they wanted to know what was going on," she said.

"Everything has fallen apart. What's so crazy is how I never saw any of this coming. I thought I had it all under control."

"Well, is it too late to pull it all together?"

I thought about her question. I had invested so much time and energy into Dax, I never considered a plan B or a backup even. I knew this was going to work, and I knew we'd make an unstoppable team. There was no way I could tell Marteen that the man I wanted didn't want me because he already had a side chick. I needed to go back to the drawing board. I grabbed my cell phone and looked up my old flame Tim's number. Nothing cleared my mind like a good, serious fuck.

JERRI

"I love you. I've never stopped."

His husky voice made me even hotter.

He suckled my bottom lip so hard I didn't know if I was in pain or in bliss. When he released me, I sucked that spot on his neck. It used to drive him nuts back in the day. His taste, his smell, his touch, it all felt like home. I closed my eyes and told myself to go with the flow, and run away with the feeling.

"When it's good between us, we're so damn good together, baby. Don't throw it all away," he whispered.

He spread my legs wider, and I accepted everything he offered.

"Uh," I moaned.

"You miss this. You miss me."

"I do, baby. I do."

Jason felt bigger and stronger than I remembered. He moved his body with the strength of someone treading in familiar territory, so that meant he was hitting all the right spots.

"Good for you?" I asked.

"Oh, Jesus! Oh, yes, baby, yes!"

His lips moved from my ears down my neck and on to my breasts. Hard and stiffened nipples awaited his attention. He suckled one while his hips remained in sync, and I loved every moment of it.

Nothing mattered at that very moment. Everything was right

between us. *My* answer would've been yes. It didn't matter the question, he could get anything he wanted.

"Damn, baby." Jason suddenly stopped and held his position. "I can't. I'm about to—"

"Come for me, baby," I moaned.

I cut him off, used my sweetest muscle and squeezed him tightly.

He was done! And so was I.

As we lay wrapped in each other's arms, and in the afterglow of amazing sex, I tried to catch my breath. Jason stroked my hair lovingly, and I couldn't remember why and how I hated him the way I did.

His strokes slowed and I heard soft snores fill the room. I was happy. I was really happy. I started thinking about how we had stumbled into bed. I had no regrets, but after hanging with the girls and drinking way too much, I was more than a little confused.

The drinking went crazy when I could no longer tell the difference in behavior between Vanessa and Natasha. It was like the two had merged into one Vanessa and I didn't know how to deal with two of her.

"What do you mean you've decided to get back with the devil?" Vanessa asked.

I turned, and they both stood and stared at me like I had suddenly developed horns of my own.

"Let's calm down." Natasha jumped between us. I wasn't sure if she thought we'd come to blows, but I didn't see the problem.

"Hey, let's go grab a few drinks and talk about it," Natasha said.

"He's not the devil. He's my husband, and we've decided to work things out," I said.

I turned to Natasha and asked, "Where are we going?"

"L.A. Live," she said.

I decided to follow them over there. I hated when Vanessa and

I got off on the wrong foot. Any time we had a war of words, I walked away and thought about everything I should have said. That's exactly what I did as I sulked toward my car.

"When we were all single and miserable together, it was all good. Now that I'm talking about saving my marriage, she's looking at me like I'm crazy?" I said aloud. I was behind the wheel, alone in my own car.

Minutes later, I pulled into the parking structure behind them and I could see Vanessa speaking in a very animated manner. I knew she had probably talked about me like a dog, but I didn't give a damn.

We walked into the first bar we saw after we left the parking structure.

Once settled inside and seated, we ordered and the waiter walked away. That's when Vanessa lit into me.

"Look at all he's done to you! He's has cheated from day one; he degrades you; and he has absolutely no respect for you whatsoever. Could your self-esteem really be that bottom-of-the-barrel low?"

"Look, I wasn't no damn saint myself. I mean, if you wanna get technical, I probably cheated more than he did. And while he was getting down and dirty, guess who was right there in the mud with his ass, so don't be checking me because I decided to fight for my marriage!"

Our voices were getting loud, but the conversation I had with myself on the drive over had fueled my adrenaline and my urge to put her in her damn place.

"Okay, chill out. C'mon, let's get some liquor in us and talk about this thing like adults," Natasha said.

I caught my breath and held my comment. Natasha reached her hand across the table in my direction.

"Honey, I know you think you're doing what's best for your family, your kids, but I kinda agree with Nessa on this one. I mean, I think there's been so much bad blood between you two," she said.

Her comment made me frown and ease beyond her reach. It was an olive branch I didn't want. I was pissed that they wouldn't simply fall in line and go with the flow.

Four drinks later, I couldn't tell the two of them apart. I felt like I was being bullied.

"Didn't he fuck that porno chick?" Natasha snarled.

"Um, remember when you thought he had an outside baby?" Vanessa pulled her lips away from her straw to ask.

I rolled my eyes at their questions.

"All he trying to do is get you to end your quest for more money. You know what they say, cheaper to keep her," Natasha said and went back to sipping her drink.

"Lemme get this straight. So, now this is a ploy on his part. He and his entire legal team put their heads together and all they could come up beat me, was him deciding to get back with me. Yeah, that's the best way to make sure I won't get any more of his money?"

They didn't even get my sarcasm.

"I'm just saying. Why this sudden change of heart? You don't think he's got something up his sleeve?" Vanessa asked.

By now, we were all tipsy. Words were being slurred, and tempers or at least my temper was on the rise. I couldn't believe them!

The scent of bacon made my senses tingle. Then the aroma of warm maple syrup joined in on the attack.

"Hey, Sleeping Beauty," Jason's voice called.

I couldn't remember when I fell asleep, but when I woke and adjusted my eyes, I grinned at my husband who held a tray filled with a feast—maple-flavored bacon, scrambled eggs and French toast on a silver platter. I eased up in bed.

"Oh, wow. I must've laid it down last night. Breakfast in bed?" I teased.

He laughed as I pulled myself upright in bed.

"Baby, you don't even know the half of it. Had me in there cracking eggs and shit!"

"Wwwwhhhat?" I smiled. "You mean you made all of this yourself?"

"Damn right I did!"

Thoughts of the verbal battle I'd had with the girls the evening before danced through my mind. But when Jason squeezed close to me in bed and started scooping eggs into my mouth, I let that shit go.

If this was his well-crafted strategy, all a part of his evil master plan, I was all for it—at least for now.

After I swallowed, he leaned over and kissed me full in my mouth. The man was all up in my *stank*, morning-breath mouth like he was searching for cavities. When he pulled back to feed me more food, I couldn't help but think I'd have to ride this thing out to see exactly where we were going, but I knew for sure we were on the fast track to rekindling our romance and our marriage.

TATYANA

Three days after my husband left, I was all cried out. It was time for some action. He had ignored all of my calls. His cell phone went directly to voicemail just like it did hours after he had stormed out of the house. And if that wasn't enough, anytime the TV was on, I had to endure pictures of him and *her* all hugged up, or pictures of him smiling and grinning like he was having such a fantastic time with her.

"To hell with this shit!"

The last time I heard his damn voicemail message about a full mailbox, I decided to end my personal pity party and take charge of my situation. My mama didn't raise no fool, and I'd be damned if I'd sit back and let him and his bitch live happily ever after.

One peek in the mirror, and I knew action was long overdue. I showered for the first time since I got back from the airport. I changed my clothes and fixed my hair into a ponytail. I pulled out my journal and started checking the deposit records. Everything was written in code to protect the secrecy of the mission.

I had worked on this plan for years, but never suspected it would end like this. There was much to do, but first I decided I needed to get my plan together. If in fact we *were* broke like he said, that changed quite a bit.

Should I stay with him? When would I confront him about Sasha? What if this really was all a ploy on his part? So many thoughts raced through my mind. The more I thought about it, how it all went down, the more my pulse began to race. I had prepared for the worst for so many years. I wasn't really sure how to move in the necessary direction now that the worst was finally here. I wasn't ready. But the truth was right in my face. My husband had left.

Did he leave to be with *her*? She had befriended me! She plotted and pulled every trick in the book! That damn Sasha! She needed her ass *whupped*!

I pushed that thought to the back of my mind. First things first. I released a huge breath, pulled myself together, picked up the phone and called my mother.

"Heeeey," I greeted.

It was a struggle to maintain a voice that wouldn't crack. Mountains of emotions wanted to push through, but I had to be strong. The last thing I needed to do was fall apart while on the phone with my mom.

"Hey, honey, how you doin'?" she asked.

"I've been better, Ma, but I need you to do something for me. You got some time?"

I sighed.

"Yeah, is everything okay?"

I heard the worry in her voice, and I didn't mean to concern her. I needed to get it together, and it started with her.

"I'm not sure, but where are the kids?" I asked.

In California, kids didn't start school until after Labor Day, so I was grateful that they'd be in Houston while this thing blew over. I needed the time to pull my shit together.

"Oh, they're upstairs playing a videogame. Why? You need 'em?"

"No, I simply wanted to make sure they weren't around. Basically, I need to find out how much money we have in the account," I said.

"*The* account?"

"Yes, ma'am."

"Oh, okay. Well, that's gonna take me a minute. I need to pull out the computer. But while I do that, why don't you tell me what's going on?"

I held the phone as I listened to her move around.

"I'm not sure yet, but Dax is saying we're broke," I said.

My mother chuckled or nearly choked over my words. I couldn't really tell which it was, but when she spoke again, I noticed that her voice had dropped a few levels.

"Well, I know there's quite a bundle in there, but I thought that was the rainy day fund or um what did you call it again?"

As she spoke, I heard her acrylic nails as they tapped against the keyboard.

"My 'exit plan' money," I said.

She chuckled a bit.

"Oh, yeah, that's right. You New Millennium women. Oh, so wait. Are you telling me you're leaving your husband? Oh dear. Oh my. What has happened, chile?"

"Mom, it's too much for me to go into now, but I need to try and figure out my next move. And although I know this is really unexpected, I need to get an idea of how much money I have stashed. For all I know, this money could be everything we have."

I held the phone and waited as my mother continued to type.

"Dear, Jesus, sweet Jesus," she said as her fingers worked.

"Mom, I've gotta figure a lot of stuff out, but for now, I need to know where I stand financially."

"Baby, you know you always have a home right here in Houston," she said.

I laughed a little. It was more of a nervous chuckle. There was no way I was about to consider moving back home, but it was cute of her to say so.

"Okay, hold on. I'm pulling it up," she said.

We had only been on the phone for a few minutes, but still I felt like this was taking too long.

"Looks like we have a little over three million in there," she said.

"Hmm, three million," I said, more than asked.

"Yeah, honey. That's what it looks like. Now what do you need me to do?"

"Nothing yet, Ma, I'll keep you posted. First, I need to go find my husband and depending on what comes out of that meeting, I'll let you know my next move."

"*Find* him? What do you mean?"

Now it was clear that there was alarm in her voice. I understood, because in a sense, I was scared, too.

"It's a very long story, but he left. Pamela was here. We all got into it. Things got heated, and he left."

"What do you mean *we* got into it? What's Pam doing arguing with you and your husband?"

My mom was an old-school mama on so many levels. I knew her mind was filled with all kinds of crazy thoughts. She was one of those women who felt like no married woman should tempt her husband by bringing another woman under her roof.

"It's nothing like *that*, but it's too much to go into right now. Let me figure some things out, and I promise, when I'm ready, I'll tell you everything," I offered.

I heard the reluctance in her voice, but I had so many other things I needed to do. I couldn't get emotional and slip up. Once the money was counted, I needed to find one person before I tracked Dax down. And I knew exactly where I needed to go. That bitch had some explaining to do. I reached into the drawer and snatched the stack of lavender envelopes.

She may have gotten my man, and honestly, they could have

each other. But I'd make sure I did whatever I needed to make sure she didn't snatch my lifestyle. I'd worked too hard, made too many damn sacrifices for her to slide in and take my place!

I decided the studio would be my first stop. Since the bitch loved the spotlight so much, I'd meet her where the light seemed to shine the brightest.

"With three mil in the bank, bail money wouldn't be a problem!"

Everything, including that thought changed when I walked out to get to my car and another envelope was beneath my wiper blade.

ELIZA

I knew I was taking a huge risk, but before I went to the club to try and smooth things over with Sasha, I felt I needed to snoop around the office first. Poppy was on to something, and I needed to find out what the hell she was up to. I'd go and talk to Sasha and convince her that we needed to do the show, but first I had to see just how much damage Poppy had caused.

I was certain at least a couple of the security guards might still be cool with me because I had gone out of my way to treat everyone with respect. But in order to be on the safe side, I knew going after hours would be the best bet. I wasn't afraid that I'd bump into Poppy because I knew her ass would be long gone before the clock struck five.

When I entered the building, it might have been the dimmed lighting, but my heart felt strange.

"Eliza?"

Bruce, one of the security guards who came in when I was encouraged to take some time, called out to me. He and I were still on good terms.

"Hey, Bruce, how've you been?"

I decided to play it cool. If I looked nervous or like I didn't belong, he'd get suspicious. So far, he seemed friendly.

"How was Mexico? Shoot, I thought you'd never come back. I know I wouldn't." He chuckled.

"Mexico?"

"Yeah, Charlene told us you went to Cancun or the Mexican Riviera or somewhere over there." He shrugged. "Lots of beach and tequila. It's all the same."

"Oh, yeah. I did, but that was only for a few days. It wasn't long enough."

He nodded.

"Well, what'd you rush back for?"

"Some stuff I needed to do for work. You know how that is."

He sighed. "Yeah, tell me about it." He slapped his massive palms and rubbed them together. "Yeah, preseason, baby!"

His radio went off, and he raised a hand to quiet me. He pulled it from his waist and turned a button on it.

"Hey, I'm gonna run upstairs to get something real quick," I said.

He nodded quickly, then turned away from me and started to talk into his radio.

I released a huge sigh of relief the moment the elevator door closed and took off. That was easier than I'd expected. I walked into my office and felt like a stranger in a foreign land.

It wasn't that much had changed, but more the fact that I hadn't been there in nearly three weeks. I could tell Poppy had been in my space. She had several shoe boxes in a corner of my office. Her handwriting was scribbled on a legal pad in front of my monitor. There were notes that meant nothing to me, and a few scribbles.

When I saw Dax's and Dwight's names written on another page, my heart began to race. I pulled a drawer open and fumbled through some unfamiliar things. I picked up a stationery set that did not belong to me and marveled at how comfortable she had become in my space. She had even moved some of her things in like she knew for sure I would not be back!

When all was said and done, I didn't find anything that would help. I pulled up some internal emails and was about to exit out when something caught my eye.

"So, someone is threatening to break a national story about a sex scandal involving Sea Lions players?"

I tried to click the sent folder to see what Poppy said when she responded, but I accidently landed on a folder that had my initials on it. I clicked the folder titled *EC* again and noticed several emails in it. I started with one dated several weeks prior.

The emails talked about detailed proof of a sex scandal that allegedly involved Dax Becall and asked publicity to make a comment. The emails indicated that out of respect they were giving publicity two weeks to make Dax available for comment or they were prepared to break the story!

"No attribution?"

I frowned as I read the emails. What bothered me most was that there was no reply email. There was not a single reply to any of the emails. The emails seemed to originate from a personal mailbox, but it was clear the person worked for a media outlet or at least that's what the writer wanted us to believe.

As I leaned back in the chair, I wondered why Poppy would not have sent anything in response. It was clear that each email seemed to escalate. The final email indicated that since we had no comment, no response, and would not confirm whether Dax would be available, they would move forward with the story.

Again, no reply email was sent from Poppy.

I considered typing something up myself, but knew that would probably cause problems. So, Dax was involved with another woman? I wondered whether his wife was aware. This was bound to blow up into something nasty and explosive.

The last thing the team needed was a bitter wife at the start of the season. Sideline scandals were never welcomed, but it was not the way to kick off any season.

I sighed.

"So, Poppy wants this blowup to coincide with my return. That's why she was so confident that I wouldn't be back yet. According to Mary, no one seemed to know about it!"

What didn't make sense was why she would risk a scandal that could impact the team, affect the players, and throw everybody off. Even if it was in the preseason, those games did quite a bit as confidence builders.

Once I felt like I had enough information, I decided to check the address. I was stunned when I realized who lived at the address she had staked out. Instinctively, I checked my watch and wondered if it would be too late to pay them a visit. If there was a scandal brewing, I needed to get ahead of it and try to cut this thing off before it started.

I double-checked the address. No matter how much I looked at the address and scrutinized over it, the pieces still wouldn't fit into the puzzle. I was even more confused.

"Now this don't make any damn sense," I said.

Why on earth was Poppy sneaking around *that* neighborhood?

SASHA

If I couldn't have the one I loved, or *wanted* to love, I decided to give it to the one I was with or would be with. Reluctantly, I found my cell and looked up his number.

I dialed and waited for the phone to ring. There had to be some kind of mistake. I knew Tim was mad, but who cared about his anger? I was mad, too! I needed release, and he was acting like a bitch! I looked at my phone and wondered how it had malfunctioned.

"The subscriber isn't taking calls? Does that mean his Cricket phone is disconnected?" I laughed. "I know he didn't change his damn number. It was so not that serious."

After I redialed Tim's number and got the same message, I was fit to be tied. Because of my celebrity status, I had to be very careful who I blessed with my goodies, but I hated the situation I was in. If only I could find another Tim who understood his role and didn't mind playing his position.

These dudes tripped me out. They'd swear they could handle it, but when it came down to it, they weren't ready for a woman like me. I tried to warn them upfront just so there would be no misunderstanding. My thought was if they knew the job was dirty from day one, we wouldn't have any confusion. I wasn't looking for love unless his bank account exceeded seven figures.

It took everything in me to not call Dax. I wanted to give him another chance. The truth was, I didn't have the energy or the time to find another baller, and why did I have to put off my reality TV dreams for another year?

When I couldn't reach Tim, it made me think more and more about Dax. I hadn't been able to stop thinking about our last conversation.

"What do you mean you lost all your money?"

"You ever heard of R. Allen Stanford out of Houston?"

"What about him and what does he have to do with you and your money?"

I pulled out my laptop and decided to look up this R. Allen Stanford guy. It wasn't that I doubted Dax's story. Who would make up some shit like that? I simply needed to try and figure this thing out. He and Tatyana were all but over. I wasn't the least bit deterred by the side chick, but it didn't hurt to check things out and see exactly what I'd be dealing with. Who knew, if it wasn't that bad, I might actually be able to stand by my soon-to-be man.

Besides, I knew he had to have a plan. You're not an NFL star quarterback without a backup plan. In the days since our time together, I decided to do my own homework.

It didn't take long to get the goods on the creep. So, this guy was convicted of charges that his investment company was a massive Ponzi scheme and fraud. Stanford was the chairman of the now-defunct Stanford Financial Group of Companies.

"Now ain't this some shit! What black man in his right mind gets caught up in some Ponzi scheme type of foolishness?" I shook my head as I read about how the man cheated people out of all that damn money!

"See, Dax needs a woman like me so badly. Ain't no way in hell a husband of mine would've been investing *our* money with this kind of foolishness. Damn, Tatyana, you plain and dumb? What the hell was she good for?"

After I had taken in all that I could stomach, I checked my Facebook page and started thinking about Dax again.

"I wonder what he's doing over there in that hotel room all by himself."

Maybe I needed to see him again now that he was sober. With all that liquor he had in him, I wouldn't be surprised if he even exaggerated the entire story.

I closed my eyes and smiled when my phone rang. I didn't even want to look at my caller ID because I was so happy. Maybe Dax sensed that I had been thinking of him. Our connection was really something fierce.

"This is Saaasha," I said sexily.

"I'm not calling you again," the voice threatened.

The smile fell from my face; I rolled my eyes and was pissed at myself that I had forgotten to talk with McKenzie about limiting access to me!

"Well, that's good 'cause I don't think we have a damn thing to talk about," I snarled.

"I tried to tell you about a huge story, but your ass don't want to listen."

"I told you. This is not the way for you to reach me if you have a story idea to share!"

The disappointment I felt that Dax wasn't the one ringing my phone was just exacerbated by this stupid bitch. Not only did her country twang get on my nerves, but I thought after the last damn phone call, she'd gotten the message. One of the things I loved most about TV was also the same one I hated most. Too much TV made everyone think their story was unique. And everybody under the sun thought they had a story. And of course they just knew their story was the bomb that was sure to make my ratings skyrocket. Trust me, I had heard it all before, and I was more than sick of it.

At a time when I needed to think of a way to get back to the Ritz and back to Dax, I was dealing with some freak who refused to take no for an answer.

"Look, lady, I don't have time for this game with you. Call the offices, and you can talk to one of the many producers who are waiting to talk to people just like you."

"Your sarcasm is so not funny. I should've known not to try and help your dumb ass!" she screamed.

"What the hell is your problem? You don't know shit about me. How you gonna dial my damn number—"

"I know you bat-shit crazy! I know you ain't nothing but a two-bit groupie who lucked up after that scandal with those coaches' wives a few years ago!" she said.

I was pissed and about to hang up when her next words caught and held my attention.

"I don't have to work this hard to offer a tip about a sex scandal involving Dax Becall," she hissed.

And that's when the earth stopped moving, and I damn near stopped breathing my damn self.

JERRI

I couldn't believe we were already gearing up for the first preseason game. I felt all giddy and young again. It had been like the good ol' days with Jason and me. We behaved like horny teenagers, especially in the days before the kids got back.

Everyone thought I was crazy. Natasha and Vanessa acted like they couldn't understand what had gotten into me, but I didn't care. At times, I gave life to their crazy thoughts. What if he really was trying to play me? But the minute thoughts like that clouded my mind, I thought back to some of the dirt I had done. The memory was as fresh as if it was weeks, instead of nearly five years ago.

I had waited nervously by the phone all day. When it finally rang, I snatched it up quickly.

"Hello?"

My voice was so shaky I fought back tears as I tried to be strong. I was on the edge and knew two wrongs couldn't make anything right in our marriage anymore. I felt used and worthless, so while hanging out with the girls, we picked up a couple of dancers.

"Have some fun!" Natasha yelled.

And I really was overdue. The rumor mill was running wild with all kinds of shit about what Jason may and may not have been doing. I felt like the worst reject ever. So, when that guy started gyrating his glistening six-pack all up in my face, and I inhaled that coconut oil, I was on fire! I used my tongue to trace along the ridges of his well-defined six-pack, and it was on!

"I can make you feel good," he whispered.

Of course my girls were cheering me on!

"Do that shit, Jerri! Do that shit!"

Next thing I knew, I was gyrating right along with him. We were in a private room being entertained like the ballers do, and it was all good.

Sexual Chocolate wasn't shy at all. Somehow my top was worked off, and he was removing my bra with his teeth. Everything he did was done to music, and he didn't skip a beat. The man was talented and moved his body in unnatural ways that turned me the hell on. The girls couldn't cheer me on too much because they were busy getting it in themselves.

"I can do anything you want," he promised. "Take you all the way to ecstasy and back."

He didn't move me from the chair. He tilted it back against something firm and started working on my nipples.

I was in ecstasy.

"You want this?" he asked.

"I want it all!"

"Tell me you want it."

He clamped on to one nipple and sucked like I was his favorite flavor.

"Yes, I want it all," I moaned.

He moved back and helped remove my skirt. He didn't bother taking my panties off, but I peeked over to see what everyone else was doing. We were all in the same room. It was going down in that room.

"Lemme get a condom," I managed.

Three days later, my coochie felt like it was on fire! I was burning.

Unfortunately for me, Jason and I had gotten drunk the day before and we had fucked like rabbits. Two days after that, the fire between my legs would not stop. I kept my thighs tight because the irritation was so unbearable. Unable to stand it anymore, I grabbed the phone and called for a doctor's appointment.

"Hi, this is Mrs. Nelson. I have a horrible yeast infection, wondering if I can get Dr. Baldwin to call in a prescription for me," I said.

"Oh, okay. Let me check with her. Do we have your pharmacy's number on file?"

"Yes," I said.

When the nurse came back to the phone, I didn't like her tone.

"Uh, excuse me, Mrs. Nelson, Doctor Baldwin says because she hasn't seen you in the last six months, she won't be able to call in a script. Is there any way you can come in?"

I sighed.

"Does she have any openings this afternoon?"

"We'll fit you in. When can you come?"

The doctor did give me more than one prescription, but it was because she felt sorry for me. That yeast infection turned out to be gonorrhea. I was stunned.

"I'm going to double the prescription," the doctor said after she confirmed my diagnosis. "Because I need you to take them and Jason has to take them, too."

I wanted to die right there on the spot.

"Jerri, you there? Did you hear me? I said two prescriptions—one for you and one for your husband."

"Okay," I said meekly.

I had gone over the fling a million times in my mind. Why did I have to screw Jason so close afterward? I knew the condom had broken, but I thought he was safe. He looked so damn good and near perfect. Of course I knew how ignorant that sounded, but there should've been a law against any fine person like that being dirty. Who took that kind of care of their body on the outside and not give a damn about their health?

When I called to tell Sexual Chocolate that he slipped me the claps, he had the fuckin' audacity to act like he couldn't be sure he had.

"Yo, I don't usually get down like that," he said.

I hung up the damn phone. *Dude, you're a damn stripper. For an extra fifty dollars, you would've tossed my salad!* I was more pissed at myself for fucking him, but the damage was done.

The wait for Jason to come home had to be the absolute longest ever. I rehearsed what I was gonna say over and over again, but it never sounded quite right. I talked myself out of telling him. Maybe it would be best to mix the pills up in his food or his drink. But damn, what if the food tasted funny? I went back to rehearsing what I should say.

Hey, um, I know things aren't like really good between us right now, but the doctor called and said you need to take these pills? The doctor said this could lay dormant for something like fifteen years?

You could've picked it up from the toilet seat in the locker room?

Nothing I said sounded believable. I couldn't remember a time when I was more afraid of my husband. He had accused me of stepping out before, but he never had proof. Up to that very moment, I enjoyed the upper hand because I had pictures to prove what he had done. He had lashed out at me over anger, but never had any proof.

Unsure of how to handle the situation, I jumped up from the table when he strolled in. It was really late, and I thought about trying to use that to my advantage, but couldn't work it out in my head.

"What's wrong with you?" he asked.

"Why something gotta be wrong with me?"

I knew I was wrong, but I felt like throwing him attitude was my best option. If I was lucky, we'd get into it, and I could throw the bottle of pills at his head. But he didn't take the bait.

"The kids down already?" he asked.

"What you think? Look at the time!"

"Yeah, practice ran long," he lied.

I didn't know if he was lying, but I needed to believe he was. His food was covered on top of the stove. Jason glanced at me, then headed for the stove.

"Thanks for dinner," he said.

I barely responded. In my mind, I kept trying to think of the best way to drop the bomb. I no longer had the stamina for lying.

Finally, I grabbed my purse and took out the pill bottle. "I need to go outside for some air," I said. Before I walked out, I walked up to him and put the bottle of pills down.

"Doctor Baldwin says you need to take these until they're all gone!"

I didn't wait for him to respond or ask any questions. Before he could notice the frightened look on my face, I stormed out of the back door and found a dark corner near the far edge of the pool.

He slept in one of the guest rooms that night, and that began our downward spiral. Sounds of the front door opening and closing snapped me back from that painful memory.

"Baaabe," Jason called out to me.

When he rounded the corner and looked at me with pure love in his eyes, I wondered how I had been so lucky. I was even more convinced that his feelings were genuine.

I couldn't care less what Natasha and Vanessa thought. When that man wrapped his strong arms around me and squeezed me tight, I was so glad we had decided to try again.

TATYANA

It wasn't the envelope that stopped me cold this time. My cell phone rang, and it was a call from my mom. I answered before I moved the envelope.

"Are you okay?" she asked the moment I said hello.

"Yeah, why wouldn't I be?"

"That crazy woman called here. She called Junior!" my mother screamed.

"What? What are you talking about?"

"Tatyana, I waited for you to call back and tell me what the hell was going on, but when you didn't I figured you had things under control. But some strange woman calls your son's cell phone and starts telling him all this craziness about how she's going to be his new mom, and how you decided you didn't want them, so she and his daddy were getting married!"

"Mom! No!"

"Chile, it took me quite a while to calm these kids down. They were bawling and carrying on, asking whether you two were getting divorced."

"Mom, I'm so sorry," I cried.

"Where's Junior? Let me talk to him," I said.

"Not a good idea. I finally got them settled down. I just wanted to tell you I think you need to call the police. This is crazy!"

"Yeah, I know you're right. I do. I was about to go and confront her, but this time, I think she's gone too far. Letters are one thing, but when you reach out to my kids—"

"So, you mean to tell me you know who this hussy is?"

"I do. And I was about to go and give her a piece of my mind, but I think you're right. I need to call the cops!"

"Call right now. I don't want to hang up because I'm scared for you," my mother said.

I knew there was no point in trying to tell her I was gonna be okay. So, I put her on hold and dialed 9-1-1 on the other line. I clicked her on three-way when the phone started ringing. I also grabbed the envelope that was beneath my windshield wiper. I quickly put it back. Since I was calling the police, I needed to leave things right where they were.

"Nine-one-one, what is your emergency?"

"My daughter is afraid for her safety," my mother blurted out before I could speak.

"Ma'am, where is your daughter?" the operator asked.

"I'm right here," I said.

I rattled off my address once I realized I was on my cell phone.

"Ma'am, is this a medical emergency?"

"No, a crazy woman is stalking her, and she threatened her son!"

"Ma'am, who am I talking to? I need to talk to the complainant," the dispatcher said.

"I'm sorry. I think she's in a bit of shock," my mother explained.

I looked around for anything that might seem out of place.

"Ma'am?"

"Yes, my name is Tatyana Becall," I said.

When she repeated my name, I felt like recognition had settled in. She probably did that to everyone, but I felt odd about it.

"Mrs. Becall, we are sending a cruiser to your home. Are you inside, and do you fear for your immediate safety?"

"I do," my mother chimed in. "People are crazy nowadays. This woman been stalking her with letters, and now she's reaching out to her kids! I want an officer posted outside her home!"

"Ma'am?" the dispatcher said.

"You can't play it safe these days. People will shoot you in a heartbeat!"

"Mom!" I yelled.

"I'm sorry, Tatyana. I hate this is happening to you."

"I know, but let me handle it, okay?" I said.

The dispatcher interrupted. "Are you inside the house?"

"No, ma'am. I was about to leave when I got my mom's call and noticed another envelope on my car windshield," I said.

"Did you touch it?"

"Yes. I mean no," I said.

"Which is it?" the dispatcher asked.

I heard sirens in the distance, and I started to feel better.

"I saw it and grabbed it until my mother told me about the threatening phone call," I said. "I put it back where I found it and called you."

"Okay, you should hear sirens," she said.

At that moment, they got louder.

"Yes, I hear them."

"Well, I'm going to stay on with you until the officer arrives," she said.

That made me feel better. Part of me felt foolish, but my mother was right. You couldn't trust people these days. This chick found my child's cell number.

My knees nearly buckled when I thought about the fact that Dax might have given it to her.

"Oh, God!" I said.

"Ma'am," the dispatcher said, "are you okay?"

"I see the cruiser now," I said.

"Okay. Great. The officer will make contact with me, and I will hang up."

"Thank you," my mother told her.

"Ma, I need to get off, so I can talk to the officer," I told her.

"You can't keep me on the line?"

"Ma, let me handle this. I will call you right back."

"You tell them everything, Tatyana, you hear me? I don't want nothing to happen to you. I want them to go and arrest this crazy broad." My mother was fired up.

"Okay, Ma, the officer is getting out of the car. I need to go."

"I'm calling back in fifteen minutes," she said.

I ended the call and looked at the officer as he approached.

"Mrs. Becall?"

"Yes, sir," I said.

He looked at me, but his eyes quickly swept the area around me. "What seems to be the problem?"

I took a deep breath and told the officer everything from the first letter to the last.

He had pulled out a small notepad and jotted down things as I talked.

"Did you touch this letter here?" he asked.

We moved closer to the car.

"I did, but then I put it back," I said.

"Okay."

I watched as he grabbed a handkerchief and removed the envelope. He used a pen to open the back and placed the letter and envelope onto the hood of the car.

I wasn't as embarrassed as I thought I was going to be.

"You did the right thing by calling this in. You can't take any chances these days, especially since your husband is so high profile," he said.

This letter was far more aggressive and angrier than any of the others. *She* was mad at me!

I WILL KILL YOU IF YOU RUINED THIS FOR ME! HE IS EVERYTHING TO ME, AND NOW HE WON'T EVEN TALK TO ME, AND I KNOW IT'S BECAUSE OF YOU! I AM NOT ABOUT TO TAKE THIS LYING DOWN, YOU STUPID BITCH! ALL YOU HAD TO DO WAS LEAVE, BUT YOU HAD TO MAKE IT HARD!

The officer looked at me.

"Do you have any idea who this woman is?"

"Yes, sir," I admitted.

He looked like, okay?

"She's Sasha Davenport," I said.

His eyebrows went up.

"The talk show lady?" He sounded surprised.

"Yes, I think she's plotted this out for months. My husband left days ago, and I thought he was with her, but now this letter has me thinking maybe he's not there," I said.

I felt such incredible shame. But I knew I had to suck it up. You don't play with anybody's kids.

"How do you think she got your son's cell number?"

I shrugged. I felt like I had said enough. I needed to know what he was going to do. Because if they didn't go and pick her ass up, an ambulance or the coroner would have to get what's left of her damn body.

He turned away from me and pulled the radio from his shoulder and spoke into it. At that moment, my mom called back, just like she promised she would. I had no choice but to answer because she would call every sixty seconds until I picked up.

ELIZA

I wasn't sure where to go first. I didn't know if I needed to go by the club, the studio, or by the address. I left the office and decided to pass by Poppy's place to see if she was at home.

There was no way I was ready to confront her, but I needed to keep better tabs on her. I felt it in my bones. I had no idea what she was doing, but I knew she was up to something, and because that something was bound to impact my career in a negative way, she became the enemy I needed to keep close.

Why would she purposely allow a scandal involving Dax to break? Maybe she thought she'd go in and clean up the mess after the fact. The more I considered that idea, the more it made sense. If she headed off the drama before it broke, there would be little acknowledgment for her professionally.

But if the shit hit the fan, she'd be all over the place, cleaning up the mess. The more I thought about her wickedness, the more I saw what the fool had planned.

I wouldn't be surprised if we later learned she was behind the emails. It wouldn't be hard to create a fake account and send those threatening emails. When the shit began to fly, she could make it seem like I had known about them all along and did absolutely nothing, and I could see her trying to use that as a basis to get me fired!

"That bitch!"

I wasn't sure what all was missing from her life, but I would be damned if I would sit back and allow all of my hard work and career to go down the tubes because she was bored.

Once I had it all figured out, I decided to call Mary before doing anything else. I was not going to play my hand too soon. But I still needed to gauge the temperature in the office even though I wasn't there, and Mary was my thermometer.

I dialed Mary's number as I passed Poppy's place. I slowed, pulled over across the street, and looked up to see lights on in her place. I felt comfortable enough that she was home. After a few minutes, I pulled away and greeted Mary when she answered the phone.

"Hey, how are you?"

"Hey, girl, I'm tired, but good. What about you? You talked to Charlene yet?" Mary asked.

"No, not yet, but I'm good, too. I think Poppy was simply running off at the mouth. You know how she can be."

"Yeah, well, we can't wait for you to come back. It's just not the same when she's in the office. You know she spends so much time in your office these days," Mary said.

"Really?"

"Yeah. She's weird. She will come in and lock herself in your office and not come out until she's headed out the door."

"That is weird," I said.

"So, when you coming back again?"

"I talked to Charlene and looks like I'll be back day after to-morrow."

"Oh, okay. Well, I can't wait to spread the word. I'm sure everyone will be stoked!"

"Don't spread it around too much," I said.

Mary's voice lowered. "Yeah, that's a good point. Besides, I don't want her to know we talk, so I think I should let it come as a surprise to the rest of the team, huh?"

"I think that's a smart move."

"I, for one, cannot wait to see the look on her face when you come strolling in. You've got to text me. I want to make sure I'm on the floor—front and center," Mary said.

"I promise. And, hey, Mary, I need to take this call on the other end, but I'll be in touch," I told her.

"Okay, well, good night."

My next drive-by involved going to the address I had scribbled on a piece of paper. Slowly but surely, this plan was becoming very clear. As I steered my car off the main road and turned to the street that led to the subdivision, black-and-blue strobe lights lit up the dark night sky.

"Whoa." I nearly rear-ended the vehicle in front of me.

Hmm, a *sobriety checkpoint*? I thought that was odd, but maybe it wasn't. This was not my part of town, so I had no idea how they got down over on this side. From what I could see ahead, I was the fourth vehicle in line. Officers stopped each driver and said something before the person was waved through. I waited patiently and scooted forward as another car in line passed.

By the time it got to my turn, it dawned on me that I hadn't thought about what I would say. As I pressed the button to lower my window, I realized it was too late. My eyes could hardly adjust to the bright light that flooded into my vehicle.

"Good evening, ma'am, are you a resident of this subdivision?" the friendly officer asked.

"Uh, no. Um, I'm not," I stuttered.

The bright light went from my face toward the backseat of my car, and then over me and beyond the driver's seat. My heart was pounding so loud I feared he might hear it.

I didn't even bother to wipe the bead of sweat on my forehead. I had not done anything wrong, but my mouth got dry, and it felt like my throat was about to close up and cut off the air circulation. My hands were unsteady and I could imagine how suspicious I probably appeared.

"What kind of business do you have here?"

"It's not business, but I was um, about to visit a friend of mine," I said.

However, this time when I tried to answer, my words sounded strained like I was trying to think fast on my feet. The gesture was subtle, but I noticed it because the bright light was no longer shining directly in my face.

Out of the darkness, a couple of uniformed officers appeared at the speaker's side.

"May I see your driver's license?" the officer asked.

One of the other two began to walk around my car.

"Sure." I sighed. "But can I ask what this is about. Is this private property or something? I can't even be sure that this is where my friend lives because I always get lost when I try to come out here," I lied.

"Oh, okay. Well, here's what we're going to need you to do." The officer looked up and made contact with his colleague. He nodded slightly, glanced at my driver's license then lowered his head to speak to me.

"That's Officer Andrews over there." He pointed ahead to the right side of the road. "I need you to pull up over there, because the officer has a few additional questions for you."

"Okay, did I do something wrong?" I asked.

"No, not at all. He will explain once you get over there."

I didn't move right away, and he tilted his flashlight back toward my face.

"My driver's license," I said.

"Oh, yes, Officer Brown here is going to walk it over there. Don't worry. You'll get it back," he said.

After I raised my window back up, I steered my car to the right side of the road as instructed. The two officers met me at the side of the road. One tapped on the window, and I lowered it again.

"Sorry, I don't know what this is all about," I said.

"One of the residents in this subdivision received a credible threat, and we're taking extra precautions. The reason you were singled out is because you seemed very unsure of the nature of your visit," he said.

"Oh, I'm not threatening anyone. It's like I told the other officer, my friend recently moved somewhere over here. The only time I've come was during the day. I'm not even sure that this is the right subdivision."

"Well, you see that's a part of the problem, too. I heard you talking to my colleague over there, and that wasn't exactly what you said."

My ears began to burn. Hadn't I said I was there to see a friend? Maybe I didn't. This was going in the wrong direction really fast, and I wasn't sure what I needed to say to make this all go away.

"He asked if I had business here, and I said no. I really was trying to visit a friend, but now I'm all confused and turned around."

"I know. I know. Do you mind if we search your car?"

"Search my car?"

"Again, a resident here was threatened. We don't consider you a suspect, but honestly anyone who doesn't live here is somewhat a person of interest. You don't have to let us conduct the search, but since you gave such conflicting information, we're hoping you won't mind helping to bring some clarity to this matter."

He hadn't been nasty. His colleague had been just as polite, and I felt like my odd behavior was probably what got me into this situation. I didn't know whether it was a bad idea to agree to the search. I knew that I needed to get my ass away from them and all of this madness.

"What happens if I don't let you search my car?"

The officer shrugged and pursed his lips. He glanced away like the answer might be a few feet away from us.

"Well, we'd consider that a reason to call up a judge and get a search warrant."

"Okay, look it's not that serious. I know I seem a little nervous—"

"You're nervous? Hmm, we weren't aware of that," he said.

Oh shit!

SASHA

Two days after the stunning phone call, I felt lost and confused. I wasn't sure what to do with the information I had received. People who hid behind anonymous phone calls were really a risk because they had a hidden agenda.

"You never know whether to trust their information. I just sat there and listened."

McKenzie looked at me, but she didn't say anything at first.

We were in my dressing room. I sat on a chair, and she was on the sofa. She rubbed her temples.

"So, you're telling me that this woman called with information about a sex scandal involving Dax, and you didn't ask *any* questions?"

"If I went off all emotional, that would've made her clam up. I wanted to see what she was talking about. You and I know that I've been working my jelly during the entire off-season. The Sea Lions are on the road this week, but she says she's about to go public when they get back, and I believe her. I'm not sure if I should do or say anything. Hear me out," I said.

The expression on her face told me she didn't agree with my decision. I crossed my legs and released a huge sigh.

"Okay, I think he and this Pam chick have been fucking. I think Pam thought she was gonna slide in to replace Tatyana. Then out of nowhere, Pam starts to see these pictures of *us* all over the place. All of a sudden, she's pissed, and she's like, 'Hold up a damn minute. I didn't do all this hard work, playing the bottom chick only to get trumped by someone new!' So, she decides she's going to try and sell her story. Now you already know, everybody tells their business to *somebody*! Who knows? Maybe Pam's best friend decides it was all good when Pam was his little secret, but now that there was trouble in the Becall household, it looked like her girl was about to move on up. You know how many females *hate* in secret! So, she decides she needs to slow her girl's roll, and she starts trying to sell the story herself."

McKenzie looked confused. She raised her hand like we were in a classroom.

"No, wait, so I have this information. Do I break the story, or do I sit back and let the chips fall wherever? I say I sit on this and let the scandal break. Tatyana and his sidepiece can get into a nasty and very public catfight that will play out all over the press. When the dust settles, I come out looking sweet and pretty on Dax's arm," I said.

I blew at my manicured nails and blew on them as if to say, Now what?

"Ummmm..."

I expected more of a grand finale reaction from her, but she sat there like she was still trying to absorb all that I had spelled out.

"It totally makes sense to me. Now here he is, Sea Lions star quarterback, making all the right moves on the field, while being that rich handsome playboy off the field. Everybody secretly loves a bad boy, and it just so happens that's exactly what I need to get *Seriously Sasha* off the ground. BAM!" I exclaimed.

"Okay, it took a minute, but I see how you brought it around full circle," McKenzie said. "It's like you're channeling your Tom Brady, Gisele, and *his* baby-mama drama!"

I snapped my fingers and jumped to my feet.

"See, now you feel me! That's exactly what the hell I'm talking about. Look at how that drama raised Tom's stock. Now it definitely helped that he is a gorgeous star quarterback, but what I'm saying is, let Tatyana's dumb butt get into a catfight with the side chick, I'll be chilling in the wings and ready to walk off with the prize in the end. When the cameras are rolling on our lives together, those two trolls will be hating from their living rooms."

When McKenzie's hand went up in the air for a high-five, that sealed the deal. My lips would remain sealed about Dax and his sidepiece.

"Okay, so let's talk real business now," McKenzie said.

I looked around the room. My eyes grew wide. I was playing with her, but not really.

"Umm if plotting to take this show to the next level via my new high-profile boyfriend isn't business, I don't know what is," I said.

McKenzie started to laugh.

"Oh, trust! That is business for sure. But what I meant is the drama that has come from the canceled show with Dax and Dwight," she said.

I sat back down.

"Well, yeah, but considering all that's going on in Dax's personal life right now, I can't say I blame the man." I shrugged. "He's got tons on his plate right now!"

"Eliza called and wanted to see if we could meet. I need to make sure we're on the same page. I don't wanna meet with her and she's pressing me about something that I have no control over."

"The ball is in their court. Carlos is the one who pumped the brakes on the interview. If they want to come together and get it done, then I'm all for it," I said.

"Okay, that's all I needed to hear. I'm gonna meet with her after work today and hear her out. I won't make any decisions until

I run them past you of course, so keep your phone on and close," she said.

My eyes scanned upward as she got up from her seat.

"I have faith in you, Sasha. I know you're gonna come out on top. At first, I wasn't following your logic, but I can't wait to see how this all plays out."

We giggled like devious schoolgirls.

"I know, riiiiight?!"

When McKenzie left, I got up and moved toward my mirror. I stared at my reflection and saw nothing but a bright future in my eyes. The days I had spent away from Dax were for the best. I needed to give him some space to figure things out. While he was in the midst of the storm, I didn't want to be anywhere around. I couldn't wait until he needed a shoulder to cry on, and I couldn't wait to be the strong woman he would need to upgrade him.

The buzzer on my phone went off, and I instinctively looked at the seat McKenzie had just left. I figured she may have forgotten something.

"Ah, Sasha, you in there?" one of the guys asked.

My cell phone rang at the same time.

"Yeah, hold on a sec."

I got up to grab my phone. I thought it was strange that McKenzie's number popped up. I wasn't sure who to answer first, but the booming knock on my door trumped both calls.

"McKenzie, hold up. Someone's at the door and on the phone," I said into the phone when I answered her call.

"But, Sasha!"

"Just a sec!" I screamed.

I pulled the door open and was surprised to see two uniformed officers.

"May I help you?"

"Are you Sasha Davenport?"

I looked between the two, but slowly brought the cell up to my ear.

"Umm, McKenzie, what the hell is going on? Why are two officers at my dressing room door?"

"That's what I was trying to tell you."

"Ma'am, we need you to drop the cell phone," one of the officers said.

"Okay," I said slowly.

Black men had been shot for much less. I didn't even say bye to McKenzie. I slowly extended my arm and showed them that I was about to follow their orders.

"Putting down the cell phone," I said, "but can someone tell me what this is about?"

"Ma'am, we have a warrant for your arrest," one of them said.

"Excuse me?"

"I need you to put your hands on top of your head and turn around," the officer said.

I stood stunned temporarily. It made no sense. I was being arrested, at work? It had to be a serious mistake.

The ruckus coming up the hall was McKenzie flanked by a couple of my male co-workers.

"What's going on? Why is she being arrested?" she huffed.

"Ma'am, we need you to stand back," the other officer said to McKenzie.

His tone was hard and cold. It was clear he meant business. McKenzie stopped in her tracks.

"You are being charged with three counts of making a criminal threat!" the first officer said.

I swallowed hard and dry, then he began to read me my Miranda Rights.

"In California, when you threaten to kill or physically harm someone and the person believes you and is afraid, that's all it takes," the officer said. "That threat can be communicated verbally, in writing, or through email. It's that simple," he said.

"I didn't threaten anybody, and I'm not no damn criminal," I muttered.

"Sasha, this has to be a misunderstanding!" McKenzie yelled.

I put my hands on top of my head and turned around. The feel of cold, hard steel handcuffs that clamped down on my wrists was nothing nice.

The officers were unmoved. It was very clear, they had their marching orders and nothing I said was gonna get me out of this one.

JERRI

I had tons of decisions to make. Jason came to me with what I considered a valid point, and I wasn't sure how to handle it. Also, I kept calling the club, and still, there was no answer. I needed to find out what happened, and why no one had been there. Each time I thought about my probation officer, Big Bertha, I pushed that thought to the back of my mind.

I knew I'd have to fess up and tell her what was going on. Two weeks had passed since I'd last checked in, and my time was coming faster than I wanted.

Jason walked out of the shower and the sight of his glorious body literally made my mind go blank. He wore a white towel wrapped around his waist, and he used another one to dry his head.

"Baby, you never dry completely off," I said.

He smiled at me and said, "I simply touch up the crucial spots. Everything else can air dry."

Jason moved closer to the bed and sat down next to my feet. *My* mind couldn't stop thinking about how happy I was—or we were. But my girls and their nagging concerns wouldn't leave me either.

"Real talk," I said.

My husband turned to me.

"My girls are worried."

I looked at the droplets of water that still sat on his back. His body was remarkable, still.

"They should be," he finally said.

I wasn't sure what to say, so I kept my mouth shut. My heart raced like an out-of-control locomotive. I didn't want to be made a fool after all that had been going so right. Instinctively, I pulled in a deep and ragged breath. I braced myself for the worst.

"You're not single anymore, and you know misery loves company, baby. I ain't got nothing personal against your girls, but when females are thirsty for so long, they can't see a good tall glass of water even if they was stranded in the Sahara Desert."

I started cracking up.

"You sure know how to paint a picture," I said.

"But on the real though, I know where they're coming from. They probably like, 'You and that fool been on some serious war of the roses type of shit. Now all of a sudden, y'all trying to make up.' Listen, if they wasn't looking out for you, they would roll with whatever," he said.

"But, babe," I whined.

"I know, but think how I feel. You think you got it bad?" Jason blew out a breath and shook his head. "I'm like the laughing stock of the locker room!"

I frowned.

"Nah, it's not like that. All I'm trying to say is if this is what you really want, and you feeling it like I'm feeling it, I don't give a damn what anybody got to say."

Our eyes met.

"Awww, babe."

"Real talk, Jerri. People gon' think we crazy as hell. Think about it for real. We did shit to literally piss each other off—had to share a house, took out restraining orders on each other, and all kinds of crap. And now we talking about getting back together?"

His cockeyed glance with the way he said it made a whole lot of sense.

He grabbed my knee. "All I'm saying is don't trip out on your girls too hard. They doing what they supposed to do."

I twisted my lips. "Seriously, if you had told them we was all good after all the shit we been through and they were like, 'Oh, yeah, girl.' I'd be worried about their asses!"

"I love you. You know that?"

"Yeah, and I love your crazy ass, too," he said.

Once our laughter subsided, he moved in close.

"I want you to know something. When we were separated, I did some shit that I'm not proud of. I nearly lost my mind for a minute there, knowing you was kicking it with that benchwarmer, Ed." He shook his head like painful thoughts weighed heavily on his mind. "The shit wasn't easy." He used his hand to lift my chin. Jason stared into my eyes and said, "I really want to say I'm sorry. I'm sorry for everything. I'm sorry for taking us off track with my stupid behavior. I'm sorry for pushing you to do what you did, and I'm sorry I didn't have enough common sense to value what I had with you in the first place. I'm sorry, baby."

He moved in and placed a succulent kiss on my lips. When I opened my eyes, they were filled with tears.

"You don't have to be sorry," I muttered.

"You're right. I don't have to be, but my heart is heavy. I want you to know that when I'm making love to you, and we're all smiles, I think of how much pain I caused, and I want to know that you can move toward forgiving me."

"Awwwww, babe," I cried.

He got up from the bed, but looked down at me. "I ain't got time to be messing with you, trying to tempt me when you know I need to get to practice," he joked.

"What? I'm over here crying, and look where your mind is—in the gutter," I teased.

"My mind ain't nowhere. I just know my wife. You saw me stroll out in this towel, and you probably didn't know what to do with yourself."

I threw my head back and released a hearty laugh. It felt so good to be where we were. The phone rang and disrupted the mood. It was Big Bertha. What the hell did she want?

I looked at the caller ID with horrified eyes.

"What's wrong?"

"It's my probation officer," I whispered.

"Oh, shit. Well, pick it up. What's the problem?"

I looked at the phone as it rang, then looked back at Jason.

"Everything is a mess. I don't know what's going on at the club, but it's been on lock for the past two weeks. And I keep calling and calling," I said.

My shoulders slumped.

"Look, baby, we in this together. You understand me? I want you to call her back, find out what she wants, and let's go from there."

"You want me to call her back?"

"Yes, let's see what she's talking about. It's not time for you to check in or anything like that is it?"

"No, and I don't want to be talking to her just to be talking."

"Call her back," he urged.

"I'm gonna listen to her voicemail first."

I picked up the phone and dialed into the voicemail. As I held the phone to my ear, I watched my husband's bare ass when he dropped the towel. I grinned hard.

But what really made me smile was the message from Big Bertha. When the message ended, I pressed the button to replay it again. I couldn't believe my great fortune.

TATYANA

Things had spun so completely out of control I wasn't sure how to rein it all in. We had twenty-four-hour police protection, even after she had been taken into custody. And the media circus was just that—a real circus. The cops kept them at a distance, but I saw all of the news trucks and reporters gathered at the entrance of our subdivision. It made my stomach churn. My life had become a Lifetime movie right before my very own eyes.

It was like I could tell the time when everyone learned that my husband's mistress had lost her mind and threatened my family. The calls began to pour in, and I wanted to go into hiding.

The day after Sasha was arrested, I was completely worn out by mid-day. People came out of the woodwork. I finally took a Valium and called it an early night.

I woke and nearly pissed myself when Dax walked into the bedroom.

"I'm sorry," he said.

I was speechless.

"I tried to get here as fast as I could, but I had to stay back in Dallas for a test. I suffered a concussion in the game."

Normally, I'd be embarrassed that I had no clue, but times had changed. I wasn't sure we were still on the same team. He chose to leave before the game was over, and now he wanted to come back?

"I think you should leave," I said. My anger wouldn't allow me to let go so easily.

His handsome face was a constant reminder of the torment I endured with each call that went to his voicemail.

"You don't mean that," he said.

But his voice didn't sound confident. It came out almost like a question more than a strong statement.

"Go back to your twenty-three-year-old," I said.

Dax frowned and pulled back.

"My *what*?"

"Don't try to play me, Dax. The shit is over! But don't trip, I'm gonna be okay. You see, while you were out playing *I Need a New Trophy Wife*, I was stacking my cash. I knew this day would come, and I wanted to be ready," I bragged.

His frown deepened.

"What the hell are you talking about?"

"You made me look like a fucking fool. But, hey, now you and Sasha are free to go lay up together. Oh and newsflash, the bitch ain't twenty-three!"

"You believe all that mess?"

"Believe it?" I laughed at his act.

Oh, he was real good.

"I know Sasha's not twenty-three. But what's that got to do with anything?"

I got up, grabbed the stack of letters, and threw them square in his face.

"Umph, all this time you've been stealing *our* money and stashing it?"

"What was I supposed to do? Was I supposed to sit here, give you the very best years of my life, then ride off into the sunset alone while you and your newbie enjoyed the good life?"

When Dax started laughing, I didn't know whether to slap him or check myself. What the hell did he find funny?

"Tat, when would I have time for anyone else, much less someone who is twenty-three?"

"I told you she's not twenty-three. I now know that was her way of trying to throw me off her trail. Freak!"

"What trail?" he asked.

I sucked my teeth. I couldn't believe he refused to give up the gig. It was over. Her dumb ass was in jail, but he still carried on like it was no big deal.

"She threatened us. She called your son, wrote another letter saying she was going to kill me!" I screamed.

"WHO?"

"Dax, get the fuck out! Just go!"

"Tatyana, you're all over the place. You can't believe none of this shit! Sasha *is* crazy no doubt, but she's harmless. She's all into taking a bunch of pictures and all that kind of crap. She's good people, in a weird kind of way; that's all."

"You expect me to believe that? You're gonna sit here and look me dead in the face and tell a bald-faced lie?" I hissed. "What's next? You want me to go down there with you to bail her out? Or wait, maybe you want me to go be a character witness and talk to the judge about what a good person she is."

He threw up his hands. That disgusted me. He had the nerve to act like he was upset with me? I never expected him to show up, and I never expected him to admit what he had done, but for him to try and defend her, that pissed me off even more.

"Once I saw all that shit on the news, I wanted to come by and make sure you were okay. You can't believe what you see on TV. They're merely trying to get people to watch."

"Guess I can't believe the pictures on the magazines either," I snarled.

"Actually, you can't. They're trying to sell magazines. Shit, you know Sasha. She's a little ditzy, but she's cool," he had the nerve to say.

It wasn't until I pulled my hand back that I realized what I had done. His head snapped back like nothing happened. He looked me in the eye and said, "Damn! You slapped me."

"Just go."

He looked at me for a long time, his jaw tensed. I watched as his mouth pinched into a scowl and the color drained from his face. He pulled his gaze away from me and looked down at the envelopes scattered at his feet. He never even bothered to pick them up. Dax turned and walked out of our bedroom.

But I didn't care, I clamped my lips shut to avoid calling after him. It was because of him that I was embarrassed and living in fear. I was supposed to be told when and if she made bail, but deep down inside, I was hoping she wouldn't. It wasn't only the fact that we were friends and she went after my husband, but the cold and calculating way she went about it.

Josie and Danielle let me know that the bitch had planned everything from day one. I had never been a violent woman, but I wanted so desperately to beat the shit out of her. She just didn't know. She was so much better off behind bars.

A ringing phone took on a whole new meaning since the drama had exploded. The reporters were relentless. My mother behaved like I needed to be on suicide watch, and I wasn't looking forward to ever going back outside again.

Maybe it was because Dax was back in the house, and I knew he was upstairs packing some of his crap, but I needed to do something other than sit and think.

The phone rang and the number struck me as odd. Over the last few days, it had been some of the same numbers calling over and over again.

"Hello."

"Is this Tatyana Becall?"

"Who wants to know?"

"My name is Eliza Carter. I work for the Sea Lions' publicity office."

I considered calling Dax to pick up but hesitated.

"Dax, don't live here anymore," I said.

"I wasn't calling for him, ma'am. I think I have some information that may be of value to you."

"Well, in case you haven't heard, we're broke, and I'm not in the shopping mood right now," I snapped.

"No, I'm sorry. It's not like that. Listen, I tried to come and see you in person last week, but the cops wouldn't let me in. After they searched my car and didn't find anything, they let me go."

"What do you mean you were trying to come and see me, for what? I don't know you."

"I know, but again, my information may shed some light on what's been going on."

Her comment only reminded me that everyone knew what had been going on. My life was all over the place like some cheap, low-budget film. I wiped a bead of sweat off my forehead. My mouth felt dry and my hands were unsteady as I held the phone.

Something wouldn't let me hang up.

"I know you don't know me. But I've been stumped by all of this until Sasha was arrested. They said she wrote letters threatening your family. You know, this is lots of information. If we could meet somewhere, I want to show you what I have and tell you what I think is going on."

"Lady, I don't know you! I'm supposed to come and meet you somewhere? Oh, I don't think so," I said.

"I know this sounds strange, but you don't have to come alone.

You can come and meet me or give me permission to come out to your place."

"And why would I want to do that?"

"Because I think you had the wrong woman arrested. And if the real freak is out there, you have no idea when she's gonna make her move."

I couldn't take any damn more!

ELIZA

The shit had hit the fan. Everyone scrambled for information about what was going on. I heard former teammates, college roommates, and even some former neighbors were being interviewed. It was definitely a mess, but this was what it took for me to put this puzzle together.

It took some serious claims on my part, but I finally got Tatyana Becall to agree to meet with me. And even when she did finally agree, she still had rules attached to the meeting. If I wasn't so hell-bent on bringing Poppy down, I would've thrown my hands up long ago.

As I dressed, I continued to go over everything in my mind. I planned to go by the club to see who was there before I met with Tatyana.

"This is some craziness," I said.

It was hard to believe how this thing went down, but I was on it, and if it was the last thing I got to do, I wanted to see Poppy get what was coming to her. I especially wanted that since I knew the hag had been gunning for me.

By the time I arrived at the Football Widows Social Club, I thought I might have simply missed the staff, but when I looked closer, I realized that the place was shut down.

"Wow," I said as I peeked into the window. "Since their leader went to jail, they closed the entire operation?"

"Hey, aren't you—"

I turned and stopped a woman's question. She wasn't alone. "I'm Eliza Carter. I work with—"

"The Sea Lions?" the woman I remembered from my first visit asked.

"I'm Danielle. Remember Josie and me?" She pointed a finger at her friend.

The three of us stood around and looked at each other.

"What happened?" I asked, and motioned toward the place.

"Well, if you really want to know," Josie began, "it's what you saw all over the news. Once we found out what was going down with Sasha, we wanted no parts of that drama."

"For real," Danielle added.

I shook my head.

"Everybody's got it all wrong," I said. "It's why I'm about to go and meet Tatyana Becall right now."

They looked at each other.

"We're the ones who broke the news to her. I'm glad that bitch is in jail. The press has been out here for days. We took a gamble thinking no one would be here tonight," Danielle said.

"You're going to meet with Tatyana like right now?" Josie asked.

"Yup, I am. I've got some stuff to show her," I said.

"Where are you guys meeting?" Danielle asked. "If you don't mind me asking."

"Oh, there's a sidewalk café not too far from here. She wanted to meet in public. I guess in case I was some kind of freak, but after all this, can't say I blame her."

As I stood and talked to Danielle, Josie stepped back and pulled out her cell phone. I dug for the piece of paper and told Danielle the name of the restaurant.

A few minutes later, Josie moved closer to us.

"Just talked to Tatyana, and we're gonna head over with you," she said.

"Oh, okay. Well, I was only coming by to kill some time," I said.

"We were about to trash the place." Danielle laughed.

Josie gave her an alarmed glare.

"Ugh! I hate what she tried to do to Tatyana. I mean, we're all in the same club for God's sake! I remember when wives, fiancées, and such used to stick together," Josie said.

I wasn't sure if her comment about trashing the place was a joke, but I figured that was none of my business.

When we arrived at the café, Tatyana was already waiting. Danielle and Josie rushed to her, and the three of them looked like they were at a sorority reunion. I felt out of place until I remembered why I was there.

"Hi, there." I extended my hand. "I'm Eliza Carter, and I work in publicity for your husband's team."

Tatyana was graceful and very pretty. She smiled, gave me her hand for a quick but limp handshake.

"What's this about really?" she asked.

I looked between her and her friends.

"Sasha Davenport wasn't the woman—" I wasn't sure how to say what I needed her to know. I didn't think her friends being here would be a problem.

"Listen," Danielle interrupted. "She all but told us with her own mouth that she was going after her husband! That's why we left. There's no question about what she was up to because she told us. We didn't have to guess. She didn't deny what she was doing."

"Hear me out. You're right. Sasha is very straightforward about what she wants. I didn't say she didn't want Dax, but what I'm saying is she didn't write the threatening letters. As a matter of fact, I'm willing to bet you that Poppy McDaniel is the one behind all of those letters."

"Pop who? Who is that?" Josie asked.

"She's my boss," I said.

"Your boss? I'm confused. You said yourself Sasha was after Dax, but where does your boss come in?"

"It was the stationery, and that whole line about being twenty-three. When I saw the letters on the news, I knew I had seen that stationery before, but couldn't remember where. One day, Poppy came into the office kicking up drama as usual. I was scrambling to gather my things and accidently picked up one of the envelopes. When I saw it on the news, it brought everything home," I said. "Also, she had been snooping around your house."

Tatyana looked at me like she was confused. I didn't want to have to fess up about how I knew she had been in the neighborhood, but I was prepared to do so if need be.

The three women looked at each other. They seemed like they were doing some sort of nonverbal communication.

"But the pictures, the videos, and why did she get arrested? I mean, you're only arrested if you're guilty, right?" Josie looked between her friends and me.

"Innocent people are arrested every day," I said.

"There's nothing innocent about Sasha Davenport," Tatyana said.

"Poor choice of words, but it all came to me. Poppy was having man trouble. I suspect she thought your husband was going to leave you, and when he didn't, she had a complete meltdown. She was on a rampage in the office. She even started babbling about how one day everyone would know her name," I said.

"But—"

I raised a finger to stop Tatyana.

"Listen to what I'm saying to you. I didn't say Sasha wasn't trying to move in on your husband. What I'm saying is she's not the one who was obsessing over your family and threatening to hurt you."

"How do you know all of this?" Danielle asked.

"I know it because I've worked with Poppy McDaniel for years and during that time I've been her personal whipping board. In the last couple of years, she has gone from one extreme to the next. Like I said, the stationery, the crazy comments. I think she has been plotting all along and Sasha's very public way of chasing Dax gave her the perfect cover. Look at what happened. We immediately pointed the finger at Sasha. The world thinks she's this conniving home-wrecker. Meanwhile, no one even knows about Poppy."

They studied me as if they were trying to determine whether to believe me. I wasn't about to stay long. I said my peace.

"Tatyana, I don't know or care about Sasha one way or the other. My only reason for coming forward is because Poppy is trying to destroy my credibility at work. That and the fact that I thought you would want to know you had the wrong woman arrested," I said. "I'm embarrassed to admit this, but I followed her for a few days and followed her to your neighborhood. At the time, I had no idea what she was doing, but we sat outside your house for more than an hour. At that time, I also didn't know who lived in the house. After I saw the news, heard about letters written by the twenty-three-year-old, I suspected Poppy, but when I looked up the address, I knew for certain."

The expression on her face told me I had touched a spot. I got up from my chair.

"I'll leave you ladies to talk," I said. "Oh, yeah, here's what I promised to show you."

I pulled out the emails I had printed.

"These are emails from an account Poppy created. She was trying to set things up to look like I had known all along that someone had the goods on a sex scandal involving Dax, and a twenty-three-year-old mistress. It's my job in publicity to head off anything that would put our players or the organization in a bad light. As you can see, this date, when she created the first one, was the day she had the meltdown, threw charges against me, and I was urged to take some time off. With me out of the office, she began to lay the foundation for what she thought would be a paper trail showing I learned of a possible threat and did nothing."

Tatyana took the papers and began to read. She passed them to the other ladies.

"Again, do what you want with what I told you, but Sasha didn't write those letters."

When I walked away, they were still reading the emails.

SASHA

I couldn't remember a time when I had ever been more embarrassed. As I rode in the backseat of the town car with jet-black windows, I felt so disgusted. I was glad no one could see inside, but that didn't ease my sense of shame. If I was alone, I'd tell the driver to go straight to the Becall house and commence to beating the shit out of Tatyana's simple behind.

Me, send threatening letters? Why the hell would I have to hide behind anything? When I decided I wanted to be with Dax, I didn't hide my intentions. I sized up my competition, rolled up my sleeves, and went to work.

"Yes, Neil. Thank you," Marteen said. She sat next to me and talked to my lawyer on the phone. I was glad she had come and picked me up. "She'll be fine. No. No need."

Inside, I was still on fire. I didn't get how they could pick me up at my job, slap handcuffs on me, parade me in front of cameras and toss me in jail over something I didn't even do.

"I wanna sue their asses!" I yelled.

Marteen ended her call and turned her attention to me. She sighed.

"I don't think you can sue anyone in this, Sasha."

"It seems that because people heard you speak boldly about your determination to go after this *married* man, it was only natural that you became the target of this witch hunt," she said. "Thank

God that Eliza came forward. It seems she was the one who figured out it was her boss Poppy, and she went to great lengths to make sure Tatyana knew the mistake she had made in fingering you."

"I still don't get how I got all caught up in that mess," I said.

"It's like I said, you seemed the obvious culprit because everyone was privy to aspects of your plan." Her tone still said she didn't approve of my pursuit of Dax.

"Sure, I told Josie and Danielle that I was pursuing Dax. This is a free country, but I never leveled any threats against him or his stupid wife. I didn't have to," I defended.

"I hear what you're saying, but, Sasha, he is a *married* man. I think you should take some time to cool off. And consider the fact that it was Tatyana's call that eventually freed you. At some point, she deserves credit for admitting her error and making amends."

I eased back into the leather seat. I wasn't buying a damn thing Marteen said. That bitch Tatyana knew what she was doing the moment she lied on me, and I won't sleep until I've paid her back. Not only will I take her man, but I plan to take her entire life as she knows it.

"Hold on a sec," Marteen said as her cell phone rang. She frowned at the number, but answered anyway.

"Yes, this is Sasha Davenport's agent," she said after she answered.

Marteen nodded and put an index finger up to her pursed lips.

"I think my client would love that," she said. "Oh, yes. Well, I can assure you she'd be great. I will speak with her and get right back to you," she said.

She ended that call and smiled at me. "You'll never guess who that was."

I was still quite sour over the whole day and a half in jail. I really didn't give a damn who it was.

"A producer for *The View*. The ladies want you to come on and co-host," she said.

Marteen was the happiest I had seen her in years.

"What?"

Her phone rang again.

"Yes, this is Sasha Davenport's agent," Marteen said. Her eyes grew wide.

Maybe the scandal, the arrest and everything else wouldn't be so bad after all.

"May I put you on hold for a quick sec? I've got another call coming in."

When I heard her once again confirm that she was my agent, I knew I was on my way to turning these lemons into a big ol' batch of sweet strawberry lemonade—*Seriously Sasha* style, of course.

JERRI

Strolling through the cold halls of the Clara Shortridge Foltz Criminal Justice Center wasn't as intimidating this time around. Of course, it helped that I wasn't alone.

The next time Jason and I met with lawyers, we were on the same team. It felt refreshing to have an agenda that didn't involve potential jail time, war or the division of assets.

Jason and I still behaved like we were honeymooners and I couldn't get enough of that feeling. I wasn't sure how long it would last, but I was optimistic about our future together.

"Man, I didn't have a clue that those girls were planning anything illegal. Yeah, I know 'em. They hang around the team, but I didn't know nothing about no damn pumping party. Somebody asked me about holding a baby shower or something like that, but nothing was really confirmed before I left. As a matter of fact, my wife can tell you she had to put them off the property for trespassing a few weeks before the bust." Jason turned to me.

"He's right. I think they knew he was going to be out of town and thought they could pull this off."

We were talking to the district attorney. Our lawyers had set up a couple of meetings. Once we finished talking about the status of my probation, we turned to the charges that were pending against Jason. My situation was easily resolved.

My community service was transferred to the local Boys and

Girls Club since there were issues with the Football Widows Social Club, and Big Bertha was no longer my probation officer. The funny thing about that was, *she* put in for the transfer. She had called and left a detailed message that she was switching jurisdictions.

Once we took care of the bogus pumping party charges for Jason, we'd be able to return to our normal life. We had a long talk and agreed the entire family could benefit from counseling. We wanted to make things work this time, so we were both willing to put in the work required.

"How long will it take?" I asked the lawyer as we walked out of the meeting once it wrapped up.

"We should know something in about a week or so. But I can't imagine these charges sticking."

After the meeting, Jason was heading over to practice, but Vanessa and Natasha were meeting me at the house for a late lunch. I planned to let them know where Jason and I stood and give them the option of remaining on *our* team.

If I knew my girls the way I knew I did, we'd be just fine. When it came down to it, my girls and me were and would always be thick as thieves.

TATYANA

The Ritz-Carlton Los Angeles was located on Olympic Boulevard in downtown Los Angeles. I knew exactly where I was going so there was no need to stop at the front desk. Once upstairs in the lounge, I took in the spectacular views of the Santa Monica Mountains and the Hollywood Sign.

As I looked through the telescope mounted on the windowsill I felt like I was so high up that I had a clear view above the smog that usually blanketed the city skies. I was building up the courage I'd need to make things right.

"S'up?" His voice still made me feel some kind of way after all these years. "You wanted to meet," he said.

That's when I turned away from the telescope, and saw him across the room. At three in the afternoon, the lounge was empty and I felt it would be the perfect place to meet Dax.

My eyes fell down to his designer Italian loafers. I remembered when I picked them out and thought he'd never agree to wear them. It turned out that he loved them and wore them often. I took for granted that after so many years with Dax, I thought I knew him like I knew myself, but still, I doubted him.

He approached and I felt a mountain-sized boulder that had suddenly lodged itself deep in my throat.

"I owe you such an incredible—" I blinked rapidly, and swallowed back tears.

"I know I ain't perfect, but, Tat, I prided myself on being true to you and the kids. You think I ain't never encountered women like Sasha before?" He blew out a frustrated breath.

Tears spilled from my eyes and my legs suddenly felt weak.

"Sasha don't want me. She wants what she thinks I represent," he said. "I wasn't as mad about Sasha as I was about Pamela though."

I looked him in the eyes and saw the hurt. He was right about it, about everything.

"They both had me going crazy. I should've known you wouldn't cheat on me. I know you. But I allowed Pamela, Sasha, and even my own mother to make me paranoid. I don't know how you'll ever forgive me." I glanced away in shame. "I've talked to Pamela and it's gonna take some time, but I think the time apart will do us some good."

He stepped closer.

Instantly, my nostrils tingled at his scent. He smelled good, and familiar.

"We're a team," Dax said. "You and me, we're a team. We can't let outside forces mess up what we got going. Listen, I know most players get a bad rap because a lot of us are bad. But, baby, I ain't interested in nobody but you! After the shit hit, I thought about it and I probably made things worse by running every time that batty woman called, but I swear to you, nothing was going on with me and Sasha."

"I know now, babe. I know. And I promise, I am so sorry."

Dax cocked his head to the side.

"Are you really?" His eyebrows danced upward.

"Of course."

He pulled me into his strong arms. I missed being there and being close with him.

"You really are sorry for everything?"

"Yeah," I said.

"Well, how about you help a brotha out with a loan. I can't believe you were stacking paper behind my back," he joked.

It was just like him to break the serious tension with a little humor.

"Again, my mom always said you needed to prepare for a rainy day. I suppose I took that a bit too far."

"It's all good. Actually, with all that fraud mess going on with R. Allen Stanford, we're probably gonna need that paper," he said.

"Wow. Really?"

"Yeah, Tat, it's gonna be a long, tough road ahead. And speaking of which, I need to know if you with me. It ain't gonna be easy."

I went in for a kiss and didn't stop until my husband knew for certain that I was definitely with him.

ELIZA

The conference room was close to capacity, with only a few empty chairs. The atmosphere was festive. I thought the excitement was due to the catered lunch everyone expected, more so than the real reason we were assembled.

"It is with great pleasure that I introduce the new Director of Publicity for the Los Angeles Sea Lions," Mr. Oliver said. He spoke with little enthusiasm.

Applause broke out. But it wasn't until Mary nudged me that I realized what was going on. I cleared my throat, and tried to calm the butterflies that came to life in the pit of my stomach.

"*Mija*, go on, he's talking about you," she whispered.

I stumbled forward and eased into the spotlight.

"Eliza Campbell—"

"It's Carter, sir," Mr. Oliver's secretary muttered.

"Uh, yes. Eliza Carter, we're pleased to have you lead our team here. And thank you for er, all that you've done."

That was more than an awkward moment; I figured that was his way of acknowledging the mess Poppy had created. Her eventual arrest was like the elephant in the room. I thought about the day they came and picked her up.

"Mija! Mija!" Mary burst into my office. "The policía, they're here; come!"

I jumped up from my chair and rushed out to see what all the fuss was about. Two police officers were flanked by the company's security guards.

Bruce looked at me and asked, "Where's Poppy?"

"Ah, last I saw her, she was headed toward the ladies' room," I said.

It had been more than uncomfortable when Poppy's eyes first met mine. She stopped near a cubicle and looked like she had just seen a ghost. It was obvious she didn't expect to see me. She gave me the look of death.

"Let me know if you need anything," Charlene said. I was stunned when she didn't say anything to Poppy. I knew her arrest was eminent, but I didn't know where or when it was going to happen. Instead of going wherever she was headed, Poppy pivoted and speed-walked toward the ladies' room.

Security and the officers waited until she emerged from the hall that led to the restrooms. The scene was like something out of a homemade comedy.

Confusion gave way to recognition on her face. Poppy watched the officers. Bruce pointed a finger in her direction. She looked to the left, then to the right, and all of a sudden, she tossed a slew of papers toward the officers and ran.

We were appalled.

"Ms. McDaniel! Stop!" an officer yelled. He took off after her, but she didn't get far. A heel on her shoe snapped and Poppy went down like a flimsy rag doll. Her arms flailed in the air and she tumbled hard. By now, a small crowd had gathered to gawk.

The officer stumbled to the ground. It looked like Poppy was still struggling to try and get away. Finally, the officer eased up and grabbed her arm.

"Ma'am! Stop! You are under arrest!"

"Speech! Speech!"

The chants from my co-workers brought me back from the antics of that day. Everyone had gathered to celebrate me and my new promotion. I couldn't help but think how close I had come to losing it all. If Poppy's plan had worked, my life would have gone in a different direction. I smiled and took the microphone Mr. Oliver extended to me.

"I want to first thank my wonderful team for all of its hard work and dedication. I am so thrilled to have the opportunity to lead such a talented group," I began.

THE END

ABOUT THE AUTHOR

Pat Tucker is the author of *Daddy by Default*, *Football Widows*, *Daddy Maybe*, *Party Girl* and co-author of *A Social Affair*. Many of Pat's stories are ripped from the headlines and focus on socially conscious themes. Pat's work has generated tons of media coverage and has been featured on the nationally syndicated "Tom Joyner Morning Show," Essence.com, Yahoo Shine, Hello Beautiful, *Ebony* magazine, and a slew of local TV and radio stations. By day, Pat Tucker Wilson works as a radio news director in Houston, TX. By night, she is a talented writer with a knack for telling page-turning stories. A former television news reporter, she draws on her background to craft stories readers will love. With more than fifteen years of media experience, the award-winning broadcast journalist has worked as a reporter for ABC, NBC and Fox-affiliate TV stations and radio stations in California and Texas.

Visit the author at www.authorpattucker.com.; on Facebook: Pat Tucker; Myspace: Author Pat Tucker; and Twitter: @author pattucker.

If you want to know how Sasha got her diva start,
be sure to check out

FOOTBALL WIDOWS

By Pat Tucker
Available from Strebor Books

Normally the NFL Draft weekend was a time of great anticipation, not just for the college hopefuls, but also for the wives of the coaches. Of course the coaches had a vested interest in the draft. Months of careful planning went into deciding which representative would be present at Radio City Music Hall in New York, and which would stay back to negotiate during the draft for the right to pick an additional player in a given round. All of this played out on a very public stage.

Tickets to the NFL Draft are free and made available to fans on a first-come, first-served basis. The tickets are distributed at the box office the morning of the draft. Most fans who want to get a live glimpse of their team's high-profile picks wind up waiting in long lines, but few seem to mind. Each year, the main event is hosted at New York's Radio City Music Hall, but all across the country smaller draft parties have become a tradition.

On the West Coast, none of those parties were more coveted than the one hosted by B.J. Almond and the rest of the Sea Lions coaches' wives. But this year, due to all of the drama going on, there would be no party and no celebration hosted by either of the Almonds.

The first year B.J. held the party, it was sort of a spoof on the way the men were all consumed by the importance of the weekend. But it had taken off unexpectedly, the press had shown up, and soon it became an annual event. That was, until this year, when B.J. walked in on her husband and her so-called good friend, Ella.

This year, weeks before the draft, Sasha saw an opportunity and decided to take full advantage of all the chaos that was surrounding the Sea Lions wives.

She would have the mother of all draft parties, and she knew just what to do to get the press out in full force. Sasha had noticed all of the buzz surrounding B.J.'s lawsuit, and her forthcoming tell-all, *Blowin' the Whistle*. She had been dying for a way to get in on some of that spotlight so she started dropping hints that her upcoming party would be the ultimate backdrop for what was bound to be the hottest photo opportunity for the press.

Sasha started contacting all of the L.A. sports-related blogs with what she was calling a news tip. She started name-dropping to imply which reporters had already committed; then made getting on the list seem urgent and close to impossible.

As she dialed the last number on her lengthy list, she smiled to herself, thinking how great she had been to come up with the idea.

The minute someone answered, she disguised her voice and said, "I need to speak to a producer or whoever takes press releases about sports-related stories."

Sasha knew by calling the bloggers and asking for real sports reporters that would immediately get their attention. At no time did any of the people admit they were not whom she asked for.

"Uh, okay, you're speaking to 'em," the guy who answered the phone lied.

"I wanted to follow up on the press release we sent last week. It's about the Fantasy Draft party going on at the Villa this weekend," Sasha said.

"Oh, yeah, what about it?" The person on the other end didn't sound all that interested.

"Well, we wanted to make sure you guys got it, since B.J. Almond and Ella Blu are going to be there. Security is gonna be tight, and both Fox and CBS have already scheduled interviews, so we're trying to make sure we have a spot for you as well."

"Oh, interviews?" the guy asked.

Sasha knew there was a rift between real journalists and bloggers who wrote stories but weren't held to any kind of journalistic code of ethics. In the L.A. sports world, some bloggers were feared more than actual reporters. If one of their stories went viral, it could seriously impact a player's worth. And in most cases, bloggers had no one to answer to, so they were free to write whatever they wanted.

"They'll be there? And they're talking to the press?"

"They've agreed to hold a brief presser, but if you don't sign up early and register as press, you may not get in."

It worked exactly as she had suspected when the idea first struck. By the time Sasha was done, just about every, radio, Internet, and TV station's sports department had been put on alert.

This was bound to be the most talked about party this side of the Mississippi. Sasha had it all set up; she had even secured sponsors for the event.

Just then, she had an even better thought. There was no way in hell B.J. or Ella would show up, but what if she extended an invite to the other ladies. All she needed was to be seen with them a few times. Paparazzi would be out in force. Then she could really execute her master plan. Sasha was getting tired of the way these athletes were treating her. So what if she was older; so what she had a couple of kids; her best years were still ahead.

She dialed Lawna's number and waited for an answer.

"Hey, Guurrrl, what you know good?" Sasha sang, as if she and Lawna were good friends.

"Who is this?" Lawna sounded irritated, as if she was being interrupted.

"It's me, silly…Saaasha."

"Sasha, look, I'm real busy right now—"

Before Lawna could finish, Sasha cut her off. "Oh, I won't hold you long. I was wondering if y'all had gotten in touch with Ella yet. I wasn't sure if you had, but I wanted to let you know she'll be at my draft party this weekend."

Silence hung between them, but that was fine by Sasha; that's when she knew for sure that she had Lawna's full attention.

"I'm not trynta get all up in y'all's business or nothing like that, but when she RSVP'd, I instantly thought about you. I think y'all can work this thing out. Why not do it at a party? You know ain't nobody in they right mind 'bout to act a fool at a party."

"You talked to Ella?" Lawna asked.

"Yeah, not about all this stuff that's going on, but I did talk to her, told her she was welcomed and well, I wanted to let you know she'll be there."

At first Lawna didn't say anything. Sasha wasn't sure if she was losing her. But suddenly, Lawna asked, "Where'd you say this party was being held again?"

Sasha grinned as she rattled off the information. Before long, she'd be coasting along on Easy Street, and she didn't have to keep chasing these damn athletes to get there either. Besides, deep down she realized that she was getting too old for that.

"Guurrrl, I'm so glad you could make it!" Sasha squealed like a robot programmed to deliver those exact words. She wore a royal blue, barely there, sequined tank mini-dress that made her legs look like they were extra long. Her look was topped off with a pair of five-and-a-half-inch, come-hither stilettos.

On draft night, 8623 Melrose Avenue in West Hollywood was the place to be. The crowd was a mixture of young Hollywood stars and professional athletes. And although she was neither, Sasha Davenport greeted each guest personally with a set of air kisses to their cheeks, whether they wanted them or not.

With help from her sponsors, Sasha had transformed The Villa, a dual-level nightlife hotspot with an exclusive A-List guest list, into the mother of all draft parties.

The Villa had a stucco façade with dark wood and marble floors, as well as a long, marble-top bar and a fancy centerpiece of a golden globe, meant to resemble a library of the old rich with hundreds of books stacked on wall shelves. For tonight's event, a long table was moved into the center of the first level.

On either end of the nightclub were huge football goalposts made of colored, sculpted ice. Between them was a spectacular sea-food wonderland. Massive appetizer trays were stacked in a series of cascading towers. Each contained an array of chilled colossal king prawns, clams on the half-shell, mussels, and lobster tails, along with oysters and crab. There were also boneless, wild Copper River salmon fillets, caviar, and Alaskan king crab legs. Scallions, along with lemon wedges and herbs, nestled in the crushed ice bedding that lined the edge of the display.

Most of the crowd was gathered in front of the seventy- five-inch, double-sided plasma screen that hung from the upper level.

"Could this place be any more fabulous? This party, it's so live. I can't take it!" Sasha yelled at one of her friends as she looked around the room.

"How the hell did you get all this press out here?" the girl asked through her fake smile.

Suddenly, a group of people cheered at the announcement of another draft pick.

"OHMYGOD! Is that the sports reporter from Fox?" the girl asked.

"Yup, all the stations are going live from here tonight," Sasha bragged. "I've already been interviewed twice." She winked.

"Okay, Sasha Davenport, what the hell did you do, and how come you didn't hook me up?"

Sasha hunched her shoulders and started dancing around seductively. "Don't you wanna be me right now?!" Sasha teased.

"Sasha, you tell me what you did. How you got all this press here? The way paparazzi has the place staked out, you 'bout to be in *People* magazine or something!"

Sasha grinned a toothy grin, and started wiggling her hips. She loved being in the spotlight. Talking to her friend, Gigglez, kept her mind off the fact that she hadn't seen any of the Sea Lions coaches' wives and she needed those bitches to at least show their damned faces.

She already had a photographer lined up to take as many pictures as he could. The plan was for her to leak them to the tabloids the next morning.

"I need to go mingle; more people are coming in," Sasha said as she danced away from Gigglez.

Her timing couldn't have been better. Just as she arrived back at her post near the door, Lawna walked in.

"Lawna, guurrrl, you look delicious! Just fab as always. Didn't you use to model?" Sasha asked.

Lawna was wearing a dusted gold-colored Gucci shorts set. The single-button jacket revealed just enough of her full breasts and a hint of her flat stomach.

"Thanks, and yeah, I did," Lawna said. She wondered where this sudden interest had come from, but this wasn't the time to talk about it. "Sasha, looks like you've got quite a crowd here."

"I do. Come on in and enjoy yourself." But as soon as Lawna stepped all the way inside, a photographer seemed to appear out of nowhere.

And if that wasn't strange enough, Sasha shoved a chilled champagne flute into her hand, grabbed her by the shoulder, and said, "Say cheese!"

It all caught Lawna completely off-guard. She didn't have time to smile. Instead, she gave what must've been a deer-in-the-headlights glare as the camera's flash clicked off continuously.

"What the?"

"Oh, gurrrl, be careful. Paparazzi are all over the place. They're like cockroaches," Sasha whispered to Lawna.

The photographer was still snapping away.

Lawna quickly rushed away and tried to find the others.

When Mona arrived, she received the same treatment as Lawna. When it was over, she looked down at the text message Lawna had sent.

I'm upstairs. Where's Jewel?

Mona rushed up the stairs and found Lawna who looked more like she was hiding out than having a good time.

"You seen B.J. or Ella yet?"

"No, but everyone else and their mamas seems to be here," Lawna said.

"Yeah. How the hell did Sasha pull this off?"

Lawna shook her head. She had been wondering the same thing from the moment she walked up and noticed paparazzi lined up like they were at the Shrine Auditorium for the Grammy Awards.

"I doubt Jewel is coming," Mona said.

"You know if she told Davon?"

"I asked her to give me a few more days. I gotta tell you something," Mona said.

"Oh, God! I can't handle any more bad news," Lawna said.

"No, nothing like that. Well, not completely. I hired a private investigator to find B.J. She's staying downtown at the Four Seasons."

Mona rattled off B.J.'s room number and what appeared to be her daily routine.

"Wow! You actually hired someone to find her? So, now that you know where she's staying, you going over there?"

"I am now; especially if she doesn't show up here to-night," Mona said.

After sitting around for nearly an hour, Mona and Lawna started to think that Sasha had just said Ella and B.J. were coming. They couldn't imagine what would've been taking them so long to get there if they were really coming out.

"You think Sasha lied?" Lawna asked.

Mona turned her head. "I didn't want to say anything, but I was thinking the same thing!"

"You know what, before we go jumping to conclusions, let's move around a bit. We've been sitting here in this one spot. For all we know, they could be downstairs mending their differences and doing the Cupid Shuffle," Lawna joked.

"I seriously doubt that," Mona said, laughing as she got up.

Downstairs, the party was in full swing. But Mona did notice a couple of the reporters huddled in a corner. They didn't look too happy and the target of their anger seemed to be Sasha. Sasha moved around the room, apparently oblivious to the reporters' building fury.

Mona wondered what was going on, but she was more curious about whether B.J. and Ella had finally made an appearance. She had been calling Ella ever since she had heard she was coming to the party, but there was no answer. Mona turned to Lawna and said, "Let's break up. You go over to that side. I'll take this side. Let's meet back here in fifteen minutes. We know neither of them are upstairs. If we can't find them down here, they're not here."

"Okay, cool."

By the time Mona and Lawna met back up again, they had already figured out the truth. Neither B.J. nor Ella had promised Sasha they'd come to her party.

"That lying...she's such a social climber," Lawna said.

Mona frowned a bit. She noticed two of the people who had been near the reporters were now looking around as if they were searching for someone.

"Wait here. I'm about to go find out what's going on," she said.

As Mona approached the two young ladies, they looked at her like she was crazy.

"Hi, I'm helping Sasha. She asked me to make sure you guys had everything you needed. Is everything okay?"

"Absolutely not!" one of the women yelled. Her complexion

started to redden. "We were told the wife of the Sea Lions head coach was going to be here and she and the woman she's suing were going to make statements! We've been here from the beginning; this is nothing but a party promoting Sasha Davenport!"

"Well, let me go find out what's happening and I'll come and let you guys know what's going on, okay?" Mona smiled.

"That would be so helpful. Every time we try to talk to her, someone comes and rushes her away."

"Yeah, I could see how that would be irritating."

Mona walked away from the women, who turned and headed back to the corner where the reporters were still huddled. They looked even more pissed than before.

"Let's go," she said to Lawna without even stopping.

"Wha-what's going on?"

"Put the drink down and let's get the hell up out of here. I don't know what kind of game Sasha is playing, but we don't need to be any part of it!"

Lawna put down the glass of Nuvo she was drinking, grabbed a crab leg from a platter, and rushed to catch up with Mona.

"Bye, ladies. Thanks for coming," Sasha had the nerve to say on their way out.